The Sun's Warmth

A Dauphin Island Story

Vaile Feemster

DEDICATION

WITH SINCEREST LOVE

TO MY MOTHER, RITA MALLON GEORGE,

TO MY GRANDPARENTS,

CHARLIE AND ORA LEE MALLON

WHOSE LOVE AND COMPASSION IS

GREATLY MISSED,

AND TO ALL THE MALLONS

OF DAUPHIN ISLAND

The Sun's Warmth is the first of two books in the Dauphin Island Series. The sequel is expected out in the summer of 2015

The Sun's Warmth can be purchased at:

Amazon.com

through local merchants on Dauphin Island

and through other distribution channels

It is also available on Kindle

This book was written as a hobby and was independently edited and published. If you wish to purchase additional copies; or if you have questions, reviews, or comments (good or bad), please contact me at vailefeemster@yahoo.com

Please look for The Four Holy Martyrs, which will be my next release, expected out in the spring of 2014

Chapter 1

Dauphin Island, 1941

Jake Cullen stared out the window, his forehead beading with sweat, his neatly starched shirt clinging to his body. The high ceilings and open windows of the small schoolroom helped, but it was as it always was in south Alabama at the end of May, hot and humid. But thankfully a breeze off the water made it somewhat bearable as it blew steadily from the southeast and across the slightly cooler Gulf of Mexico. And thankfully a hint of that breeze made itself known to the room, and Jake smiled.

The class teacher, Ms. Irma, faced the chalkboard, perspiration providing a skunk like stripe down the back of her blouse. The short stocky woman was talking, or muttering, all the while scribbling on the board. Whatever she was saying didn't really matter to Jake, since he wasn't listening. He simply didn't care to listen as he was preoccupied with much bigger things than learning. There was something important that was going to occur today, he was sure of that, and it made him nervous. So he sweated from more than just the heat inside the small room as he gazed out the window while the teacher mumbled something about "liberty or death."

Like nearly all the other students in the class, Jake was born and raised here and attended every year of school in the small, two roomed, plank sided building. Up until two years ago the school had been painted white, but that changed. It was now a bright shade of red. Jake wasn't sure who picked the color, "but damn they liked red!" The tiny desk that Jake had long since outgrown and now seemed tethered to, sat in a tiny room of the tiny school at the base of what everyone knew as the

1

Shell Mounds. As its name suggest, the Shell Mounds were mostly made of shells (oyster shells) with earth mixed in, and had been constructed by Native American tribes who inhabited the region centuries ago. And generations of Islanders believed their intent, long since quieted from beating drums and medicine men, and now resigned to the goats and cattle that freely roamed its landscape, had been for tribal rituals and burials. The mounds were mystique in nature and as many islanders believed, haunted.

The Shell Mounds rose quickly above the flat landscape of the island and into the shape of a manmade bowl, its form heavily banked by huge oaks and cedars. Silvery Spanish moss dangled from the trees, lying motionless and asleep, awaiting a breeze to stir it to life. And although the moss seemed to serve no other purpose than stuffing for a bed or pillow, it was without doubt both delicate and beautiful. To the east of the mounds, and school, Dauphin Island Bay sat in a tranquil state of deep blue existence, its waters rarely venturing from glistening smoothness. The landscape was stunning, perfect in fact. And although it was God who created this splendor, somehow it was the little red school that made it whole; and the beauty was piercing.

Jake leaned back in his desk, the two front legs edging their way from the floor. The breeze, his friend throughout the morning, slowed and then vanished. He shrugged his shoulders as if to say it would be okay, before turning away from his studies, which had been the sight of a school of mullet (a type of fish) jumping about in the nearby waters. Though the room was brightly lit, the afternoon sun doing all the work, it took a moment for his eyes to adjust to the shadows. As he scanned the room, studying the faces he knew so well, he noticed that everyone was here today; three sophomores, four juniors and seven seniors, and they were all crammed into the small room like fish caught in a net. This was to be an important day, and he wished some of them had decided to stay home. Discouraged, he shook his head in dismay.

"You don't understand?" the teacher asked.

Jake's glare found his best friend, Will Burton Jr., who was staring back at him. Jake nodded in understanding while arching a brow. And just behind Will was Pate Carter, without question not his friend, who also stared back. Jake scowled a bit and again shook his head as he lowered a brow.

"What don't you understand?"

Jake teetered in the desk, a smile now crossing his face as he found the lovely Mira Lea. His heart skipped a beat as he realized she too was eyeing him. He couldn't believe she was taking such a keen interest and felt this bode well for what he had to do today. "Yea, today's the day," he thought as he gave her his best, although nervous, smile.

The ruler; a thick, eighteen-inch long slat of wood crashed across the desktop. It was a blur as the hand that held it flashed before Jake's eyes, followed by a heavy "thwack!" Jake was caught off guard, his state of daydreaming interrupted, and the teetering desk slipped from beneath him. He let out a yelp as his hands flew above his head and his legs sprung outwards in an attempt to keep his balance. It was no use though as he realized he was going to crash to the floor. The room instantly filled with laughter as Ms. Irma's hand caught the front edge of the desk and brought the legs, and Jake, safely back to the oak floor.

The teacher hovered over Jake, inches from his face, everyone else laughing. "I said," the teacher said rather deliberately, "do... you... understand?"

Jake's face reddened from the embarrassment that hadn't yet subsided, though it could have been much worse. He could have fallen to the floor and rolled around while trying to free himself from the entanglement of the desk. Thankfully that didn't happen as it would have completely wrecked the day. So he looked into the eyes of the woman standing over him, and while seeing her as his aunt (she was married to his father's brother), thanked her with a gentle smile. Then, as she morphed back into the teacher who caused his near collapse and undue embarrassment, presented her with a scathing frown. "Yes Ma'am," he muttered hesitantly.

"Yes Ma'am, what?" the teacher echoed.

Jake shrugged and cocked an eye. "Yes Ma'am... death?"

Everyone again laughed.

Ms. Irma allowed the class to take an early break while Jake stayed behind. The teacher may have been Jake's aunt, but she showed no favoritism. The lecture was stern and by the time Jake finished sweeping the floor and cleaning the chalkboard and erasers, recess was nearly over. But he was finally excused and raced from the building. There was still time to make this the most important day of his life.

Chapter 2

Jake knew exactly where he was going as he ran from the
school house and headed for a thicket of trees and "the oak."
The oak was the place where the older kids met whenever they
had a break in studies. And the oak was probably the oldest
tree on the entire island, it was certainly the largest. As Jake
rounded the tree he was pleased to see Mira… very pleased.
She was standing alongside Will, John Gardner, and Lisa Cole,
and this group of people, this backbone of Jake's social
existence, was more than just friends. The five had grown up
together, went to the beach and played in the heavy surf when
the Gulf became ornery, and attended every year of school as a
unit. They were family, and in fact most were related as only a
handful of islanders weren't kin through extended generations
of brothers and sisters, aunts and uncles. And this fact, this
kinship fact, was something that a young man couldn't ignore
on a small island with limited suitors. It was a complex
dilemma that at one point reflected considerable angst for Jake.

* * *

At twelve, when Jake first realized the difference in boys
and girls, and more in particular, he and Mira, he rushed home
from an afternoon of swimming with the gang. He needed to
talk to his mother, and boy it was important! You see, Jake had
always loved Mira, but on this day, he LOVED Mira!

Overnight she went from one of the guys, someone he played games and joked with, someone he dunked beneath the waves or tackled in the sand, to someone who made him feel as if he was riding the wind. And it stirred him like never before.

On this particular day, Jake looked peculiarly at Mira, tilting his head with an unknowing regard. Her hair was wet and matted, her face dripping with saltwater. She wore cut off denims and a loose fitting tee shirt that clung to her body... to her curves. He was puzzled, fascinated; she was different, captivating. And although he'd seen her like this hundreds of times before, today... today she was pretty, and exciting, and unimaginable. Jake took his time sizing her up, studying her features, her form. "Who is this wondrous person," he thought to himself... and "who is this" scared him to death. And like a flash, he ran.

Jake gasped, trying to catch his breath as he slammed open the screen door and ran into the house. He had run the entire way home, leaving Mira and the rest in the far distance. Still panting he found his mom preparing dinner. Jake's Mom, Laura, went about her chores as Jake chased from behind, tugging at her apron. Sand desperately clung to his feet, fighting the moment when it would dry enough to fleck off and abrasively settle to the floor. He left a trail of grit in his wake and knew he'd have to get the broom once he asked what he had no choice but to ask.

"Are we kin?" Jake yelled with panting exasperations, his heart aching as he awaited the answer.

Laura hesitated and then smiled as she continued to work.

"Are we?"

Laura shook her head, knowing exactly what and who he was speaking about. She then gave him a brief genealogy lesson on the Lea's and Cullen's.

Things changed on that day. The world collided with that immovable object thing, a force that couldn't be budged or conquered, and Jake and Mira's friendship, in its former tense, ground to a halt. There would be no more games, no more joking or poking fun at, and only on rare occasions would they go for a swim together. Mira was now special. She was suddenly pretty, and not like any of the other girls or his mom. It was difficult for a twelve year old to pin down, but she was… well; she was just different!

***

Ever since that day at the beach, Mira had been Jake's girl. Well, technically he hadn't yet made it official with a date, or by even telling her she was his girl. But he had chosen her all the same. He had whispered her name a million times and wrote it a thousand more, and that pretty much sealed the deal. So, here he was, puffing and panting as he rounded the huge oak, his gaze fixed on "his girl".

To Jake, Mira Lea was to die for! Her skin was tanned, and she had gorgeous shoulder length hair that set Jake's heart racing every time he was close enough to catch a scent. He had even convinced himself, long ago, that love smelled like Mira's hair. It was the sweetest scent. But that wasn't what made her so incredibly attractive, because nothing could compare to her eyes. They were soft and beautiful and honest. In all the movies he'd ever watched, even those starring Rita Hayworth and Ingrid Bergman, he had never seen eyes so wonderful. They were as green as the deepest waters off the western tip of the island, and when you looked into them as longingly as Jake often did, there was compassion, and love,

7

and hope. Yea… Mira was magnificent, perfect in every manner, right down to her gentle smile.

Jake began to sweat, and wiped his forehead and the side of his face with his hand. He felt a trimmer pulse through his body. There was no going back. It was time to leave some new footprints along the shore and he needed that perfect wave to wash over the sand, leaving a smooth and pristine beach in its wake. He just didn't want the wave to be too big.

Chapter 3

Will Burton struck a match and placed it to the tip of the Camel. He breathed in, exhaled slowly, and the air immediately reeked. His eyes squinted as he held the butt of the cigarette between his fingers and looked at the fiery glow of its tip. And it was obvious that he was miles ahead of the rest of his peers. Will had worked in his dad's bar since he could walk and had heard it all; all the racy jokes, all the vulgarity and stories that men quietly talked about amongst themselves, and all the gossip that wasn't "fit for children's ears". And all this left him believing that he was as much of an adult as anyone on the island.

Jake grimaced as the air around him filled with smoke, though he did well to hide it. Smoking was something he hated, and he often tried to judge the others to see if they felt the same. He despised the way it burned his throat and made him choke. It should have been easy to just lift his hand and refuse the gesture, but he didn't. He didn't want to appear unsocial, especially in Mira's presence. So he reluctantly kowtowed to the pressures of being trendy, just as he imagined the rest of the group did, and painfully awaited his turn for a puff.

John and Lisa eased off into a conversation of their own and away from the smoke. As for Jake, in spite of all that had gone wrong on this morning, he felt extra chipper and displayed a genuine bounce in his step. There was no disguising his high-spiritedness as his face was beaming. "Life is good and the time has come." And it did seem to be the right time. Days of school were all but gone and an opportunity to ask Mira to next week's graduation dance was growing scarcer by the day.

Jake stole a quick glimpse of Mira without moving his head. "God she's gorgeous," he thought, and again his nerves returned. His stomach railed against him, knotting and growling, and he was sure the others could hear it as well. His face and neck became flushed and turned a beet shade of red as he smiled uncontrollably, nervously, all the while repeating the mantra he had carefully scripted and religiously rehearsed over the past months. So, with his blue striped white cotton shirt pressed and starched into obedience, and his hands deeply entrenched in the pockets of his khaki slacks, his decision was made. The time had finally arrived.

Chapter 4

The cigarette in Will's hand stunk, but Mary Gorman, the girl who poked her head around the tree, stunk more. The Gorman's, Mary, her dad, and an older brother, moved to the island in 1939 and lived in the last house on the eastern edge of the village. And they were; drifters, gypsies of sorts who mysteriously and magically appeared one day, out of the blue and not knowing a single soul. Well, it was certainly mysterious how they came to be here, though the magic part is up for debate. In any instance the Gorman's were unlike all other drifters, because they stuck!

Now it wasn't uncommon for folks to be passing through, think the island was paradise and all they had ever wanted, and then settle down. But once the novelty of living in the middle of the Gulf, and more in particular the difficulties of living off the water became an unquestionable focus, they would disappear and never be seen again. It had happened countless times though that wasn't the case for the Gorman's.

The Gorman's came to the island with less than most, which only included a few housewares, some clothes and a ratty boat. And being the drifters they were, they settled into an abandoned house that had been gutted years earlier by the floods of a hurricane. The house was decrepit, the Gorman's seemed inept, and from the beginning it was obvious that their life here was going to be a chore. Not one of them was very good at fishing… or crabbing, or oyster tonging, or poling their boat; which were necessities of living on an island. Yet, they could grow a little garden here and there and shoot a few ducks in the winter, but it was scarcely enough to survive on. But none of that seemed to matter to the Gorman's because here they were, two years passed since their arrival, gnawing away at survival. And so, for whatever reason… well, the Gorman's stuck; like mud!

Mary, also a senior, attended school with the rest of the kids though she was a loner. As for her older brother Jeff, he'd never been seen near the building. And truth be told, no one was sure if he had ever attended school anywhere, at any time. In fact, he was more of a loner than his sister and typified the Gorman clan with his silent stares and disheveled appearance.

Mary's face peered around the thick gray bark of the oak, no smile, no frown, no brow curiously arched; nothing but distance in her glare. And she was as she always was, just plain, dull, Mary. On top of that, Jake could cross another day off the calendar that he wasn't sure she had any teeth because he had never seen her smile. Mary was a full two years older than any of the rest of the seniors, and looked it. The rumor, and this came straight from Pate Carter (aka the ass, troublemaker, agitator, and further known as a "real shit"), was she failed a couple of times in another school, went insane because of it, and was later put in a mental hospital. And although Mary never confirmed any of that, the rumor was still as good as truth in the eyes of teenagers. Freckled faced and tall she was also bigger than the other girls, but in a stout manner, not fat. Further adding to her distress was that she never made any attempts to make herself pretty, although her features weren't unattractive.

Mary's body language always radiated caution, warning others to stay away like a light house near a rocky shore. And other than Pate giving her the nickname "Scary Mary" on her very first day of school, no one tended to delve into her business because they knew. They knew she'd set her gaze upon you, that her eyes would glass over and that you'd fall under her spell. It was voodoo (see Pate's gossiping again) and she didn't try to hide it. You could feel her glare like you could feel the first sunburn of summer on the back of your neck. It was uncomfortable and it seared eerily and feverishly within your body. And her eyes were filled with something Jake had never seen, something... well he didn't know how to explain it since he had never seen it before. But he didn't like it, that's for sure! It gave him the impression she didn't care about anyone or anything, including herself.

The day was hot, too hot for the dress Mary was wearing. The thick clothed, long sleeved, light brown dress flared outwards just past the knees and was buttoned firmly up to her neck. It was worn, tight, and aged; with obvious seams that needed stitching as well as two missing buttons. Mary only wore two different dresses, both in need of repairs, both designed for winter. She never wore anything that seemed well kept, and it left a person thinking that the lack of a mother to take care of such details, to be the reason. And as for her mother, that was someone that not even the rumor mill could confirm to exist.

Having peeked around the tree and studied the group, Mary flicked a glance at all of them, a silent warning, as she stepped over the roots of the huge oak and came into full view. She had never been a part of the close knit group, never talked to any of them as normal schoolmates would, and never met with them at the "oak" or anywhere else... so this was special. Mary immediately turned her attention to Will, who had been amused by Jake's mannerisms and jerkiness on "his important day." The unflappable Will took notice of the lurking Mary. His smugness vanished and his spine snapped straight as Mary's eyes met his. Mary continued her quiet prowl in his direction.

Will was tall, thin, and pale, his life in the bar and absence from the water obvious. But however pale he had previously been, it was nothing compared to now. It was as if death was coming… correction, death was upon him and no one could stop the shadow that moved ever closer. He wanted to scream, to say stop, to say anything… but couldn't. He was frozen solid with only his eyes twitching back and forth, silently begging for help; Mary, Jake, Mary, Jake… Mary!

Mary hesitated, her moves calculated; deadly. She seemed more tense than normal, maybe angrier. But, she appeared in no hurry. She was like a large cat of prey, patient and undaunted.

Jake noticed Will's eye movements and felt bad for whatever he had done to provoke Mary's ire. The silence, as everyone focused on the two, was as relentless as the afternoon heat. Even the breeze vanished, its very life sucked from it, leaving the afternoon heavy and thick.

"Boy, he's gonna get it" repeatedly shouted in Jake's mind. And he knew there was nothing he could do to help; more likely, there was nothing he wanted to do to help. "Besides, it may be a good laugh," he thought as a slim trace of a smile crossed his face.

Jake watched intently and with a bit of delight as Mary, clearly stalking Will as her prey, moved in for the kill. And in a brief glimpse he thought he saw a fang emerge from the corner of Mary's mouth. Jake turned his eyes to Will, who was now grimacing, the frantic and fear filled throws of death near.

Jake's focus came back to the carnivore and he was dumbfounded as he noticed a faint semblance of a smile on her normally pursed lips. He was intrigued as to where this was heading. He tilted his head, quickly realizing that Mary's manner toward Will wasn't threatening, but rather sincere in nature. Maybe it was the company of Mira that steered Jake's thoughts to a happy place, like a child waiting on Santa. But for whatever it was, at least at this moment, Scary Mary seemed almost decent.

Mary said something to Will, whose face took on a nervous twitch as his left brow rose sharply. He squinted with his right eye, that continued to twinge, and frowned ever so gently as his face went blank and his head tilted as if Mary were speaking a different language. Will looked uncomfortable and perplexed at the same time.

It took only a couple of seconds before Will's body began to relax, his shoulders releasing to a more natural state and his face demonstrating the well liked smile he always offered. Mary even managed more than her normal rigid expression and their conversation; well… it became a conversation. Looking at them both standing there, Jake thought they somehow seemed to fit; oddly albeit.

Chapter 5

Jake's eyes didn't stay on Will and Mary for long, not with the beautiful Mira standing so close. The assembly around the tree was strangely complete, everyone now paired off and engulfed in their own conversations. And it was almost too perfect as Jake found himself in a fortunate position. He and his girl were all but alone. Jake rubbed the back of his neck and tried to correct his posture, which had become tense. He straightened his back and forced his shoulders backwards. He was standing mostly on his toes, bouncing, his hands continuing to dig deep into his pockets.

"Mira," Jake muttered. He realized he sounded stupid, his voice cracking. He paused long enough to catch a breath and began again, this time with manufactured confidence. "Mira, would you…." Jake never finished the sentence. From behind someone shoved; heaved his body in the direction of the oak tree. Jake was unable to halt the momentum of the thrust and crashed into both Will and Mary, causing the two to stumble and fall onto the huge coarse roots of the oak.

Jake quickly turned to see Pate Carter laughing; begging for it. "You little bastard," Jake fumed! But before Jake could react, before he had time to even think, from his backside a heavy blow from a clinched fist caught him square in the right ear. Falling to his left knee there was a thunderous ringing that scrambled and mixed with the thought of having to fight both Pate and Jimmy Clark (Pate's crony and ever-present best, if not only, friend). His head was spinning from the punch as anger blared through his mind. "They're going to get theirs" he abruptly concluded through clinched teeth.

As Jake spun around, ready to unleash his anger, there was only Mary standing there, white knuckled and red faced. Blood streamed from her elbows and knees where the harshness of the roots had torn her skin. Mary had taken the liberty of striking Jake from behind, and every ounce of stored anger in her body uncoiled for another shot to his chin. And boy, did she ever connect! Dazed, Jake's eyes crossed and he staggered back with Mary's body in close pursuit. He felt as if he were drunk, his mind and vision trying to focus, his legs wobbly and heavy. He somehow managed to push her away. A couple of feet now separated the two, as well as a couple of seconds for Jake to formulate a plan.

Jake's instincts told him not to strike her, simply hold her down until she cooled. He hastily assessed the situation and realized he needed to be decisive! "She's a girl" entered and then left his mind as Mary's tight fist drew back for another assault. Jake knew what he had to do, no matter how disappointed his Dad or anyone else would be. At this point, self-preservation was all that mattered. So, with unbridled concern, he threw a punch with his entire body's weight, landing flush on the girl's cheek. Mary crumbled and fell back into the tree again. Her body, now lifeless and limp, appeared frail. Suddenly, she became this feeble and innocent creature.

The entire class had now gathered at the sight of the fight, but not a sole spoke as Jake struggled to catch his breath. He was panting and sweating profusely as panic wrenched his conscience. He was horrified that he may have killed her! Jake looked around at the other kids, his expression begging for their understanding, begging for them to understand why he did what he did. But he was alone; stunned and mortified. His hands remained tightly balled, the knuckles on his right hand throbbing in pain. He brought his fist up to meet his eyes and glared until he could finally unclench them. The stored energy and adrenalin that had thickly coursed through his body moments earlier, eased. He then headed toward Mary, he needed to save her!

Chapter 6

Mary roused and lumbered to her feet.

Jake, who was about to come to her rescue, halted.

Mary, who was almost as tall as Jake, now seemed to tower over him, her chest heaving with a frighteningly deep rhythm as the muscles in her arms and neck bulged. It was an unmistakable display of might.

Mary smiled and it overflowed with disdain. And her eyes... her red and fiery eyes never moved from Jake's.

Jake was unable to look away, unable to beak the voodoo curse.

Mary wiped at the trickle of blood running from her bottom lip and then shook her head like a champion boxer who was about to show an underling what it was all about. And with renewed fervor Mary sailed headlong into Jake's stomach. My God the rage! Jake felt the hatred, the true and exhaustive loathing of a beast; and he knew. He knew this wasn't going to end well and that it was going to be brutal!

It seemed Mary Gorman had sharpened her nails to a razor's edge as she scratched like a wild cat at Jake's face. And yes indeed, Jake now knew she had teeth; lots and lots of sharp, fang-like-bloodthirsty-eat-you-alive teeth. And as proof, blood covered everything as she dug them deep into the flesh of his chest. Jake screamed like a woman, his voice rising higher than any soprano could envision. His mind was frantic as he couldn't react to the onslaught. He screamed again; bloodcurdling! He tried to fight back, but every blow he delivered was returned with more hatred and greater infliction. No doubt about it, the sharks were out and Jake's flesh and blood had become the perfect bait.

The fight raged, for what Jake believed to be hours, until Ms. Irma pried at Mary's arm and mercifully pulled the girl off his body. Ms. Irma tugged as hard as she could, trying desperately to pull the bullheaded Mary away, Jake continuing to suffer as kick after kick was delivered to his ribs and stomach. The teacher stammered as she wrestled with the girl, "Jake, you should be ashamed of yourself for fighting with a girl! Your father is going to hear about this!"

By the grace of God, and Jake would not forget God as he vowed to say ten Hail Mary's and twenty Our Father's the next time he was in church, Mary was dragged beyond reach.

Jake lay flat of his back, on the grass and dirt, his hands pressed to his forehead, his eyes closed as he tried to collect his thoughts and catch his breath. The situation had been bad, but it was now desperate as he realized the worst wasn't over. For a moment he thought it may be best to just lay there until dark and then sneak home under the cover of night. But he realized the ridicule would still come and that the verbal assaults would be more brutal than the fight itself. And so, he sat up, resting on his arms that he extended behind him. He looked down and his once pressed shirt had disappeared, his chest full of drying blood.

Every kid in the school gawked at Jake as Ms. Irma corralled the cursing Mary toward the school house. Suddenly, and quite alarmingly, Mary broke free of the teacher and headed back to the fray. Jake's entire body winced with every step she took, each foot hitting the ground like thunder; enormous, directly overhead… thunder! Jake made an imaginary sign of the cross as his mind raced faster than Mary's long strides. He was frantically searching for a way out.

"Maybe if I play dead, she won't beat an unconscious man!" he thought. He was eternally thankful he didn't have to find out as Ms. Irma grabbed hold of Mary's arm, and with words Jake was unable to hear, calmed her enough to head inside the school.

Jake never really noticed just how many kids there were at the little red school. But for now it seemed like thousands, and every single one of them was standing at the site of the worst massacre since the Battle of Little Bighorn. He searched for Mira, through swelling eyes, but only spotted a grinning Will. Jake's eyes rolled as the smirk on Will's face said it all. And as if on cue every person began to laugh, hysterically. Jake twisted his body, searching, and caught a glimpse of Mira heading into the classroom as the rest of the children continued to laugh and point.

The school bell rang, and again Jake added a few prayers to his growing list as all the kids grudgingly headed back to class, except for Will.

Will approached Jake and while towering over him, shook his head in dismay. A moment later he extended a hand so as to help him up, and quipped, "Nice scream, your mom teach you that?"

Jake moaned from deep within and fell back. He lay flat of the ground and cursed the events that had just occurred.

After a few more seconds of self-pity, Jake managed to his feet while Will walked about and picked up the shredded remains of his shirt and both shoes. He placed all the pieces in Jake's palms.

"Is that a bite mark on my shoe? And where the hell's the rest of my shirt?" Jake asked.

"That's everything!" Will was clearly amused as brief moments of laughter mixed with each word.

Jake shook his head. "I don't want to know, but what the hell happened? Did I black out? Did I faint?" He paused as his eyes took on a hopeful, yet pitying expression. "Did I win?"

Will couldn't stop laughing. His side began to hurt and he doubled over and placed his hands on his knees.

Jake wasn't amused.

The two looked in every direction, and amazingly that really was all the clothing. Jake firmly believed that Mary had eaten the rest.

Jake paused and rubbed the back of his neck with his left hand while stretching. He craned his neck, to help ease the stiffness that was beginning to set in, and his eyes became fixed, skyward. Will followed his gaze up through the limbs of the giant oak. "Now how the hell did that happen?" Jake's voice was genuine as both stared at the shirt.

"I don't know, but you need to count your blessings that it wasn't worse."

"Worse! How could it have been any worse?"

Will paused for a while and offered with a chuckle, "You're absolutely right, it couldn't have."

Their eyes came back down and they glared blankly at each other for a moment. Both burst into uncontrollable laughter. And with Will putting an arm around Jake's shoulder, they headed for home.

Chapter 7

The long arching white-sand beach was so bright in the mid-morning sun that it was difficult to see. Jake held a cast net in one hand and a croaker sack in the other as he walked along the shore, small waves lapping at his ankles. He squinted, his eyes scanning the sandy bottom of the gulf, searching for areas where the water suddenly deepened and grew dark. Having eyed a shadowy spot, a wash out caused by the rip tides that frequented this side of the island, he stopped. Already in the sack were four mullet and a flounder, but he needed a few more. He dropped the sack where the sand and water merged and stood perfectly still while fixing the net, readying it for the next throw. He draped the net in front of him, his hands clutching large wads of webbing. He lifted a section of the heavily weighted lead-line that runs along the bottom of the net, and pinched it between his teeth. His mind became focused, his thoughts clear and attentive. He did his best thinking when he was fishing, and today was no exception. "The fight of the screaming man," came to mind. He shrugged, thinking it likely that Will had dubbed the fight and then spread the word like wildfire. In any case it didn't matter, because nothing mattered.

For Jake school had come to an abrupt conclusion, the last four days of his high school career not ending as he had wished. Instead of enjoying the moment, the celebration and privileges that go along with being a senior, he idled his time away, alone and out of sight, while waiting for the scratches and bruises to heal. Truthfully, he'd shaken most of the fight off, the physical effects at least, but felt strolling into school wouldn't be worth the teasing he'd have to endure. Even the younger kids had a leg up on him at this point, and that was something he couldn't bear. Above that, there was Mira. The embarrassment of the fight paralyzed him and he just couldn't face her... he just couldn't. Not returning to school was the hardest decision he'd ever had to make, because he knew it was over. Just like that, in the blink of an eye, his opportunity to love the one he loved; vanished. And it had been stolen by Mary; nooo...... it was Pate, and that was something he could never forgive.

The ten foot net opened perfectly, as round as a silver dollar, and Jake pulled on the hand line that was attached to his wrist. He felt at least one fish struggling to get free and eventually placed two more in the sack. He realized he had enough for dinner and that it was time to find a shade.

The sand was cool beneath the cluster of pines and Jake settled in. He thought about school, and the kids. He thought it likely they were just sitting around, talking and laughing at him and the stupid fight, while waiting on parents to bring fresh baked pies and cobblers for the evening celebration. Based on past years, he figured they'd be let out early and then return around dark for the party. And it would be a party, with punch, leftover deserts, and music. His stomach growled, or perhaps that was his mind. He told himself everything would be okay because he had his net, seven nice fish, and a tree to sit beneath while looking across the open gulf. A smile briefly appeared before it vanished. His thoughts, once again turned to Mira and what her evening plans might be. "Would she go to the dance..." he asked himself. He paused, taking a moment to watch a line of pelicans, gliding no more than three feet above the gulf waters. The pelicans were majestic and efficient, riding the upstream of air that rose from the gulf.

The pelicans soon disappeared and Jake returned to his thoughts, a rush of panic flooding his body. "She was going to the dance?" he realized as his face reddened. "She's going to the dance and she's going... oh my God she's going with someone!" He hadn't thought of that until now, and the alarms sounded. "Damn it!" he said out loud. Well, if she was going to go, which he was sure she was, then he hoped it would be with Will, or somebody who wasn't Pate Carter! "It better not be Pate Carter!" He lingered on Pate Carter and figured he would have to move away from the island and never return if Mira ended up dating and then marrying Pate Carter!

Jake rued, and then pondered before ruing again. The anguish made his head ache, and he realized he had to let it go. So he calmed his mind as he thought of other things, such as fishing, and... more fishing. But it was no use, as he knew the most beautiful fish out there was Mira and that she was about to be caught in someone else's net.

Chapter 8

Jake sat on the lone wooden pier that jetted a short distance into Dauphin Island Bay, his feet dipping in and out of the warm waters. Small waves rolled beneath his toes and onto the beach, each fulfilling their destiny. The nearly full moon, rising in the east, illuminated a soft hue of golden tranquility. The evening seemed content as the breeze merged with the night and both became delicate and gentle. Summer nights, the pulse and rhythms of the island, is always the first love for those that come to know this place.

The pier was a few hundred feet from the school, and the music and laughter coming from inside the building drowned out the usual sounds of the night. Jake loved the sounds that normally echoed in the dark, but loved the rarity of music and dancing even more. So he listened, and missed being with his friends, of being one of the ones who laughed the loudest and danced the most. But mostly, he missed Mira.

Jake tossed key shells at something that wasn't there, each splash causing small shock waves to ripple across the water's glass-like finish. The glow of the moon reflected off each tiny ripple, a display of a thousand shimmering lights sparkling before him. He was mesmerized by the spectacle, though it was the school that fascinated him the most. He repeatedly glanced over his shoulder, taking in the sight of the warm and familiar glow of kerosene lamps that glimmered in the open windows. He looked on as shadows chased shadows throughout the building and realized he'd give anything to be in there. The thought, the dream of being a part of the senior celebration toyed with his mind and tugged shamelessly at his will. It forced him to slip on his shoes and start toward the school. He walked no more than ten feet and stopped. He shook his head and shuffled back to the beach.

Jake circled to the side of the wharf, the tips of his shoes pressing into the soft sand where the beach and water merged. "There's nothing to stop her. Besides, it's not like I ever told her how I feel," Jake said in a long sustaining murmur. His voice trailed off as he draped his arms on the pier and laid his forehead against the wood.

"Jake?"

Jake was motionless, afraid to lift his head.

"Jake?"

"Yea," he said, his voice as shaky and frail as an old man's, "it's me."

"Are you with someone, or do you always talk to yourself?"

Jake's body trembled as the weight of the world was placed upon him. He lifted his head and turned to look at the shadowy figure. He closed his eyes for a moment, though he needed more than just a moment. There was no mistaking the scent, the outline he knew so well. "Just one more embarrassing moment in the life of Jake," he offered softly. Desperately, he needed to get past his embarrassment. He needed things, at the very least, to be what they were before the humiliation began.

"The life of Jake seems to be interesting these days."

He smiled, "You know me… never a dull moment."

"Nooo, you're not dull! Just look at how you impress the ladies." Mira's brow lifted as she moved close enough to make out the features of his face.

"Some may only look, like a..." he hesitated, "lady."

"Awful brave when she's not around." Mira's tone became more hurried as she changed her demeanor to suit the moment. "Bet you won't be so brave in a few moments. You do know she's on her way out!"

"What?" Jake's voice was much higher than he wanted and his face reddened, although Mira was unable to see the change.

Mira smiled slyly, and Jake was wonderfully misplaced.

"Why aren't you inside dancing?" Jake asked, finally breaking the silence. "Who did," he paused as he steeled his nerves. "Who did you end up going to the dance with?" He braced for the worst.

"Pate..."

"Son of a bitch," Jake said louder than he wanted and as he gritted his teeth.

"What was that?" Mira asked as she smiled. She decided to let him off the hook. "......I didn't go with Pate. I never even made it to the dance."

"God she's lovely," Jake thought.

"I guess I was never asked by the right guy." Shyness dripped from every word she uttered as her body twisted from side to side.

To Jake, Mira's glow, her radiance, was gorgeous. She was special, and not just because he loved her. She was going to be someone, go somewhere and be important; and he wanted to be a part of it. The door had swung open and Jake mustered the nerve. "Mira, will you go to the dance with me?"

Jake was tender and honest and sweet, and it made Mira's heart ache. She breathed deeply; taking in the night air, the feelings of first love and the nervous energy that it created. She made him wait through an insightful yet painfully long pause, she too gathering her emotions. "No, I won't." Her voice was not cynical and Jake was deflated. "To be honest… well, to be honest I like it right here. Besides…… you're the only one I wanted to dance with."

Jake looked longingly at the moonlit face of the girl he loved. He smiled as he took her hands and the two began dancing to the distant music, beneath the canvas of a glowing moon.

Throughout the evening their hands never parted. They danced to every song played and talked like the good friends they were. The laughter came easy and often as the night moved slowly, deliberately… expectantly. Whispers filled the sky as two hearts sailed on a breeze that gently stroked the night. And as the conversation ebbed, Jake leaned over and pecked his girl on the cheek.

Things changed by the water's edge, and it seemed this one night now controlled a lifetime.

Chapter 9

It was nearly dark; a long summer day coming to a close by the time Toke Cullen walked up the steps, opened the tattered screen door, and entered. It marked the end of Toke's day, and the end of his visit to Mr. Willy's. With long standing resolve and devoutness that a nun would envy, Toke patronized Willy's bar three nights a week and didn't arrive home until around 10 pm. But not tonight; tonight he was home early... because tomorrow was mail day and Toke was the mailman.

Toke accepted the mailman position when old man Lander called it quits more than four years ago. And it fit him and his relaxed schedule nicely. Toke's job was unique in that he didn't stuff boxes, open the bags he was charged with carrying, or drive along dusty country roads with a car. Instead, he plowed through waves, and could very well have been the only mailman in the entire country who used a boat for delivery.

The task of delivering mail required navigating nearly three miles of open water (a bay known as the Mississippi Sound), twice a week by boat. The nearly three mile trip was even more challenging since Toke had no motor on his nineteen foot skiff, meaning he had to either pole or row the entire distance. Poling was the preferred choice of the islanders and fortunately the bulk of the distance across the bay was shallow, no more than six feet deep. A man, who was keen to the bay and adept at poling, could easily propel their skiff across the Sound in a few hours, with the only rowing coming at the ship's channel. The channel was only a few hundred feet across, but was deep and beset with rapid currents when the tide was rising or falling. Crossing the channel was a sobering experience for even the best of hands.

You have to recognize the rarity of crossing the bay to the mainland when considering the true scale of everything Toke's job entailed. Most people ventured to the other side less than once per month, some once per year, and this left Toke with a bigger role than just handing over a bag of mail. On most mail days he'd have a list of things that had nothing to do with his postal duties. Oftentimes he'd tote personal items across and then wait for someone's family member to either come by and pickup whatever it was, or bring something to him for the return trip home; a prescription, fresh bread, kerosene, etc. And Toke always waited, making the best of his time by fishing or cooning (walking about and picking up oysters in the shallows); no matter how long it took! And when it called for it, he was a ferryman as well, transporting those who wished to come and go; those who needed to check on someone who was sick or who simply wanted to go see their family. It was something he enjoyed… loved, and he was happy to be the mailman.

Laura, Toke's wife, wasn't shocked when he happened in early. She knew his habits and dinner was prepared. She looked at her husband as he entered, and it was obvious that he had only sipped on a couple of beers this evening. Toke may not have been aware, but when he left the house and headed to the bar, his ever present cap sat squarely upon his head. From there it was all up to Toke, and depending on how much he drank the further to the left it rode. And as for those special occasions, when the night ran long, keeping his hat atop his head appeared to involve magic; it was an amazing feat! Tonight though, as he sat for dinner, his hat rested just a tad off center before he removed it and threw it across the floor.

Laura placed a bowl of white oyster stew with corn bread fritters on the table to cool. She kissed Toke on the forehead and in turn he gave her a loving pat on the rump. She smiled as she retrieved two more bowls and placed them on the table as well. Seafood, every way you could think to cook it, was an undeniable staple and the center of every islander's existence. You would think a person couldn't eat the same ingredients twice a day, seven days a week; but in the middle of the gulf there weren't many options. And this wasn't always a bad thing as a fellow could do a lot worse than fresh seafood. In fact, seafood was so abundant that even the years of the Great Depression weren't entirely devastating. They were all poor as dirt back then, still are, but they had something to eat and even the Great Depression couldn't take that away.

"You see Jake today?" Laura asked.

Toke nodded.

"And?"

Toke was leaning into the table and blowing at the hot stew. "We herded the cattle back from the fort and then went to Willy's and drank a few. He said he was going to see Mira."

The fort Toke referred to, was a fort; Fort Gaines. The fort was built in the early to mid-eighteen hundreds, and during the Civil War it protected the mouth of Mobile Bay (the whole "Damn the torpedoes…" thing). The cattle made an almost daily trip to the fort because of a nearby artesian well that flowed unabated.

Encircling nearly three acres, Fort Gaines has brick and mortar walls of more than fifteen feet high. Inside the walls are cavernous hollows that were once confederate barracks, stables, and positions that housed cannons, black powder, and kilns. Further protecting the fortress, along the south and east parapets, are large boulders that had been put into place over the years so as to slow the effects of beach erosion and washouts.

Without question the fort is unique, as well as enticing, especially for children. Here, the kids play army or hide and go seek, and search out lead balls or shots (ammo used during the Civil War) that they now use in their homemade sling shots. The fort is an alluring giant, though there's danger in the temptation. The high walls have no protective railing and are less than two feet wide across the brim, making for a precarious perch. And the boulders beneath are craggy and always wet and slimy from the gulf's spray.

Laura raised a brow and let out a soft and thoughtful "mmm."

To Toke, the "mmm" that eased from Laura's lips was... remarkable. He forgot about the bowl of stew as he stared at his wife. She was lovely, very lovely. She was his girl and he wouldn't change one single thing. Well, there were a couple of things, minor in detail, but at this moment he couldn't think of anything but that wonderful "mmm."

Unknown to Toke that "mmm" was nothing more than the inner Catholic in Laura coming to the surface. The only church on the island was the Catholic Church, and most everyone on the island was Catholic. And as a Catholic you're either on one end of the devoted spectrum or just a pretender who sat in a pew, then stood, then knelt, then stood again before kneeling, sitting, and then standing so you could walk to the altar for communion and respectfully kneel while making a sign of the cross. And this was after confession, where you knelt. But Laura was not a pretender and spent many days standing, kneeling and going to confession. She was serious when it came to the Church, to God, and in being so made sure Jake endured all the rigors that encircled the faith. She conceded early on that Toke wouldn't look after their son's spiritual wellbeing, since he had a hard enough time looking after his own. So, from baptism, to catechism, to first communion, to altar boy, to confession, to confirmation.... and as was her unrealistic goal of priesthood, she made sure Jake followed the entire Catholic structure. And in the course of her actions she did her best to prod Toke along as well. To completely understand Laura you have to realize how devoted she was and the enormous concession she made when she married Toke. Because there was never any doubt that Toke was entrenched on the other end of the spectrum.

"He drank a few, did he?" Laura questioned as if drinking would soon be an issue.

All of a sudden, the "mmm" that had passed from Laura's lips didn't seem so alluring. Toke frowned as he remembered that that was one of the "minor things" he disliked. "I think they're getting serious," Toke responded, deciding to change the subject. Too much focus on drinking, he thought, may lead to some woes of his own. And that was one area he'd like to leave as is.

"That'd be ok, she's good for him. She won't put up with his foolishness like I do," Laura added as she aimed a glare at her husband.

"Yea I guess, but ya never know where life will lead ya."

"Here it comes," Laura thought as she stopped what she was doing and placed a hand on her hip. She didn't have to wait long.

"Maybe he ought to date a little more before settling on one girl," Toke said, clearly angling in a silly direction.

"He should date more than one girl? You think so?"

"Yea, I hear that Gorman girl is nice," Toke said as he blew at the hot stew that pooled in his spoon.

Laura tried to suppress a smile but failed for the most part. She turned her face from the table. She thought of Jake ducking and hiding, and all the excuses of why he couldn't join them for meals while his scratches and black eyes healed over the past two weeks. And even though it was her child and it shouldn't have been funny, it was. "Okay Toke, that's enough," she said with a softhearted giggle.

"I didn't mean anything by it, I'm just thinking out loud." He acted more innocent than he could ever be.

"You always mean something! And you're always thinking about something you shouldn't." Laura gazed with fondness at Toke, who ate his stew while glancing up without moving his head.

"Love you," he replied as he swirled the spoon in the bowl.

The screen door opened and Jake strolled into the room. He took his usual spot at the table, to the right of his father. He arched his brows. "So ya'll been talking about me," he said, though it didn't come out as a question. "It got awful quiet when I walked in." He dunked his cornbread into the steaming stew and took a bite.

Laura quickly recovered. "We were just talking about you and Mira. How is she this evening?"

Jake shrugged his shoulders while nodding his head. "Yea that's it?"

"Well she's very sweet," Laura said, "and the two of you make a wonderful couple."

Normally, Toke would allow Laura to continue her mother hen dissecting but decided to change the topic for his son's sake. "You want to go with me in the morning?" he asked Jake.

Jake knew what he meant. He had made the trip plenty of times and there was nothing else he'd rather do. "Heck yea," he said emphatically.

"Feels like it's gonna be foggy tomorrow so you two be careful," Laura interjected. Although Toke had spent more of his life in a skiff than on land, she still worried about her boys.

Chapter 10

Two hours before sunrise, Toke and Jake pushed off from shore, from a spot on the island's north side known as the Shell Banks. The beach was a natural haven, well sheltered from winds, and dotted with a majority of the island's boats. Two boats were tied to the pilings of the lone pier, while the remaining anchored along the half-moon shaped beach. The beach was littered with oyster shells, masking large swaths of sand that lay beneath.

Laura had been right, and the fog lay heavy in the early hours of the moonless morning. And it was an ominous start to the day, the fog having fused with the blackest of nights, consuming any hopes of the two seeing their way to Cedar Point. It was an agonizing state, as the loss of sight toyed with Jake's mind, replacing his senses with anxiety and numbness. If it weren't for his feet being firmly planted in the skiff, he wouldn't have known which way was up. He didn't like it, and the feeling that knotted in his stomach was as relentless as the morning was eerie. But Jake did his best, putting on a good face as he stood next to his Dad; amazed at how his father could be so adept in these conditions.

Earlier in the night, around midnight, the rising tide had pushed water high onto the banks, flooding the surrounding marshes. It was now beginning to recede, and Toke was discouraged. The daily ritual of retreating waters would soon rush from the bay, leaving soggy spits of land, exposing enormous oyster reefs and sandy shoals.

Toke eased the small boat along the shoreline as reed grass brushed the white washed sides of the wooden craft. A Blue Heron fishing nearby, squawked, further rattling Jake. The fog was dense, and within minutes water ran from their slicker suits (long rain coats with hip-wader boots) as if they were in a downpour. Toke plied onward, and within moments they exited into open water. Jake stumbled to the bow as they left the marshes, and took his position. He turned to face his dad who appeared without worry, navigating from the consistency of the bay's sandy bottom, rather than from sight. They moved along, like a bat in search of food, completely blind but using their own measure of radar. They traveled slower than usual, Toke gauging and calculating, measuring every thrust of the pole and feel of the bottom against his previous trips across.

More than an hour passed and neither said a word. Toke was concentrating on the task at hand while Jake fretted about more than just the weather.

"Dad,"

Toke dug the pole into the sand and heaved, but before he made another stroke and as the skiff glided ahead, he turned his attention to his son. He waited.

It was vague, but Jake could see his Dad standing there, looking back at him. "You know I've been seeing Mira." It took so long for Jake to say what he wanted to say that the boat had turned sideways because of the falling tide, and now headed due west.

"Yea," Toke said irritably. He had to right the boat and once again set it in motion. And it took a lot of work. The next time Jake opened his mouth, and he would, Toke decided he'd keep poling while he listened.

"I really like her… in an awful way," Jake said with hopes that his Dad understood that he loved her, without having to say so.

"There seems to be a lot to like about the girl. She reminds me of your Mom."

Jake rolled his eyes. Although he realized how much his parents loved each other, it was unimaginable that Mira reminded anyone of his mom. Mom was Mom, and Mira was young and outgoing and beautiful, in a sexy way. "Mom may still be pretty, but she is neither sexy nor young," he thought. He shuttered at the thought of sexy and pushed it from his mind. "Dad, she starts college next week. And she'll be living in the Bayou (Mira would be staying with her Aunt in the Bayou, Bayou La Batre, a coastal town across the bay from Dauphin Island and on the mainland). It's the only way she can get to school." Jake's voice took on a sound of urgency.

"I take it this bothers you?"

"More than I can stand. I don't know what I'll do without her."

"Will she be coming home from time to time?" Toke understood the problem but wanted to hear it from Jake.

"I don't know. She's taking a double work load so she can finish early. It won't leave much time for coming home…… or me."

"You know what I think?" Toke didn't allow time for a reply as he peered through the fog. "I think you're being selfish. She has a chance to do something special. She ….." Toke stopped talking in mid-sentence, causing the hairs on Jake's neck to stand.

The water had deepened and the pole in Toke's hands had to be extended further with each thrust. They were at the slope that led to the channel, and the familiar sandy bottom of the shallows changed to mud and muck. The deep trench that split the island from the mainland was getting ever closer as the skiff continued its forward motion. Toke lifted the pole out of the water, and listened. The night was as silent as it was blinding.

"The quieter the better," Jake said softly.

Crossing the channel at night depended on what sounds drummed in the dark. Motor yachts, sail boats, and ocean going ships traversed this waterway, and the real danger, more so than being hit by one of them, was being broadsided by a wave from one of their wakes. If that happened the boat would be swamped, and it'd be over in a matter of seconds.

Chapter 11

Jake listened for boats, for any sounds, while watching his dad. And he struggled to do both. The morning, less than an hour from daylight, was murky, creepy in respect and filled with dread. Jake prayed for the fog to lift and for them to be safely on the opposite side of the channel.

Jake's head jerked sideways; there was something, a sound, faint and distant. His distress surged within, his blood pressure increasing to the point that the tips of his ears burned. He was out of sorts, unable to calculate how far they had drifted into the channel; perhaps to the deepest point. He had never been so afraid.

The noise also found Toke's ears. He turned his head from side to side, tilting it at times as he tried to figure where it was coming from, or what it was. The sound was foreign, as the normal knock of a diesel, or putter of a gas engine, wasn't there. Nor was it under sail. No, this was smooth and it hummed with perpetual ease, like an oscillating floor fan. It purred with a constant and measured pattern and was much closer than it sounded!

Toke jabbed the fifteen foot pole toward the bottom, his hands nearly reaching the water's surface before it found its mark. The pole lodged itself into the thick, black, mud. He thrust, using all his might to push the bow of the skiff toward the east, into the direction of the noise. If whatever was making the noise didn't make a direct hit on their boat, then he needed the bow to meet whatever wave this vessel would produce.

The sudden movement jolted Jake, causing him to lose his balance. He fell hard onto a wooden bench that ran the width of the boat as a wave capped into the tiny vessel. The boat rocked viscously, filling with water, the edges tipping in the balance, inches from going under.

"Bail Jake, bail!" Toke yelled. Toke struggled to right the boat that had been tossed about from the impact of the wave. He also knew what else was coming.

Jake reached for the homemade bailer and was frantically swiping the water from the skiff's bottom when another wave broadsided them. The eruption of the powerful wave flung Jake over the edge and into the blackness of the channel's depths.

Jake's hands grasped for the boat's side, his nails clawing the wood. "Dad!" Jake screamed in horror, his waders rapidly filling with water and dragging him to the bottom.

Toke raced from the stern, hollering "Kick off your waders! Kick off your waders!" He reached for Jake's arm but only found his fingertips. Both fought to hold on, their fingers perilously interlocked. Jake's hand slipped from his Dad's hold. The salt water had made their skin slick to the touch, and neither could hang on. Toke watched as his son's open eyes slid below the surface. Toke stabbed an arm into the water, his face and upper torso submerged below the choppy waves. He was about to come up for air and dive overboard when he found Jake's hand. "Get the waders off!" Toke yelled as their heads surfaced and both drew in deep breaths.

Jake was frantic, his body ridding itself of precious energy with every kick of his legs, his hand once again sliding from his Dad's grip.

Toke cursed as he fought to hang on, rage welling up inside him, his face contorting with a blood red strain. Every muscle in his body bound tightly, knotting with energy and fear. Finally, one of Jake's legs was out of the waders, followed by another.

With the waders gone Toke was able to pull Jake into the skiff. Both lay on their backs, exhausted, their bodies limp and floating in the nearly submerged boat. The waves subsided nearly as fast as they had begun, and the waters once again smoothed to a polished sheen. Adrenaline pulsed through their veins, and with every breath their hearts pounded as if they'd burst from their chest. Jake's adrenaline slowed and he felt sick. He sat up, leaned over the side of the boat, and vomited.

"You alright," Toke gasped.

"Tired," Jake muttered as he wiped his mouth, "and my ribs hurt." Deep breaths came desperately and with tremendous labor between every word he spoke.

"I'm sorry. I'm so sorry. Sure you're ok?" Toke kept repeating. Clearly frustrated with that fact that his son nearly drowned, Toke cursed himself while turning his attention to the nearly sunken boat. He began to bail.

"What the hell was that?" Jake asked as he rubbed at what could be broken ribs.

"Don't know; never saw it, never heard anything like it either. It just appeared…. I don't know." Toke's breathing was slowing though he continued to bail. By the time he removed the water from the boat's bottom, he had regained his composure.

If not for his Dad calming so quickly, Jake would still be panicked. And even with his Dad now rowing the width of the channel, looking like nothing had happened, Jake's mind fought to hold his emotions in check. Neither said a word the rest of the trip over as they concentrated on getting to Cedar Point.

Chapter 12

Anxiety over the trip home had stung both Toke and Jake, and neither could quell the emotions that robbed them of their once spirited confidence. They spent half a day at Cedar Point waiting on the postman and a coal truck, and by the time they swapped mail bags and later filled five sacks of coal, they pushed off from the mainland. It was past noon and the high sun dried the air, dissipating most of the fog. The rain suits were no longer needed. Toke and Jake agreed to keep the morning incident from Laura's ears, allowing everything to move along as normal. They conceded that nothing good would come from making her worry.

The second trip across the channel presented little fanfare, though both men were happy to reach the homeward side. Having crossed over, Toke laid the oars down and again turned to the pole, but he didn't head for home. Instead, he changed directions, setting his sights on a school of mullet to the west. He picked up speed and allowed the boat to glide into the center of the large gathering of fish. The silvery fish jumped in all directions as both father and son manned their nets. Most saw throwing a net as work; but for the two, catching mullet further soothed the strain of a difficult morning. Order, they felt, had been restored. It took less than ten minutes before they had what they needed, making sure they could feed Mr. Willy's family as well.

The cloudless day turned out to be spectacular, as Dauphin Island basked in the afternoon sun. The blue waters closed tightly around the island in a shimmering reflection of beauty, tall pines arching to a skyline more stunning than that of any city. And the sight lifted Toke's spirits as he put the morning behind him. He stood with his all too familiar stance, his weight resting on one leg with the other cocked outward, and marveled at his son who sat on the bow. Jake was scaling and fileting the fish they'd just caught. Toke chuckled to himself as his boy made sure to leave the bellies in, even though there was little to no meat on them. It was a silent tribute, for Jake knew his Dad liked the bellies the most, having once heard him say, "If it weren't for mullet bellies, we'd have starved to death as children."

Toke smiled as he laid the rod in the bottom of the skiff. He took off his shirt and cap, and dove overboard. He swam around the boat once, before rolling to his back and closing his eyes. The bay water was warm and salty, and his body relaxed and eased with comfort. His muscles loosened as his thoughts grew gray and blank. His heartbeat became the only sound that existed. Jake noticed his Dad's mind drifting as aimlessly as his body, and couldn't resist. He sprang from the side of the skiff, bundling his body into a tight ball. The splash broke Toke's dreamy state, instantly bringing him back to the present. Toke ducked Jake back under as soon as he came up, and they played as they had when Jake was a child. Both smiled and laughed as they flung water in each other's direction. It was pure elation, and Toke prayed he'd always remember this moment. He needed to remember more than he needed his next breath.

Jake found it difficult climbing back into the skiff, his ribs aching. So Toke climbed up first and then pulled him aboard. Jake may have been sore, but still grabbed the pole that lay in the bottom of the boat and moved to the stern. He began moving them south, closer to home. As he stroked the boat along, managing rather gracefully with his injury, Toke marveled in both sight and thought. And pride overcame him. Jake was special, Toke had long since realized that. And though they had just played as they did when Jake was a child, Toke now saw his son as a man. It saddened his heart like he'd never known, but somehow lifted his hopes at the same time. It was an emotion he would never again experience.

Jake continued to move them forward as Toke turned to the bow. And with the breeze in his face and the sun's warmth gazing upon his body, smiled broadly.

Late that night Toke and Laura lay in bed. A thin sheet covered them as a light breeze blew from the south. The curtains softly bellowed and the room filled with the scent of the gulf.

"Is everything okay?" Laura always sensed when something bothered Toke.

"I'm okay." Toke's instincts drove him to tell her about the ordeal. "Laura, we had a little trouble today."

"Everyone ok?"

"Yea, but I doubt," Toke stopped talking, his eyes drifting as he relived the moment. "I don't know if I did everything I could have. It was so fast."

"Everyone's ok," Laura said again, but as a statement this time.

"Yea." Toke rolled onto his side and faced his wife. He draped his left arm across her waist while folding his right beneath his head and pillow. It was so dark he could barely make out the features he knew so well. Toke brought his hand to Laura's face and let his finger trace her beautifully shaped nose and lips. "I know you know this, but that boy of yours is quite special. I'm not sure what I'd do without him."

"Me either," Laura whispered. And although she worried, she also trusted Toke without limits. And that was all she needed.

Chapter 13

Cold marble lay beneath Mira's feet. And to her left and right, rows of books rested in neat order on mountainous shelves. She sat at a table in the East Mobile College Library, her head skewed by a large stack of books beside her, her cheek perched firmly on her left palm, her elbow balancing stiffly against the table. She flipped through a basic human-anatomy book, her mind grappling with the weariness of an increasing work load. If nursing had not been her dream, all she ever cared to do, she thought "now would be the time to walk away."

Nursing, as a course, was new to the College and had not yet been honed to a science. And as proof, Mira's summer, now passed, had been consumed by a chaotic flood. For three months she struggled with a course that had no introduction, no defined prerequisite, and no orientation. It was the first year the curriculum existed here, and it was as if it were an experiment of sorts, an attempt to institute an unfamiliar discipline with never before seen material. It's as if the college faculty randomly selected books and threw them in her lap.

Research, and memorizing the syllabus set before her, had stolen Mira's every waking moment. Long days became nights, and weekends drew to an end before she realized they ever started. And now that summer was over and school had begun in earnest, the burden increased. As Mira finished high school and set a course for college, she decided to cram the entire eighteen month course into less than one year, realistic or not. It meant double courses, double class time, double time studying, double this, double that, double, double, double,.....she wanted to scream, but didn't. She had done this to herself, and so, she would double or even triple her efforts to make sure she fulfilled her dream.

Many, many students, seemingly more fascinated with the opposite sex and freedom from their parents, tended to drift when it came to school and studies, like a boat that had broken free of its moorings. They only wanted to talk, to philosophize about life and love, as if they knew anything about it. And they were nothing more than hounds, trailing the scent of the opposite sex that lay thick and heavy upon the desks and stairs and quad. But not Mira, she wasn't like most of the rest. Even though she loved Jake and often thought romantically about him, she wasn't throwing herself at him or anyone else. She came here to learn, and Jake was but a dream, a bottled emotion that quietly entered her mind, causing her to stir.

Luckily, and the only thing that kept her sanity, Mira wasn't completely alone in this world of ailing commitment. Sherry Larson, a petite blonde with bright blue eyes and a brilliant smile, was the only thing that separated Mira from total seclusion. And from the first time they met in a stairwell, they had been inseparable. Remarkably pretty, thin and tan, the boys always took notice wherever Sherry presented herself. And although they did the same when Mira made an entrance, they weren't nearly as ambitious in their efforts. Even to Mira, Sherry was pretty, and spectacular!

"So this is where you've been hiding," Sherry whispered as she took a seat, her smile instantly saving the marble columned room from its own boring death.

Mira never moved her head but looked up through hair that dangled haplessly across her eyes. "Yea, I've been hiding. Everyone knows I'm so smart that I don't have to study. So I figured who'd look for me in a library?"

A "Shish," came from the librarian, who like an eagle on a high perch, sat behind a raised podium no more than twenty feet away.

Neither Mira's sarcasm nor the librarian's shish was lost on Sherry who brazenly stared at the woman before turning back to Mira. "Well I know you're brilliant, that's why this was the last place I decided to look. I've been all over God's creation."

Mira smiled, nearly to a laugh, and now gave Sherry her full attention. "Thanks. So, what are you into today?"

"Just checking you out... and avoiding the fact that I have my own studying to do."

Their conversation moved swiftly, some of the talk centering on school work, some on a beautiful, and quite stylish, white collared blue dress that Sherry purchased earlier in the day.

"Ahem."

"Ahem," came again, slightly louder this time, but not too loud.

The girls looked up, across the table, and took in the sight of two boys. The boys stood there, leering, both wearing navy blue dress-coats, khaki slacks, and red and blue striped ties. They dressed like five year old identical twins heading to a funeral, right down to their black, wingtip loafers. But they weren't five year olds, though they were unmistakable. They were frats; boyish, full of themselves, frats!

"What's buzzin," one of the young men whispered now that he had the girls' attention. He made a point to show a winning smile.

Mira rolled her eyes at the choice of words while Sherry looked straight at him, undaunted by what she knew to be the beginning of a pickup line.

"I'm John and this is my friend Perry," John said with a voice that struggled to show confidence. He raised his brows and tilted his head sideways, toward his friend. He added, "We've been sitting across the room and noticed you two are cooking with gas."

Again Mira rolled her eyes, and again Sherry did or said nothing.

John's left hand nervously pressed his tie against his chest, smoothing it in a downward motion. "You know you're the hottest girls on campus." He smiled again.

"Sizzlin," the other boy quickly added.

Mira laughed as the librarian gave another "shish" and stood from her chair as if she were about to come over. Mira held her hand over her mouth as the giggles subsided.

Sherry nodded, a peculiar grin growing on her face, her lips pressing to a devilishly thin line. And the smile, the challenging expression, was who Sherry was, a vixen in every sense.

Meanwhile, John glared at his friend, an admonishment for the interruption and use of the word "sizzlin". He turned back to the girls. "What if we give you two a chance to join us and have a ball?" John's voice was gaining steam.

"We have some real killer-dillers," Perry chimed. He spoke as if he were trying to coax a child into taking their first step.

Sherry's eyes deepened to a sultry glean as she turned and glared longingly at Mira.

"Did the boys vanish," Mira thought as the stare from Sherry continued. It was such a long and intense moment that Mira began to feel self-conscious and found herself checking the buttons on her blouse.

Sherry eased from her seat and slid her chair next to Mira's. The girls now sat next to each other, both facing the young men who hovered on the opposite side of the table and whose hands moved with agitation and nervousness.

"You boys think you have killer parties?" The way Sherry spoke carried a distinct tone of carelessness and sexuality. You could literally hear the boys gulp as their eyes widened with both fear and interest.

Mira briefly glanced past the boys and to the librarian whose keen interest in the four remained fixed.

"Well, you gonna answer or just stand there?" Sherry asked after the two failed to give a reply.

"Yea, we um, we think we have killer, I mean we have diller......" John's voice trailed off now that he realized he wasn't making any sense. His face turned as red as a beet.

"What he's trying to say," Perry said, now picking up the pieces while elbowing John in the ribs, "is we know what dolls like you want, and if it's wild you want, it's wild you'll get. I'll personally make sure the two of you have a good time." He smiled and then released it. It was an obvious attempt to mollify the ladies.

Sherry grinned and her eyes again narrowed. "Sooo... you believe you're wild?" Sherry was already attractive, heavenly in fact, but the way she tilted her head, inviting yet submissive, made the boys melt with yearning fascination. "Well maybe you're not ready for dolls like us." Sherry turned her face toward Mira. Mira continued to look straight ahead, though aware that Sherry had now focused on her. Mira jumped when Sherry laced a finger down her arm, goose bumps racing up her arm and to the back of her neck.

Mira had always been quick witted, able to give a retort in any situation, but her mind went blank as her body surrendered to the touch.

Sherry leaned even closer, her mouth flirting inches from Mira's neck.

Mira could feel the warmth of her friend's breath as chills ran the length of her spine. The delicate hairs on her neck, stood.

"Well we know what women want," Sherry said with a low sexual tone, her lips nearly grazing Mira's neck.

Mira squirmed in the chair. Her breaths became shallow and she could feel herself losing control. Her hands trembled with edgy excitement.

Although Mira's eyes never turned from the direction of the boys, she never saw them. She stared through them, her mind focused on a world where Sherry's actions thrilled the senses and made her feel things she never knew she could.

"Well, we don't think we need any boys," Sherry said as she stared at the soft features of Mira's outline. "What do you want?" Sherry asked with a whisper. It wasn't clear who the question was meant for.

Mira's mind scrambled to reason the emotions that poured from her core. Her body burned and ached.

Sherry blinked, sobering to the surroundings. She turned her face from Mira and looked at the two young men. She couldn't help but gawk.

Mira, clearly flushed, snapped from the spell she'd been placed under. She tried to focus as her heart raced.

Sherry nodded in approval as the boys stood; both of their mouths ajar and their bodies clearly aroused.

The two lads were enamored and didn't grasp their current conditions until Sherry extended a finger and began to snicker. Mira looked at what Sherry had so deliberately pointed to and laughed as well. The boys became aware of their situation and quickly covered themselves with their hands as they turned away. Their faces red and egos damaged beyond repair, they raced for the door.

Mira and Sherry lost it. Laughter from the two erupted, prompting several threatening "shishes" from the librarian who eventually walked over and placed an index finger on the table. The librarian tapped the finger against the wood as she spoke. "That will be enough!" She then turned and headed back to her perch.

Mira's eyes filled with tears as both girls tried to stifle their outburst. By the time they had regained their composure, the boys were no longer to be seen.

Mira was still reeling from the experience when Sherry finally spoke. "So, we did a number on those two, didn't we?"

Mira held a long breathe before letting it out, "Yea, we taught them." Her voice was more timid than she could ever remember. "You were.... well...." Mira was unable to put things in order, her mind trying to separate innocence from curiosity.

Sherry smiled like a kid in a candy shop. "I'm sorry if I got to you too, but I guess my sexuality has no boundaries." She was clearly pleased with her efforts.

"No, I guess you don't," Mira agreed. She was unsure if Sherry was acting or if she enjoyed the moment as much as she did, but would never admit... to anyone, ever!

The two seemed to be gauging the others' intentions, and after a long pause Mira's body jerked sideways as if a revelation from heaven had just occurred. "Sherry, you want to stay with me this weekend?" She placed both hands on Sherry's arm before continuing. "We always have this baseball game between the Island and the Bayou and it's this weekend. It'll be fun. And you can stay with my parents and me at my aunt's. And on Sunday we can go to the Island! Please... there's nothing I'd like more." Mira hesitated after the long plea. "God I miss the island."

Sherry was excited at the prospect, but realized she had her own issues. "I can't. Dad's coming and I'm sure he'll want me to go home."

Sherry's dad, Ted Larson, came for his daughter once a month. And the two always left for an extended weekend at home. Sherry never denied her father's request, realizing that when her mother died several years back that she was all he had. Her mother's passing had been difficult for both, but she knew the damage to her dad was different, deeper. She never forgot the sounds of sobbing that emanated from her father's room late at night, or the countless trips he made to the graveside. From then on she vowed to protect him, to never allow him to be disappointed again.

The two girls sat as people should in a library, quietly, though the wheels continued to turn in Mira's head. "We'll ask him to come," she blurted; deriding another "shish" along with a pointing finger. She again lowered her voice. "Everyone would enjoy meeting him, and we can always make room for one more. My folks will show him a great time, I promise."

Mira's voice quickened with excitement. "Besides I want you to meet Jake and Will! The two of them are a riot. And Will... mm, mmm, mmm." Mira's brows lifted and her head nodded approvingly as she spoke of Will.

"I don't think Dad would go for that. He seems to like it when it's just the two of us," Sherry said, becoming even more reluctant of the chances. "He hasn't done anything since Mom left."

Mira thought it interesting that Sherry chose to say her mother left, as if she were coming back someday. But then again, she couldn't begin to understand how hard it would be to lose her mom. She didn't have the strength to even think about it. "Please.... just ask. I'll ask with you if you want. Please..."

"Fine, I'll ask. But when he says no, that's the end of it. Agreed?" Sherry was assertive in her response, using her hands to animate "the end."

It may have only been Tuesday, but Mira could hardly wait!

On cue, Ted Larson showed up on Friday and was surprised to be met by both girls. Mr. Larson stretched his frame as he exited the car, arching his back in the process and taking in the early autumn day. Ted was a rugged individual, not bad looking for a man in his late forties, and looked every bit the part of a cattle rancher. He was a tall, broad shouldered man with large callused hands and a face as tan as anyone from the Island.

"Hello sweetie pie," he said with a deep voice as he walked to the curb where the girls stood. He gave his daughter a long hug. "Good to see you too Mira, it's been a while," he added while looking over his daughter's shoulder.

"Yes sir it has… and it's good to see you also." Mira fidgeted with anticipation, and for some reason she curtsied. She rolled her eyes at her own actions.

"So," Ted paused as he glanced at a smiling Mira who balanced on her toes, "do both of you wanna come with me?"

Getting to the point was apparently not one of Mr. Larson's weaknesses, and Mira worried that this may lead to a flat out no. She needed him to at least hesitate so she could jump in with her plea.

"Dad," Sherry's said with a childlike voice, "would you like to stay with us for the weekend? Mira's family is having a ball game against another town and we've been invited to stay with the Lea's. It's a big event for their communities."

Sherry and Mira waited, and with each passing moment they grew more astonished that Mr. Larson hadn't yet refused.

"There'll be lots of home cooked seafood… and fun," Mira said enticingly. "And you'll meet the nicest people."

Mr. Larson's face was etched with creases of hard living and outdoor life, and oddly, a huge smile. This was only the second time Mira had met him, and the first time she'd seen him smile. It was nice and genuine. She pictured him and Sherry's mom playing and laughing while cuddling in the front porch swing, beneath a blanket, and that his broad smile made the moment extra special.

"I'll do it on one condition."

"Whatever Daddy, just name it," Sherry blurted as she put her arms around his waist and squeezed.

"Mira has to stay with us next month. That's my only demand."

And before Sherry could respond, Mira agreed and hugged the man like he was her own father.

Chapter 14

The first Saturday of October brought something more important than a little game called the World Series. There were two communities and countless families coming together, and it signified a reunion of sorts that's been occurring for more than thirty years. Family, food, and community pride were all on order today.

The entire Island ventured to the Bayou and this year was different, quite possibly a banner year. It was an undeniable first as every single family member, including the perpetually antisocial Gorman's, made the trip to the mainland. Yes, even the Gorman's! Now, before we get ahead of ourselves, it's not like they rode in the same skiff with another family, poling along and singing tunes together. But in no small measure, it was a step in the right direction. After all, they traveled at the same time the rest of the community did and ended up in the same spot. They were even somewhat social once they reached the Bayou, making one think that a small miracle had occurred. Perhaps Father P.K. Malone, the priest of St. Timothy's Catholic Church on the island, had said a prayer or asked God to intervene on their behalf (even though the Gorman's weren't Catholic, which meant he probably thought twice about such an exertion of wasted effort). In any case, the

Gorman's came to the game, as did Father Malone who tagged along and rode in the skiff with Tommy and Eula Gibson.

Father Malone, a native of Ireland, moved to the Bayou with his mother, father and sister (a sister who became a Sister) when he was twenty-two. And he served the Bayou for nine years before being reassigned to the Island. The priest was a big fan of God, the sport of baseball, gumbo, and boxing; and in no particular order… after God of course. He also enjoyed trips to the Bayou and often stayed for a week at a time, which left the islanders wondering which community garnered his true allegiance. In any event, he didn't play ball for either team though most felt his close ties with the man upstairs could somehow sway the final score.

Allegiances aside, today was magnificent and special. The cloudless sky formed the perfect backdrop. And the storm front that moved through a couple of nights ago left nothing but a light breeze from the north and cool dry air in its wake. It was one of those days that started off a little chilly, but by mid-morning the sun warmed your bones, making you feel young at heart. It would be a perfect day.

The game was always played in Bayou La Batre, so named after a 1700's French-maintained artillery battery whose placement ran along the banks of the deep and well protected bayou. Now the Bayou community wasn't nearly as old as the Island's, but man it was bustling. If you were inclined to fish the gulf and needed a vessel, wanted to buy or sell seafood, or have a weekend getaway, the Bayou was the place to do it. There were hotels and nightlife, and a train that delivered people into the city for the weekend. On top of that, the seafood and shipbuilding industries thrived.

Along the west bank of the bayou, large seafood processing shops worked relentlessly at filling big-city orders, while men along the east bank crafted boats of all sizes and from various materials. Fisherman along the gulf coast entered and left the bayou's mouth, delivering their catches and then heading out for more. Even the families of Dauphin Island weren't completely immune to what the Bayou offered. A man had to either sell his catch in the Bayou, or take a sixteen mile trip up Mobile Bay to the downtown district of Mobile or head to Biloxi Mississippi. And when you added it all together, it meant the Bayou stood tall as the place to do business.

Yes, the Bayou and its bayou were vastly different from the Island in many respects. The bayou had no sandy beaches, just huge bulkheads that held back the earth where large seafood processing shops draped the water's edge. The buildings jetted out and rested on enormous wooden stilts so boats could dock and unload their haul. Large wooden shrimp boats, their nets hanging from their erect outriggers, cluttered the bayou in an array of color and strength. Wide avenues spiraled through the city, connecting businesses and homes, the roads filling with people and cars who bustled in every direction during the work week. Profit and money dug deep into people's lives here, fueling a need for more. They had electricity and running water, a bus line and train station, and the ease of life this created was undeniable; enviable in fact.

By contrast the Island offered none of the modern things the Bayou did, but it didn't matter because some things you just can't put a price on (at least that's what the islanders told themselves). The islanders cherished simplicity and the soft underlying gentleness of their remote world; and that was as defining for the Island as the waters that surrounded it. There was no frantic pace and no particular place or time to be anywhere. It was peaceful and untangled; a place where birds, and the waves that lapped upon the shores were all that bothered you. The Bayou and the Island were very different, and both communities wanted it that way. They may have all been kinfolk somewhere down the line, but the Island and Bayou agreed on little.

In terms of money the Bayou had it. And they demonstrated the fact by building a ball field without rival, complete with dugouts, a fence that circled the entire field, and bases; real bases! Large picnic tables littered the surroundings, and wooden bleachers stood six rows high for those not wishing to sit on blankets. And to top it off, a beautiful scoreboard that read "Welcome to the Bayou" had been erected in left field for everyone to see. It was a baseball mecca, a place for everyone to gather!

By mid-morning the ball park was nearly full and the women took to cooking and socializing with the kin they hadn't seen in quite some time. Hugs abounded as did kisses and fat little cheeks that got pinched. There was also plenty of food. Every kind of seafood you could imagine was either simmering, boiling, frying, or in a smoker. Every family cooked, and every family shared whatever they conjured. It didn't matter what community you were from, you shared and you were glad for it.

The men from the Bayou toted tubs of ice from the seafood shops that quickly filled with beer. Kids laughed and played as they sent homemade box kites of every color and size high into the air, using fishing rods to raise and lower them. Young ladies made off to themselves and giggled at awkward young boys, as the old timers sat in the shade and told war stories; some speaking of World War One while others talked about the important one, the one between the States. For now the two communities were as close as any family, but once the game started, the line was drawn and alliances went to their teams.

Chapter 15

Car after car arrived at the ballpark, Jake inspecting each one closely as they pulled onto the grounds. He had become impatient as the lot was almost full and there had been no sign of his girl. The food was cooked, the ball players were here, and the morning was giving way to mid-day. The torrent of vehicles had slowed to the occasional straggler, and with what seemed like the last car to arrive, a black Buick rolled in and found a spot beneath a shady oak. The vehicle idled, the windows dark, its occupants invisible. The back door opened and Mira stepped out. She wore a blue and white dress that draped her long lean body to perfection, and her hair, longer than Jake remembered, was pulled tightly to a pony tail.

"Always the tom boy" Jake thought.

Mira scanned the surroundings before turning back to remove an armload of items from the car.

"God she's beautiful," Jake said, unable to take his eyes from her, his heart pounding as he took in every move. She was graceful, sleek… gorgeous.

Mira peeked about expectantly as she said something to a girl that had also stepped from the car. She then pointed in the direction opposite Jake. The girls only made a few steps when two young men, two Bayou boys, cut them off. The boys tried to relieve the girls of the dishes they were holding while smiling and chatting. The amorously stubborn boys were persistent and didn't take the hint until a rather large man moved between Sherry and Mira and put an arm around each, drawing them next to him. The message was unmistakable and the boys apologized as they respectfully stepped aside, though both turned to enjoy the view as the girls sauntered away. Mira smiled as she led the Larson's, Ted's arm now around her and Sherry's waist, toward her parents. The strong manly figure of Mr. Larson was everything her father wasn't, and truth be told she was a bit smitten.

After a long hug with her Mom and Dad, Mira introduced everyone; her parents, Toke, Laura, and her Aunt Rebecca. Ted was quickly swamped in conversation and he and the other men walked a few feet away. Laura and Rebecca returned to the simmering dishes as Bess watched her daughter. Mira scurried about, doing what she could to help, doing her best to live up to that "good daughter" moniker she'd so carefully constructed.

"Mira… that's enough, we've got it under control," Mira's mother said. Bess cupped both of Mira's arms, just above the elbows, and with a warm motherly smile she stared at her daughter in amazement. Her daughter was grown, a woman who made her own decisions, good decisions, decisions she was proud of. "I think there's someone else you may want to see. He's been moping around all morning like a lost puppy. Now go enjoy the day!" Her mom was right, there was in fact someone she not only wanted to see, but desperately needed to see, and her mother didn't need to say it twice.

Mira turned to her right and took a step toward the ball field, and then turned in the opposite direction. She looked out across the picnic tables, studying the faces of those gathered, mindfully discarding man after man from the cheerful crowd until she spotted a beaming face. Her heart began to race. She started toward him, picking up speed with every step, her eyes never moving from his. She sailed into his arms. Enthusiastic little kisses were planted all over his face until she found his lips. And then, with the heat and need from being apart for so long, their mouths met. Jake lifted her feet off the ground, their arms holding on for dear life. As the kiss ended, the two stared into each other's eyes. And the moment, softly and beautifully, warmed their bodies like the morning sun. Mira smiled as Jake remained fascinated. A moment later Mira pushed back, conscious that she wasn't acting much like a lady, and Jake eased her to the ground. She stepped back, their bodies separating as she gripped his hand, pulling him towards something neither could see. And as a gift for the man she dearly loved, she dared not take her eyes from him.

"Is this Jake or Will," a spry voice from behind uttered. Sherry had to be in the middle of everything. "I'm guessing it's Will from the way you two kissed. It'll be interesting to see how you greet that Jake fellow?"

"Very funny," Mira added as she faked a laugh. Mira turned to face Sherry as Jake stood at her back, his arms wrapping around his girl's waist.

"Oh, well," Sherry said, sounding exhausted, "in that case it's good to meet you Jake Cullen. I've heard so much about you."

"Jake, this is Sherry Larson," Mira said, trying her best to be the good hostess while restraining the giddy feeling that had taken her over.

"Good to meet you," Jake said as he eased to Mira's side and gave Sherry a one armed hug.

Sherry's head turned in all directions, "So Jake, where's the girl who pummeled you?"

Jake shot Mira a glance, his lips pressing into a hard thin line. Mira knew the look, pulled from his grip and bolted away in a full sprint. Jake took after her and soon caught up, his arms again wrapping around her, her angelic laughter chorusing through the air. They played for a moment, Jake tickling at her ribs until she demanded he quit. Then, as if they finally remembered Sherry existed, they headed back to Mira's friend.

"You're right Mira," Jake said, deciding to take some revenge of his own. "Sherry is the prettiest girl I've ever seen." Jake's body flinched from the elbow Mira delivered to his ribs. And in return, he hugged her even tighter and smiled with content. Jake jutted a chin toward a crowd of people. "If you must know, she's over there," he said, referring to Mary. "She's over there with her family... the big brute! And hopefully she'll stay over there. I still haven't gotten over the nightmares," he quipped. "And you," now turning his full attention to Mira, "you don't need to be telling people my life story!"

Mira only chuckled and rolled her eyes while giving him a salute as if he were an army captain barking orders.

"So Sherry, what do you think?" Mira asked as a general question about the festivities.

"Mmm, I see why you said you love him so much."

Jake froze while Mira clinched her mouth and balled one fist. There was no movement and no sounds from any of them. To Jake, every emotion he'd ever known collided.

Mira dared not look at Jake as she continued to glare at her friend. "So your Dad seems comfortable," Mira quivered while trying to act unfazed.

"Oh no… I don't think so! Let's go back just a second," Jake said, firmly applying the upper hand he now held. "What's this you said about love?" He gestured a nod toward Sherry who looked as innocent as a new born calf.

"Well, my work here is done. I think I'll go check on Daddy." Sherry hummed an upbeat melody as she disappeared into the crowd.

"Mira,"

"What Jake?" Her eyes were soft, deep. Her body gently swaying before she laid her head against his chest. She listened to his heartbeat as her eyes closed. She shrugged her shoulders as if she were talking to herself, trying to decide what she should do, what she should say. "I love you Jake Cullen."

Mira felt warm to Jake, even as his body burned hot as coal. Her whispers stole his breath as his thoughts slowed, pacing steadily with that one sentence; that one thought. He had finally heard the one thing he craved most in life.

"I love you too. I've always loved you." He had said that to himself a thousand times and always thought that when the day finally came to say it to Mira, he'd be nervous. But he wasn't. It was as he never imagined and his body and mind relaxed. He had spent his whole life loving Mira, and now, well now he had all he ever wanted.

"I know," Mira said softly as she put her arms around him.

Lately, the world seemed crazy, out of sorts with itself. And Mira and Jake needed this moment, this time in their lives where they became joined in spirit and trust. After all, it had been a difficult three months for both. From the time they could first remember they had never been apart for so long, nor had they needed each other so much. The words were now spoken, and it left them knowing that they would make it through this world together.

Chapter 16

Will strolled toward Jake and Mira, his face chipper, his charismatic smile beckoning attention.

"You get lost?" Jake asked.

"Sort of," Will replied with a sheepish grin.

"What do you mean, sort of?" Mira questioned.

Will cut his eyes at the girl that not only held tight to Jake's arm, but also seemed to be crossing an unspoken boundary. "Um… Jake! If it's okay with your mom here, we'll talk later." And with that, boundaries were reestablished.

"That's fine," Mira stated coldly, "you little boys can keep your little secrets. I have other things to take care of." Her voice was as snooty and uppity as she could manage. "Besides, Will… you may want to thank me instead of keeping stuff from me! I brought an extremely sweet friend with me and she is very eligible. And if you don't behave, I won't introduce you."

Jake raised his brows and nodded approvingly.

"And you can quit agreeing so easily Jake Cullen! Now give me a hug," Mira said as she wrapped her arms around Will and squeezed tightly. She smiled prettily and then strolled away.

"Her friend is pretty," Jake uttered in a low voice so that the exiting Mira wouldn't hear. With what just happened between the two, the whole "I love you" thing, he decided it would be unwise to rock the boat.

"That's good," Will said distantly.

"You ok?"

"Yea I'm fine. We'll talk later."

The picnic area rested beneath a dozen or more massive oaks, a haven for those wishing to sit in the shade and relax. Mira and Sherry were giggling, and whispering, and placing bowls and plates on the table when Will and Jake walked up. It was an obvious attempt to get the boys attention and hopefully serve up their own brand of mystery. But it failed, miserably, as Jake's only response was, "this is nice."

Mira shook her head and let the rouse go, figuring it'd take an oak limb to the back of Jake's head for him to catch on. But for Jake, he was in a world he'd always longed to be. He envisioned this being the norm for years to come; two couples, four best friends, and lots of beautiful, wonderful love.

"Well, well, you must be the infamous Will Burton," Sherry said as the two boys walked up. She never took her eyes from Will's as she extended a hand. "I'm the equally infamous Sherry Larson." She liked the first impression; his look, his demeanor. It was the way he smiled more than anything; genuine, glowing, and with a touch of something else hiding beneath.

Will ran his hands though his wavy blonde hair, while the smooth character of his carefree life patiently hid behind long lashes that blinked innocently before his dark brown eyes. He took Sherry's hand. "You'd think one of these two yucks would've introduced us. I swear, all they think about is each other."

"It's because we love each other and we don't keep secrets from the ones we love." Obviously, the snubbing Mira endured earlier had left a mark.

"Love? Boy, I must have been gone for some time. The last time I saw you two you could barely hold hands!" But Will smiled as he spoke, pleased that the two had progressed so far.

The four sat at the furthest table out, the shadows of an oak draping their forms. It was cool enough in the shade that Mira snuggled against Jake for added warmth. The breeze was light and precarious, and wafted with the scent of spicy boiled shrimp and fried oysters. The group told stories as they dined and laughed, and everything seemed natural, fitting together like a puzzle with no missing pieces. Will and Jake drank a few beers as the easy afternoon leisured along like a sailboat with a windward breeze. Jake looked at the faces around the table and smiled. It was the best day he'd ever known and he didn't want it to end.

For Sherry, she enjoyed food she never knew existed, and didn't hesitate to try anything and everything. Her favorite was the flounder stuffed with crab meat and topped with a thin tomato sauce. Mira's Aunt Rebecca had baked it that morning at her home a few blocks away, and it was a delightful dish. She also enjoyed the company at the table and found herself fancying Will, more and more. He was sweet, and untamed. She imagined he had the ability to turn on a dime and that he'd never be satisfied with the ordinary or stay the expected course. A wild gleam hid behind those beautiful eyes, and she wanted to see more. But that wasn't the most pleasant surprise, not even close. As refreshing as the company was, it was her dad that made her the happiest.

Ted Larson sat at the table with Jake and Mira's parents and Rebecca, and Sherry was amazed at how much he laughed and offered conversation without reluctance. She couldn't recall the last time she saw him open up or joke. It was unrestrained and honest. Toke, and Mira's dad Peter, told stories unending, and the group boisterously responded. Her father drank beer as Rebecca, a widow herself, made sure he always had plenty to eat. She peeled steaming shrimp for him, and retrieved a cold drink whenever he ran out.

Sherry knew little of Rebecca, only the few things Mira had told her, but the woman looked like she hadn't had the opportunity to take care of anyone for a long time. She appeared to enjoy it. For that matter, Sherry's dad hadn't had anyone take care of him for a long time either, and "maybe he needed that also."

Game time was approaching and the men hastened their meals. Their full stomachs hindered their desire as the sun gleaned its warmth, temporarily masking the faint signs of fall. An afternoon nap appeared more appropriate than a ball game. But the two-game losing streak the Island was in the midst of made the boys that much more determined. And after having stretched and loosened up, they headed for the field.

Chapter 17

A man in his prime... mmm... doubtful; old... not quite there either; and certainly not a spring chicken. But the team coach as well as the tenth man, now that's who Toke Cullen was. He was there... ready, but not necessarily raring to go if someone was injured or thrown out of the game. Now he used to be one of the best players around, a shortstop that had acrobatic skills and always made the game saving play. But presently in his mid-forties, Toke didn't move as well as he used to and found it difficult to bend all the way over and scoop up grounders. And if he participated too much, the next day was achingly miserable. But he could still manage at playing first base although he prayed the entire time, hoping they wouldn't hit the ball in his direction.

Toke strolled to the pitcher's mound where Nolan Manier, the Bayou's coach, and Jim Cowl, the lucky devil and lone man who would umpire today's game, waited. And it was easy to tell, even before the first pitch was thrown, that Jim had his hands full.

"Well, if it ain't Mr. D.I. Dynamite (the island team was known as DI Dynamite). So you swim over this morning?" Nolan Manier (a besmirching little bastard whom Toke had always known as a besmirching little bastard) said.

Toke almost gave a reply, but decided not to. He thought it best to just let Nolan stew.

Laura had five siblings, four of them taking a liking to Toke while one of them, Nolan, not so much. To Nolan, Toke was beyond flawed as he wasn't from the Bayou, didn't take a shining to steady work, and was born of "disgraceful Irish and Sicilian descent." And all of this left Toke Cullen well below the Manier name. But it wasn't just the Cullen's, because in Nolan's mind no one could ever live up to, "the oldest and most honored family along the coast."

***

The Manier's, the forefathers Avenall and his brother Jean Batiste had been a part of this coast since the beginning of the eighteenth century. The two brothers first sailed into the waters off Dauphin Island with Baptiste and Pierre Le Moyne, who claimed the region in the name of France. The Island, originally named Massacre Island because of the large number of human remains the landing party stumbled upon, was later dubbed Dauphine, for the long line of French Kings.

The Manier's were ship builders, master craftsmen in fact, and after having satisfied their obligation to the Throne, they elected to stay. As a reward for service, King Louis granted them lands. And from these two brothers, Laura and Nolan's ancestors spread throughout the gulf coast. It was even rumored, something Toke probably started, that Nolan had married his first cousin from Pass Christian Mississippi just so he wouldn't blemish the Manier lineage. But that was just a rumor.

Lineage and first cousins aside, to Nolan, Toke's flaws were unacceptable. He wasn't of French descent, he was insulting, he married his sister, and he never did what Nolan told him to do. And above that and on one occasion in particular, Toke went too far.

It was Christmas and the only year in Toke's life that he didn't spend it on the island. He and Laura had recently married and she was terribly homesick. She had been on the island and away from her family for more than three months, and wanted to see her momma. Now she loved Toke, wanted nothing more than to spend the rest of her life with him, but she was just eighteen. Besides, it was Christmas and she wanted nothing more than to be home; to be at home. Toke understood and happily agreed to a trip to the Bayou for the holidays.

The two set out on Christmas Eve, with Toke poling the skiff while singing Christmas carols the entire way. Laura occasionally joined in, but left most of the singing to her husband who was pretty good, especially the ones that the young Bing Crosby crooned.

Toke and Laura were welcomed by Laura's parents and the four siblings who still lived at home, Nolan being the only exception. Nolan was the oldest. He was grown, with a wife and child of his own, and lived on the other side of the Bayou in one of the newer, booming subdivisions. But even he came home for Christmas.

Christmas day, although long, had been mostly enjoyable, and Nolan and Toke were fast becoming friends. They even threw horseshoes earlier and were on the same team more than once. It seemed the Christmas spirit was upon them all as the afternoon settled in and gave way to a cold night. After dinner, Nolan called everyone's attention and removed an object from his pocket. As the custom, Nolan hand carved a decoration for the family tree every year. Most men carved ornaments, and many were quite artful. But for Nolan, well, he wasn't the best whittler although much love had gone into his creation. His entire family looked on, parents and all, and they "oohed and aahed" and fawned all over him for the fine work. He sure was proud of the two little Christmas balls he carved for this occasion, his face beaming and his smile unabashed.

Now Toke didn't mean anything when he walked up, inspected the ornaments, and remarked, "Now that's some fine little Noleyballs." Looking back, he was sincere although it may have come across as condescending.

Nolan was embarrassed by what could only be perceived as crude ornaments. Most men carved intricate ducks, or boats, or every kind of fish there was; while Nolan carved… circles, and not very good ones at that. Nolan's face reddened, no longer beaming with pride, and the misunderstanding escalated as he snatched the ornaments from the tree. After giving Toke a what for and then demanding to Laura that she leave him and that his parents kick his ass out, he stormed from the house, wife and child in tow. But that's Nolan. Like most eldest children he was used to getting his way, used to bullying not only his younger siblings but to some degree, his parents. And although he may have been the oldest, he was the least mature!

Obviously Laura never left Toke and her parents never kicked him out, which didn't sit well with Nolan. Several years passed before he and Toke spoke a single word, and even that remained unfriendly. But after a while egos eased and most of the quaff seemed repaired, at least when Laura was present. In front of her, both managed tolerable pleasantries.

* * *

Nolan glared at Toke while trying to decide if he should punch him, or punch him! He did neither, and instead opened his fat mouth. "When you going to move my sister to civilization?" Nolan began with the same old rhetoric he used every time he saw Toke. "She's not as young as she used to be. And for once in her life she deserves nice things." He paused, "hell, she at least deserves basic things like running water and electricity! And for that matter," Nolan was now stepping onto his high horse, his speech increasing with speed, "the Bayou could even teach you how to be a respectable citizen. I don't think you realize how much the Bayou has grown and how important we are. Why you're probably looking at the next mayor of this town."

Toke squinted into the afternoon sun, the cap on his head lying well left of center. The extended lunch had been filling, in more ways than one, and Toke didn't mind stating his thoughts once his cap began to move like the sun settling to the west. After a long and insightful pause, Toke replied in his usual carefree and drawn out tone. "You know Noley, if I owned both the Bayou and Hell... I'd live in Hell and rent the Bayou out."

Nolan's plump round face reddened, and then turned purple. "Let me tell you what, you little smartass!" A finger was aimed at Toke's chest, which Nolan wasn't much taller than.

"Calm down Nolan," Jim Cowl, the third man on the mound interjected as he put an arm into Nolan's chest to keep him from advancing toward Toke. "What good's it going to do getting your ass beat before the game even starts?"

Nolan's head jerked around, his mouth agape. He stared bitterly at Jim, embarrassed and speechless. Now furious, his face raged to a deeper shade of purple as he muttered a stream of obscenities while stomping toward his team's dugout. He stopped midway and turned to face the two men. "Don't worry Toke, you'll get yours soon enough. And as for you Jim, when I become mayor, I'll take care of you too. I promise you both!"

Jim looked to Toke, his head cocked to one side, his lip curled upward on the right edge. "I think he's upset. We may have pissed him off," he said with a bit of a laugh.

"I always liked you," Toke stated with an emphases on the word "always". "You tell it like it is."

But Nolan's threat wasn't completely lost on Jim, although he hid it well. Jim had reason for concern; after all he was the sheriff in the Bayou and not a local, which meant he had two strikes against him. He had come from Pascagoula Mississippi about five years ago and brought changes along with him, which some of the affluent didn't like. He was fair and honest, and tried his best to help everyone by doing the right thing. He would even go to the Island when rare trouble occurred, even though he had no obligation to do so. It was his decency that shone through and Toke, as well as the rest of the islanders, greatly appreciated him as a man.

In any case, Jim knew Nolan would likely be elected mayor and that he would in fact cause him trouble. But today, well, that didn't seem so important. The sky was high and baseball and food was all that mattered.

"Well Toke, ya'll ready to play," Jim said with half a smile.

"We're ready," Toke said as the two shook hands.

And with that Jim shouted, "Play Ball!"

Chapter 18

The Bayou boys took the field. Victorious in last year's game, they now enjoyed the privilege of being home team. And it was like watching the Dodgers or the Giants, or some other major league team heading out to the green manicured grass on opening day. The boys moved in harmony, had matching uniforms, and looked sharp. Red numbers blazed like fire on their navy blue jerseys and contrasted perfectly with their sparkling white pants. Everyone donned a blue cap with "Bayou" stitched cursively across the front, and they all wore steel cleats. The young men exhibited grace, poise, and confidence as they strutted to their positions.

Most notably, the tall pitcher that hustled to the mound exuded a supreme sureness that would rival a Greek god. As he stepped onto the mound he pulled the brim of his hat down low, and had to tilt his head upwards to look out. His eyes squinted towards home plate, and it only added to the persona. He stood atop and dominated the mound, just as a king would his court, daring anyone to defy the control he wielded.

Toke glanced at the pitcher as he walked to first base and settled in. He scratched his head as he turned his attention to the boys in the dugout. The boys hungered to swing the bat. The crowd became raucous and everyone, and I do mean everyone, was eager to get started.

As the pitcher completed his warm up tosses a heckler from the bleachers yelled insults. "Go home you bums! Go back to that pile of sand and stickers (sand spurs) you call home!"

The voice was irritatingly loud as it blared through Toke's head. He was standing next to the home team's side of the field, way too close for the voice that screeched septic insults. But Toke decided from the beginning that he wouldn't think of turning around. He wouldn't give them the satisfaction of knowing it bothered him, no matter how much it really did.

Fast balls, curve balls, sliders; Toke blinked twice and then rubbed his eyes thinking he even saw a Noleyball or two thrown in there. The Bayou pitcher was better than he remembered from the year before, which was great, and the boy quickly disposed of the first three batters. And as if all three batters striking out weren't irritating enough, after each third strike, the heckler walked to the fence next to Toke and laughed a sinister laugh. Every damn time!

And so, having failed to reach base, the Island boys took the field. And in their own way they too were colorful. In an assortment of tee shirts with numbers scribbled on the back, bare feet, cut off slacks, and a multitude of cap colors, they were independently unique. They weren't nearly as organized as the team they had just replaced in the field, but they had a savvy look about them, a gleam in their eye and confidence in their ability. They moved like graceful deer, gliding about in a remarkable display of athleticism and poise.

Ralph Cullen, a southpaw who could fire a ball like no one from these communities had ever seen, took the mound. He was one of the eleven Cullen kids, and Toke's youngest brother. Twenty years separated the two and the youthful Cullen demonstrated greatness. In fact, he was so good that if only the right person could see him pitch, a scout perhaps, then

82

he would certainly make the majors. He had an unbelievable arm, was incredible with the bat, and could have… should have pushed himself harder. He should have sought out scouts and traveled wherever was needed to tryout in front of the right people. He should have worked harder at being noticed, at being great. But he was a Cullen through and through and never worried about making the majors or anything else. He simply wanted to be like his brother. Having grown up in Toke's footsteps he idolized him, still admired and believed in him, and knew his brother's days in the sun weren't over, not just yet.

Ralph's stride was long and deliberate, his delivery starting from way outside before it circled toward the plate with speed, accuracy, and something that could only be described as punishing hatred. Most batters saw few lefties and none ever saw one as great as Ralph. When he let go of the ball it looked like half an aspirin coming straight at you, forcing most batters to duck as if the ball was going to hit them. He had talent, and it showed as the three batters he faced in the first inning struck out as they swung clumsily at the pitches. And yet, the strikeouts carried another round of shouts from the heckler in the bleachers as the teams changed positions.

"They're all cheaters ump, you better check the pitcher!"

Toke again camped at first base. The little patch of red clay, just outside a white, lime powdered stripe that signified play and foul, was his base camp, his stop on the way to the top of Everest. And although a climb up Everest was frigid and lonely, the quietness would have been welcomed. The steady spew of insults continued, and making matters worse, his cap rested squarely on his head. And he wondered "how in the hell he let that happen!"

Like the amount of alcohol in Toke's body, his resolve to ignore the troublemaker lessened by the moment. The refrain, "remain calm, don't let 'em get to ya," repeated over and over in his head. But he was sober, and he murmured "God bless it," with every irritating shout that was rawer than the last. He was losing control.

Both teams' pitchers dominated the game, their control as constant and unyielding as the obnoxious fan; the game marching forward with spectators living and dying on every pitch. It was a great match up, and a great game.

The bottom of the sixth found the Bayou's Mark Seamon reaching first on a single up the middle. And it was the first base hit Ralph allowed on the day. There were two outs and he now faced the number nine hitter, who hadn't managed a decent swing all day. The first pitch; the batter never offered a swing, and Ralph jumped ahead in the count with one strike. As Ralph poised, ready to deliver the next pitch, he flicked the ball to first. The runner was leaning toward second but recovered and dove safely back to the base. Everyone knew the runner would be on the move with two outs, and Ralph wanted to slow his jump. Ralph reaffirmed his determination to end the inning by striking the batter out and readied again for the pitch.

The ball hid in Ralph's glove. He rolled it around, gripping it just right in his hand. He wound his body as tightly as a top and delivered a pitch to home plate. The batter swung and the ball jumped off the bat and toward right field. The base runner bolted as Jake sprang in the direction of the line drive. Jake was making up ground on the fast moving ball that was tailing away from him and dove at the last second, stretching his entire frame as his arm and glove extended for the ball. The ball rapped against the heel of his glove and deflected toward the fence. Jake's body pounded onto the ground.

Jake peered, shockingly, into his empty glove before jumping to his feet. He chased the ball that rolled against the chain link fence. With his right hand he grabbed the ball, turned and flung it hard and flat toward Will, the second baseman. The ball lined to Will's glove and he in turn heaved it toward home plate. The ball and runner reached the plate at the same time and a collision of bodies and dust erupted. The ump stood over the tangled boys, searching. "Safe! Safe!" he yelled with his arms waving in a crossing motion as he glared at the ball lying on the ground. In all the confusion the batter decided to try and swipe second, but Ralph quickly reached home, picked the ball up and fired it to the base. Will snatched the ball up after one skip and swiped at the approaching runner, easily tagging him out. The score was Islander's-0, Bayou-1.

The Island boys headed to the dugout. Jake paused, his body bent and head down. He put his hands on his knees and rested his weight. He felt sorry for letting the team down and said a few curse words beneath his breath.

"Boy that's a good player in right field. He's the best player we got," rang loudly from the Bayou's bleachers. "Instead of DI Dynamite, you should call yourselves DI Duds!"

Toke looked at his son as the voice from behind scalded him. He couldn't take it anymore and marched toward Laura, Father Malone and Father Young (the Bayou's priest), who were sitting and watching the game together.

"Damn it Malone," Toke ranted, "for God's sake will you please go ask your sister to shut her mouth!"

Laura and the Priests looked at each other in amusement, and that amusement in itself irked Toke to no end.

Father Malone looked back in Toke's direction, "now why you have to be bringing God into this" he said with an Irish lilt. "Besides, I'm not sure the Lord wants to be involved in baseball?" He smiled. "Or tangle with my sister. She's a hard woman, I promise you that."

Toke remained determined, and glared at Malone.

"Fine Toke, but I can't make any promises you know. She has a mind of her own."

Toke got what he wanted and didn't know what else to do. "Bless you Father," was all he could think to say.

"You look a little irritated," Laura finally said as Father Malone strolled off while whistling an Irish melody.

Toke stared at Laura, not amused in the least. "Start your shit why don't you. That's all I need is more aggravation!" He threw up his arms, turned and muttered under his breath as he walked back to the dugout.

The Island managed little as they failed to score in the top of the seventh, the score frozen at 0-1. But it would be okay, at least for a while, as the middle of the seventh couldn't have come at a better point. The "stretch" was about to begin, and it would be a dandy. And once again, winning and losing took a backseat as both communities headed for the shades of the oaks.

Chapter 19

The first person to greet Jake as he walked off the field was Father Malone's sister. She gave him a lengthy hug and apologized. Jake smiled at the nun, whose black coif atop her head stood out in the crowd. He thanked her for the apology, and in a way it made him feel better.

"It's been a good game, win or lose," Mira said to Jake as she walked up from behind.

Jake turned. "Yea, it's been fun, but maybe we can pull it out." He was trying to convince himself he hadn't cost them the game.

Mira frowned. She had always been confident, always known what she wanted. And she didn't take kindly to self-pity. "Damn it Jake, you still have two at bats and their pitcher is tiring. And in case you didn't notice," she drew close and murmured in his ear. "When he throws his fastball," she cut her eyes from side to side to make sure no one was listening, "he always nods his head before his windup. It's the only pitch he does it on. And he always does it; always!" She pushed Jake away, hard, and he stumbled a few steps. "Now quit being such a baby and do something about it!"

Jake was amazed, and stunned… and terribly in love. He couldn't begin to describe his reaction. "Was there no end to what his girl knew?" It made him proud that she was so astute to a game most women simply watched to keep their husbands and boyfriends happy. But more importantly, he was proud that she "slapped him around" and made him stand up straight. "She's just like mom!" he thought, and "you're the best," he added out loud. Unable to hold back, he kissed her on the cheek.

The break lasted for nearly an hour and turned into a seventh inning party. People dined on leftovers from lunch, enjoyed a sack race, and bobbed for apples. It had been fun, but baseball was the business. So the teams headed back to the field and the excitement roared to life.

Chapter 20

The Bayou failed to score in their half of the seventh and the Island team came to the plate with their best hitters due. It was the top of the eight and the score remained 0-1, Bayou's favor.

"Will," Jake said as he nodded for his friend to come close. Jake put an arm around Will's shoulder and told him what Mira had so masterfully noticed. Will nodded as Jake spoke, then left the dugout and walked to the plate.

Will didn't blink. Mesmerized by the pitcher's actions, he studied every move, every pitch thrown during warm-ups. But there had been no telltale sign as the man's head remained steady the entire time. The pitcher scuffed the ground with his cleat, deepening the hole he'd used for leverage throughout the day. He planted his foot and looked to the catcher as Will stepped into the batter's box. The first pitch came roaring by. But his head never bobbed and the ball curved, missing the outside edge of the plate. The ump called it a ball. The same happened for the second pitch and with the same results. As the tall, youthful faced lad drew his glove to his face for the next pitch, his head bobbled ever so slightly. It took a keen eye, but it was there.

Jake could barely contain his excitement as the ball was released and raced across the plate, straight as an arrow.

Will never moved, never even flinched as the ball slammed into the catcher's mitt for a called strike. But he did smile, rather smug in fact, as he knew Mira was right. And he was going to make them pay!

The pitcher readied, his broad shoulders stretching his number 21 jersey to its seams. He stared long and hard at the catcher, and the nod was there. He coiled his body for the pitch.

Will waited, his hands wrenching at the bat, his time having arrived. The roar of the crowd vanished behind intensity and sweat. Will's mind slowed as a light breeze stroked his face. The ball came out fast, furious, and rushed toward the plate; destined for destiny. Will started his motion as soon as the ball left the pitcher's hand, and the wooden bat connected, catching the ball flush. The ball jumped, up and outward, and every person followed suit, their eyes trained on its flight. Everyone in the park was standing, hoping and praying, their mouths ajar.

For Will, there was never any doubt from the time it was struck. He marveled, his eyes smiling as brightly as his mouth. The ball cleared the center field fence easily, and Will rounded the bases as the Island side cheered wildly, his feat instantly becoming that of legends. The entire team greeted him as he crossed home plate, tying the game 1-1. He embraced Jake and they both turned to give Mira a huge smile of thanks with a sly wink coming from Will. Will headed back to the dugout, stopped, took his cap off and bowed before the rabid fans. He disappeared into the dugout and reemerged seconds later to give an encore salute. And the fans ate it up!

Nolan strolled to the mound. He talked for a while to the starting pitcher who abruptly slammed the ball in his coach's hand. Number 21, angry and displeased, then swapped places with the left fielder. It was the right move by the coach as the new pitcher shut the Island team down for the rest of the inning.

Chapter 21

Ralph Cullen was tired. A lot of pitches had rifled from his arm, which was nearly lifeless. But in reality he was all the Island had. He was the only true pitcher on the team and wasn't about to fail them. So he downed a cold beer, and then massaged his aching arm as he made his way to the hill. His pitching arm dangled by his side, storing the energy it would soon need. He wiped his brow with his glove before motioning to the ump that he didn't need any warm-up pitches. It was the bottom half of the eighth inning, and he was as ready as ever.

The first batter dinged a soft blooper that the third baseman gloved. And although it was an out, Ralph realized they were getting close to his timing. His arm lacked the earlier zip, and he now relied on his curve and changeup to keep them off balance. But without the threat of a lively fastball, it was becoming more and more difficult.

The next batter was old faithful, good ole number 21. He was a big boy and the plate at his feet appeared small. He clinched his jaw tightly; his eyes filled with emotion. Will had tied the game on one swing and then flaunted his triumph, embarrassing him to no end. He was determined to correct the mistake and stuff it down their throats. So with the first pitch, he swung and hit a line drive to the left field fence. It should have been an easy double, but oddly enough the batter held up at first. The momentum had swung to the Bayou's side, and both teams knew it.

The Bayou's best hitter was next, and he walked to the plate. He was hitless on the day, but his cocky attitude showed as he tapped the bat against his cleats and stared at the laboring Ralph. Toke called time before heading onto the field to talk with his brother.

"Bring me a beer will ya?" Ralph hollered to his approaching brother.

"Me too," the umpire added.

Toke circled back, and thinking it a good idea he retrieved three beers. On the way back out, he passes Jim a beer before continuing to the mound.

"You ok?" Toke asked Ralph, his head hitching upwards as if to ask the same question. He handed his brother the bottle. The entire group of infielders closed in on the conversation. Jake grabbed Toke's beer and popped it open. He took a long satisfying swig. Toke gulped as he stared at the frosty sheen glistening on the bottle's side. He extended a hand, but Jake didn't hand it back to his Dad. Instead, he passed it to Will.

"I've got enough to finish. Besides, if I get by this guy the rest will be easy." Ralph was doing everything he could to keep his teammates confident. He then downed his ice cold beer with one long drink.

"I could put Lionel in for ya," a distracted Toke added as his eyes followed what should have been his beer. The bottle moved to the hands of another boy as Toke's mouth filled with saliva. He took a deep gulp.

"You might as well forfeit if you're going to do that. Lionel couldn't get Mom out," Ralph said in Toke's direction, although Toke's gaze was fixed on the once again traveling beer.

"Hey, I'm standing right here!" Lionel chimed.

"At least he can get it across the plate, it's just not much on it," Toke said without turning his head from Pate, who was now swigging from the bottle that dripped with condensation.

"Cut it out!" Lionel whined. He was not enjoying the conversation.

"That lob pitch he has is pretty devastating," Ralph added with a chuckle.

"Look, if ya'll don't quit talking about me, I'm leaving!" Lionel was clearly irritated and to the point of walking off the field.

"Calm down. I was trying to see if Ralph had any fight left in him," Toke said as he glanced briefly from Jimmy, who now held the prize, to see if Lionel had bought into the lie. "Good talk boys. Give 'em hell Ralph and let's see what happens." Toke clapped his hands once as he hurried through the last of the pep talk now that the beer had finally made its way back to him. "Damn it!"

The disappointment showed on Toke's face as he turned the empty bottle on its end. "Damn it!" With the revelation of an empty beer staring him in the face, he grudgingly decided to continue the talk. He looked at everyone standing in the circle and shook his head as he thought. Finally he spoke. "Keep everything low and don't give 'em a chance to hit it out. The boys behind you will make the plays," he said to Ralph. "Just don't try to do it by yourself. You know they can play." Toke talked fast, his eyes moving from the players to the empty bottle. "Damn it!"

"Sounds good, let's do it fellas," Ralph said with a sense of rejuvenation as he handed Toke his empty bottle.

The group broke and went back to their positions.

"Damn it!" Toke said over and over as he headed off the field.

Jim caught up with Toke, to hand him the empty bottle. Toke looked at Jim's face, then to the bottle, and again up to Jim's smiling face. Toke's expression was deliberate and he had no intention of taking the bottle.

"Fine Toke, I'll take care of it myself. You don't have to be so sensitive you know."

Toke mumbled as he continued off the field and into the dugout. He went straight to the wash tub, ducked his hand into the icy water, and pulled out a cold beer.

Both crowds came back to life. The runner stepped away from first as Ralph delivered the ball home. The batter made contact and lined a grounder toward short. Jimmy Gardner, the shortstop, gobbled it up and relayed it to second. Will gloved the ball, stepped on second and then flung the ball toward first. As he let go of the ball the runner slid into him, his spikes high and intentionally aimed at Will. The metal teeth on the shoes tore into Will's shin, shredding the skin as the force knocked him backward. Will rolled once, sprang to his feet, and dove headlong into number 21.

Punches flew and both benches cleared, followed by the stands, followed by those at the picnic tables who weren't even watching.

"My goodness," Laura said as she shook her head, "every damn year!" She watched the melee, next to Father Malone who was throwing his own phantom punches. She wasn't sure who he would have been punching had he been out there, but she believed it would have been Toke.

For those that rushed onto the field, both men and women, some threw punches as others tried to break it up. Toke forced his way to Will and number 21, and tried to pull them apart. As he tugged at the boys, someone grabbed him from behind and inner-locked their arms with his. The person bound Toke's arms behind his back and spun his body around. Nolan was staring Toke in the face, his arm cocked and fist balled.

Chapter 22

Nolan's face said it all. His grin showed his teeth, while his head nodded approvingly. His eyes were inflamed, demon like, his lips slivering like a snake, becoming thin and long and menacing. And Toke knew without doubt that Nolan was the devil who would one day become the mayor of Hell. Toke was helpless, his struggle to escape hopeless. So he awaited the punch and hoped Laura wasn't watching. He didn't want her to see him bloodied, perhaps his nose broken. But mostly, he didn't want her to see the real Nolan. He knew she loved her brother more than he was worth.

It was vicious! As Nolan's arm started forward, his aim dead and true, the motion was violently halted. Nolan's short stubby body spun in the opposite direction, his forehead meeting with Ted Larson's chin. His eyes bulged at the sight of the large man…… with the large balled fist. It was in reality, nothing more than a short jab, a love tap from a very strong man. But Nolan's chin thought otherwise. His jaw cracked as his eyes rolled back in his head and his body snaked to the ground. He lay in a lifeless heap.

Toke gawked at the display of strength as his arms were released and the man who had been holding them backed away. Toke didn't react to being freed; instead, he looked at

Ted. "Thanks Ted, and remind me to never piss you off," he said with a huge smile.

The "bang," the sound of the gunshot that pierced the air was enormous, deafening! And before anyone could react, another shot rang out. Silence and confusion gripped the crowd. Their ears rang, their hearts pounded, and their eyes searched for the shooter as much as the one that had been shot.

Chapter 23

Jim Cowl held his 45 caliber pistol in one hand, a catcher's mask in the other, and one of them was aimed at the crowd. "Now that I have everyone's attention," he said as he raised his voice so no one would mistake what he had to say. "As much fun as a family brawl is, we have a game to finish and more beer that needs drinking. And if that ain't good enough for ya, and you don't go back to where you belong, the next time I use this gun it won't be pointed at the sky!"

They all knew Jim, the type of man he was, and the lengths he'd go to restore order. So they gathered themselves, wiped at the red clay and dust, then trailed off to their respective places.

No longer the lawman, Jim continued with the orders as the field slowly cleared. "Both runners are out and the eighth inning is over. And 21 is ejected from the game!" He used his thumb, as if he were hitching a ride, to signify the player had been tossed from the game.

Jim moved next to Ted and Toke and Nolan, and watched as the field finished clearing. "Now let's finish this game," Jim barked.

Ted and Toke started toward the dugout, but Nolan never moved; he couldn't. He was out like a light, his crumpled body lying ten feet from the pitcher's mound. Ted sidestepped

Nolan's body while Toke made a point to step directly over him, as if he were nothing more than a base pad. And as he did, he used the toe of his shoe to purposely kick clay in Nolan's direction.

Jim was amused. "And for God's sake, would someone drag Nolan's ass off the field," he hollered to the Bayou's bench as he laughed.

Doctor Meyer looked at the unsteady Nolan, and diagnosed him as being… groggy. He then made his way to the Island's dugout and examined Will's leg. "He'll be ok. And if he can play, it won't bother anything."

Will tried to stand and walk, but couldn't. The muscle that covered his shin bone had swollen and stiffened, and turned blackish in color. He plopped onto the bench, aggravated and discouraged.

"You did good," Toke said as he knelt next to Will. "That was a great double play. I'll go to first and Lionel can move to second. We'll finish this up with a win." He patted the boy on the shoulder.

Will nodded in understanding, but didn't say a word.

Pate Carter led off the top of the ninth. He was patient and ran the count full before managing a walk. The relief pitcher for the Bayou was struggling to throw strikes, and the Island was intent on ending it; now! Toke, in the dugout instead of coaching first, gave the signal. And it was the mother of all signals. He acted as if he were poking himself in the eyes with his fingers. He then flapped his arms like a chicken before pulling at his hair like a crazy person. Yea, only Toke Cullen could come up with these signals. But it was clear as crystal; Pate was ordered to swipe second.

Pate walked several feet from first base, his body leaning, his cleats digging into the hard clay. The pitcher cut his eyes to the runner and glared at him, daring him to run. The pitcher turned toward home and the motion was short, deliberate. His arm started toward home plate where the batter, Lionel, waited. Pate dashed for second as soon as the pitcher's arm began its motion. Lionel watched as the ball swooshed by. The catcher received the ball and immediately flung it toward second base, his mask contorting on his head from the violent eruption of the throw. Pate slid, the heel of his shoe edging out the glove that swiped at his foot. He was safe! Pate stood up and dusted the clay off as the Island's bench jumped to their feet, cheering and clapping with the fans.

Lionel again hovered over the plate and quickly gained a second strike. Pate remained at second. The next pitch hung, unable to cut and turn as intended, begging the batter to swing. Lionel didn't disappoint and the ball lined like a frozen rope. The shortstop dove, barely gloving the ball. His body hit the ground and the ball trickled across the clay in front of him. He quickly regained his feet, picked the ball up, and held it in his hand. He was unable to throw any of the runners out, but he did keep Pate from advancing. There were now two men on base and no outs, and momentum, the often capricious and elusive intangible that decides ball games, had now swung back to the Island.

Normally it would be Will's turn to bat. But he sat, his injury robbing him of this rare chance to be the hero yet again. So tenth man time had arrived, and the tenth man hadn't swung a bat in months. Toke thought seriously about his chances and didn't like them. So he called timeout and brought the team together, including the two base runners. After a short conversation, Pate and Lionel headed back to their bases and the team went back to the bench. Toke walked to the plate as

Jimmy Clark stood on deck, swinging furiously in an attempt to loosen up.

Toke took the first two pitches, both being strikes, and watched as the third swished by, narrowly missing inside for a called ball. He believed it should have been called a strike, and couldn't help but think he had a little help from the ump.

The pitcher was gaining confidence against the elderly batter and fired his fourth pitch in, low and tight. Toke squared his body and bunted a soft dribbler down third. The third baseman charged, picked up the ball and decided first was his only option. He flung the ball and the aged legs of Toke were thrown out by a step. But he had done his job as runners now rested at second and third with only one out. Toke remained at first, but outside the white line and again as a coach.

It was now Jimmy's turn to be the hero. He walked to the plate, his hands wringing the bat handle like a wet dish towel, his time in the sun having finally arrived.

The Bayou team called timeout and huddled at the mound. After a long while they broke, and headed back to their positions. Jimmy readied himself for the pitch, but it never came. They intentionally walked him. The Bayou had decided to load the bases and hopefully turn an inning ending double play. And Jake was the batter they were going to do it against.

Jake let out a huge sigh as he walked to the batter's box. He glared for any kind of hole on the infield, just somewhere to squeeze the ball through. But the Bayou players had moved back to double play depth, and Jake knew it'd be difficult to get a ball through the infield. As he stared toward first base, at the man standing just outside the white line, his resolve steeled. "This one's for you, Dad."

The Bayou pitcher didn't waste time. He quickly wound and threw a perfect strike. He was throwing hard and fast, and there seemed to be more on the ball than Jake noticed from the bench. Jake readied himself again.

As the ball flew from the pitcher's hand and towards Jake and the plate, Pate leapt from third base. At the same time, Jake's right hand slid up the handle of the bat. The squeeze was on! Jake bunted the ball along the first base line as the other base runners bolted. "Oh shit," the first baseman said as he tried to react.

"Oh shit," a dizzied Nolan said as he couldn't believe what was happening.

"Oh shit," Mira said…well, she thought it.

And "oh shit" was right.

Jake raced toward first as Pate hustled to home. The pitcher reached the ball just as Jake was about to pass. Jake slammed to a halt as the pitcher scooped up the ball and took a swipe at his waist. He missed. With no other choices, he flicked the ball to home plate but was too late. Pate had already slid safely for the go ahead run. The bases remained loaded, though most notably the lead now belonged to the islander's. And for the tenth man, the coach, Toke had counted on the Bayou walking Jimmy and called the squeeze play perfectly.

The Island team went on to score three more runs in the top of the ninth. And although Ralph struggled with his control in the last half of the inning, the boys played great defense and shut the Bayou out the rest of the way. It was a much needed win for the Island, and bragging rights would be theirs for a whole year. More importantly, however, the festivities were just beginning.

Chapter 24

The game concluded, the Gorman's left, and they were the only family from the Island to do so. They didn't say goodbye, or thank you, or we had a good time… or anything. They simply packed up their belongings and walked away. It seemed odd to most as it was late in the day and would soon be dark, but all the same, a milestone had been established. Everyone figured the Gorman's had taken a huge step by coming over in the first place, and believed that by this time next year the peculiar family may be inclined to stay for the night. As for the rest of the crowd, a few families from the Bayou also left early, though their reasons for parting were related to dim views of the way everyone celebrated, more than anything.

Fried mullet, grits, buttered galettes (a homemade, poor man's flatbread that's cooked in an iron skillet on top of a stove or fire), and cold beer and scuppernong wine greeted the evening. A handful of men took to frying fish while the rest gathered by a radio to listen to the World Series, which was in the second inning. The Series between the New York Yankees and Brooklyn Dodgers was tied at one game each, with the current game being played at Ebbets Field in Brooklyn New York. And it would become much like the game the two communities had just played, a pitchers' duel.

The Series moved along and drinking and eating continued at the same pace. The afternoon eased gracefully into night and conversations got bolder and louder at the same time. The Yankees ended up winning the game though it didn't matter to those listening. They merely enjoyed the game and imagined themselves in such a setting.

Will struggled with his bum leg, although it felt better now that he had dispatched several beers. He sat next to Jake and the two did what guys do. They relived the game they just played, gushing over the heroics that had occurred. But girls aren't guys and Mira and Sherry sat, restlessly, and across from the boys. And they made sure the fellows understood they weren't content. They sipped as ladies often do, drummed the tips of their fingers on the table, rolled their eyes from time to time, and waited. And what they waited for was the group of men that listened to the game. Because everyone knew nothing happened until the game ended.

"God I hope that damn game doesn't go into extra innings," Mira said.

Jake cocked a brow as he looked at Mira. "You liked watching our game," he said as a point of emphasis.

"Who told you that?"

Jake drew his chin in and wrinkled his face. He was about to delve into the mystery a bit more when finally, and mercifully, the men broke from the stranglehold the radio held over them.

"You think the music will start now?" Mira asked, her mood instantly changing, her face aglow with anticipation.

"Should," Jake's said as his eyes went soft. "Why, do you want to dance?" The answer was obvious, but he longed to hear the sweet reply.

"I do, and I will, whether Jake Cullen dances with me or not." Mira batted her sultry eyes.

"Well who am I going to dance with?" Sherry begged.

"You got Will," Mira conceded with a nod of her head in Will's direction.

Jake jumped in. "Yea, it's either Will and his bum leg, or old man Harmon who lost a leg in the war. But hey, I'd give the old man a try; he's only seventy!"

"You up to it?" Sherry asked the injured Will.

"Heck yea. This little scratch couldn't keep me down. Besides, I could dance circles around the old man… and his wooden leg!" Although still seated, Will made a motion with his arms as if he were dancing an Irish jig. The beer had miraculously healed his injured…… mind.

Jake, Will, Mira and Sherry looked on as musicians gathered with an array of instruments that included guitars, fiddles, a mandolin and harmonica, and soon began playing beneath a sparse array of street lamps. As soon as the instruments were tuned and the rhythm and sound of music echoed in the night, people gathered to dance. And these folks certainly knew how to dance.

"Come on Jake," Mira said as she took his hand and led him to the grass where a crowd moved about.

Sherry and Will looked on, clapping their hands in rhythm as the first song played to an end. But as the next song, a slower song began, Will took her hand and the two joined the crowd. Will was a better dancer than Jake, even with the bum leg, but no one cared. They were young and happy, and for now there was nothing but the moment.

For more than an hour the band played fast songs, country songs, a strange bit of twang sounding jazz, and even some gospel, before taking a break. Mira and Sherry were enjoying the night, the company, and the wine, and both had moved slightly past tipsy. Jake and Will had long since been light headed and weren't about to slow up as they continued to fuel their intoxicating state.

"I can't wait to show you the Island tomorrow," Mira directed at Sherry who sat across from her.

Sherry's eyes sparkled, the tip of her nose a glowing red. "Let's go tonight," She replied.

Jake may have been drunk, and could have even been out of his mind hammered, but some things he just wouldn't do. He'd crossed the channel many times and knew from recent experience that he'd never venture without his Dad, especially at night. "No, that ain't gonna happen," he said.

"He's right, it's way too dangerous," Mira added.

"You bunch of scaredy-cats. Come on," Sherry said as she tugged at Will's arm. "I'll get Will to take me. You'll take me, won't you Will?"

Will shook his head vigorously even though Sherry didn't noticed.

Thankfully the band began again and Sherry soon forgot about going to the Island. Mira and Jake headed back to the grass while Sherry tried without success to get Will to his feet.

"I can't do it," Will said.

Sherry's body moved to the music as she gazed at the crowd moving in all directions. The crowd laughed and whooped and continually swapped dance partners. It was a party on the grass and she longed to be in the middle of it. "It's ok, I'll just sit here with you and we can talk." She picked up her cup of wine, which was nearly full, and downed the entire contents.

"Go cut in on Jake. He may have two left feet but he's ok."

"Are you sure? I could dance with my Dad instead." But she'd have had to cut in on that dance as well since Rebecca continued to monopolize his time. Besides, having glimpsed her Dad's face, which was beaming ear to ear, she knew he was having fun. And she would never do anything to spoil it.

"Just one quick dance and I'll be right back," Sherry said as she grasped Will's hand and squeezed. "Keep an eye on me!" She added as she staggered off.

"May I cut in?" Sherry asked. Oddly though, the request was directed to Jake.

The alcohol was indulging, and the freedom of choice was easy for the taking. And Sherry, the most liberal of them all, made a show stopping choice. She quickly grabbed Mira's hand and the two began moving to the song. Jake's eyes widened as his girl, danced with a girl! The girls moved slowly, closely, Sherry's hips meeting with Mira's. Mira's hands were low on Sherry's back, and Sherry's hands held to Mira's hips, feeling the movement, guiding her along.

Jake had never seen two girls dance, well, at least not two adult girls. And he didn't know what to think or do. So he stood there, like some kind of idiot, balancing on the thin limb he had been forced to climb out on.

Will had kept close tabs on Sherry from the time she left him. And he couldn't believe his eyes. Even the pain in his leg disappeared as he climbed atop the picnic table for a better view.

Mira enjoyed the intoxication of life, youth, and alcohol that spread from her mind to her body and then to her spirit.

And it was the first time in her life she had been truly free; daring in fact. She moved her right arm up Sherry's back and put it around the girl's neck. She pulled her close, their noses nearly touching, their panting breaths coming together as one. Mira giggled while Sherry remained focused and in control. Sherry cut her eyes to Jake, watching his reaction as she too enjoyed the seduction. Jake glared back at Sherry, upon the woman that could easily unravel his dreams. A sliver of a smile formed on Sherry's face. She knew she held Jake's life in her hands, that she had won the prize. And she would soon make sure he understood his fate.

Will watched, and then gulped at the vivid display.

Mira whirled and seized the frozen Jake by the shirt, his top button popping off. Jake, suddenly in the middle of the two, wasn't sure that was where he wanted to be. The three swirled in movement, making a dizzying circle, before Mira kissed him. The kiss was long and hard. And when Mira released her mouth from Jake's, her lips were a plumb red. It could have been a dream, the alcohol forming a dizzying haze. Jake's head was swimming as Mira turned her face from his and Sherry brought her lips to meet Mira's. The kiss wasn't brief, nor did it linger. But there it was, bold and impassioned, and eagerly accepted.

Jake shook his head, fearful of what just happened, terrified that Mira enjoyed it. The girls looked as if they were about to kiss again... wanting to kiss again, when the song ended and the three, panting with emotion and sweat, stared at each other. For Jake, he couldn't understand any of this. And he wasn't sure of the boundaries they'd just crossed or what could be done, if anything needed to be done.

As they separated, Jake glared at Mira even though she was oblivious to his fears. She never turned to acknowledge him, or acted like she cared how he felt. The truth was...... he was scared. In fact, he'd never been so scared in his life.

"Wow," Will said as the three rejoined the table.

"That was a damn good dance," Mira said as she wiped moisture from her cheeks and fluttered her hands in front of her face in an attempt to cool down.

"Sorry, but I did ask for permission to cut in," Sherry said to Will. She then snatched the beer from his hand and took a long drink. As she finished the contents of the bottle she again cut her eyes to Jake, and it was more than just a passing glance.

Jake never uttered a word.

Chapter 25

The evening, the party and festivities was winding down. And most everyone packed up and headed home. Laura had danced the night away and was rather drunk, she thought, although she'd only consumed four beers. She leaned against the end of a picnic table as Toke and Nolan staggered towards her. She shook her head with confusion, now convinced that she was very drunk. Toke's hat rested on his left ear, mystically suspended like a high-wire trapeze artist on a thin wire. The two drank from whisky bottles, a free arm wrapped around the other. Fondness was written in their smiles.

"I love you Laura," Toke said as both men stumbled to the right.

"I love you too," Nolan slurred.

"And I love both of you," Laura said somewhat cynically.

"And I love Nolan, he's like one of my sisters," Toke said emphatically.

"Ohhh, that's nice," Nolan said. He appeared on the verge of crying.

Laura may have been drunk, but she knew when Toke was full of it. "Toke, behave yourself!"

"Hey!" Nolan hastily intervened as he shook a finger at his sister. "You're a lucky woman to have such a won… won… won… good husband!" He patted a hand against Toke's chest. "Ole Toke here's a fine soul. The man's a saint. A saint I tell ya!"

Toke nodded in agreement, his chest bowing, his finger also jetting out and wagging at Laura. "I am a saint," he boldly added just before Laura slapped his finger away. Toke followed the tip of his finger with his eyes as if it were the gold watch of a hypnotist, his body tilting off center. He staggered a step before Nolan was able to grab hold and prop him up.

"You watch it there missy," Nolan said to Laura, "you need… you need…… What does she need?" he asked Toke.

Toke shrugged.

"That's right," Nolan said. "You need my boy to be treated with respect. He's a saint, mind you." He turned to Toke, "If she gives you any trouble… any trouble at all, you let me know." Nolan pointed a thumb at himself as he closed an eye so he could focus on one of the Toke's in front of him. Nolan let go of Toke, straightened his back, and turned to walk away. He hesitated, looked back at Laura and again shook his finger disapprovingly. Then, like a sack of potatoes, he thudded to the ground.

Toke looked at Nolan, then to his wife. "He's a good one, but he sure spends a lot of time on the ground."

Laura didn't find any of it funny and knew from experience that Toke could take things too far. It was all a game to him, a game he usually won and a game where everyone else suffered. "Toke, you make sure he gets home okay."

Toke smiled. "I will." His voice became mellow. "And I'll tell ya why."

"It's not because you like him as much as you're letting on, that's for sure."

"Oh, I'm hurt," Toke said as if being accused of something he didn't do. He held his finger to his lips and leaned to Laura's ear and whispered, "Don't tell anyone, but I'll do it because I'm a Saint!"

Laura laughed sharply, "Yea, if you're a saint then I'm the Pope!" She giggled as Toke smooched close and the two kissed. God she loved the way he kissed! She enjoyed it more than anything in this world.

"You still my girl?" Toke asked.

"Always," she replied as she put her arms around his waist and held tightly.

Toke stole another kiss before making his way off, grabbing Nolan by the collar and dragging him into the dark.

One last song played as Laura finished a glass of water. She was ready to head to Nolan's house, where they had made plans to spend the night. She searched for Toke and the last she saw of him he was in a race. He was walking on his hands, competing against another man, and they were in the middle of a group of men with dollar bills waving in the air. She knew he'd be a while, and Laura decided to walk home in the dark.

Chapter 26

Laura awoke in a comfortable bed, though alone. The sun shone brightly through the window and a beautiful Sunday morning beckoned. "Too bad," she thought, "that her head didn't feel the same way." Her eyes ached from the inside out and her head pounded from the night before. She wondered how anyone could do this regularly and worried about Toke. He had had plenty to drink, and obviously never made it to bed. She quickly bathed, greatly enjoying the running water, and put on a pretty blue dress she'd brought for Sunday Mass. She eased into the living room, not wishing to disturb anyone, and looked at Jake lying on the couch. He must have been dreaming because he tossed and turned, almost angrily, little sounds emanating from his slumber.

Laura made her way to the screen door and silently slipped out. Her eyes squinted before the sunny day and it only aggravated her condition. She stopped on the large porch, which circled the entire perimeter of the house, and looked at her husband who sat on its edge, next to the steps. Toke had one leg on the ground, the other stretched out across the gray planks, and his back against a post. He whittled on a block of cedar, and had nearly completed a replica of a four inch long fishing boat. He looked up at Laura and held the boat out for approval, just as a child would his first report card.

Toke held an innocent expression that made Laura take notice. He may not have known this, but with that one look, that one gesture of naivety, Laura was completely helpless. She was his forever, and glad of it. "Maybe he is a Saint," she thought as her eyes watered.

"Toke, you been to bed," she asked as she wiped the tears from the corners of her eyes.

"Yea, I slept a while." He continued carving as they talked. "You feel ok? You had quite a bit to drink."

She was completely stunned. Her head beat like a drum, and yet Toke had drank everything in sight and seemed perfectly fine; perhaps better than fine. "I'm good," she lied. "What about you?"

"It's a beautiful day and I feel great!"

"I don't know how you do it Toke Cullen. You always amaze me." If nothing else she admired his strengths, no matter what they were.

The admiration didn't last long though. It was interrupted and buried deep within when she looked to Toke's right. Nolan lay sprawled out on the deck, not ten feet away from where Toke sat, in nothing but a woman's nightgown and bloomers. His face was caked with every shade of makeup known to women, with red lip stick smeared across his mouth and from ear to ear. She shook her head and turned back to Toke, who had stopped whittling and directed his full attention to her. He was expectant, almost smiling as if he was proud of what he had done.

Laura didn't say a word as she waited for a response, tapping her left shoe against the deck.

"You only asked that I get him home safely." He paused and gave Laura a wink. "Besides, all that Saint talk last night... it may not have been a true description of me." Toke raised a brow and a smug little smirk zipped across his face.

Laura was unable to suppress a laugh as she walked down the steps and to her husband. She laid her body against his and pressed her face into his neck. "Don't ever leave me," she whispered.

Toke felt his heart tug as he welled up inside, "I won't, I promise. Besides, you're my girl!"

And with that, everything was okay.

Chapter 27

Laura soaked up the morning as she walked along the barren sidewalk toward St. Michael's Church. St. Michael's sat on the bayou's west bank and welcomed everyone with a large statue of Jesus, standing with open arms, receiving everyone unto the Lord. She remembered going to service here, up until she and Toke married, and how a hundred or more people would cram into the church for mass and communion. She had always been amazed at people's faith and their commitment to Christ, and took comfort in knowing she wasn't alone when it came to worshipping the Lord.

Father Malone was moving slowly when Laura eyed him up ahead. "Father," Laura said while still at a distance. There was no reply as the man turned the corner onto Main Street, and set out on the final leg to the church. Laura stepped faster and soon caught her prey. "Good morning Father," she blurted from behind.

The Priest jumped, startled, and then stopped before turning around. His pale face appraised the intruder, who struggled to catch her breath. He covered his eyes with his right hand, as if it were a visor, and squinted at the outline before him. "Don't be too cheerful Laura," he said gingerly. "It may be the Lord's Day... but it can pass quietly."

Laura frowned. The two paced on and the church soon came into view.

"Where is that husband of yours?" the priest asked softly.

"He's at Nolan's," she replied with reservation. Father Malone had never asked about Toke, and this set off several alarms in her head.

"Well I hope he's hung over and didn't get a wink of sleep. He made sure I kept my vow of poverty last night," he said as he turned again to look at Laura. He could barely open his eyes.

Laura showed no emotion though she silently fumed.

"And God bless him," the priest gently concluded.

"You're absolutely right Father, God did bless him. In fact, he told me this morning that he was going to give all his winnings to the Church."

The priest smiled.

"To Saint Michael's!"

It was like some sort of magic trick as the smile on the priest's face disappeared, and then reappeared on Laura's.

The Church only a few paces away, as was its bell that chimed in what should have been a heavenly tune. Today, however, it was relentless and the cause of immeasurable pain.

"Well, at least I don't have to give Mass. I can simply be a member of the flock and watch Father Young," Father Malone thought as he feigned a smile in Laura's direction. He placed his fingers to his temples and rubbed.

The two headed inside the white sided sanctum, and there were only three other people in attendance. "So much for people's dedication to faith," Laura muttered as she and the priest dipped the tips of their fingers into a bowl of Holy Water. They both followed with a sign of the cross.

There were plenty of seats open, and Laura and Malone moved to the front pew and sat, awaiting the start of Mass. Nine o'clock passed and Father Young had not shown. Father Malone sat with his eyes closed and his head resting on his fingertips, as if he were in deep thought. Laura hadn't decided if he were praying or sleeping, and thought it best to leave him be. An altar boy stood next to the altar and waited for someone to give him direction.

Finally, at half past nine, Laura nudged the Priest next to her.

"Amen," Malone said in a startled motion. He instinctively made a sign of the cross with his right hand.

"I guess it's up to you Father," Laura said, her head nodding toward the vacant altar.

"The Lord's work is never done," he said grudgingly. He struggled to his feet and moved slowly toward the altar. His movements may have been slow but he hastily made his way through a few psalms, including the First Letter of Paul to the Corinthians, and went straight to communion. As he blessed the wine the altar boy rang the Sanctus bells, enthusiastically! Father Malone winced. His shoulders cringed and his head pulsed with pain. He looked at the lad whose face demonstrated an eager need to please. The priest said nothing. He continued Mass, and blessed the Body of Christ. The boy again did the same with the bells and the Priest could only endure what he had brought upon himself. Father Malone persevered through blood shot eyes and gave communion to all four of the congregation, and the altar boy.

After Mass, Laura headed back to Nolan's. She felt better than she did earlier, and enjoyed the soft breeze that swirled around her. She stopped a few times along the way, looking in the windows of shops along Main Street. Everything was closed but Laura still enjoyed her imaginary shopping spree. She was almost to Nolan's when she heard yelling and cursing, and realized their welcome had come to an end. Undoubtedly Nolan had discovered his state, and once again he wasn't happy with the Cullen clan.

Chapter 28

It looked like the Spanish Armada, but of really tiny boats, heading across the open bay toward Dauphin Island. For the most part it had been a nice venture to the Bayou, though getting home was now the goal. The cloudless sky and light wind that kicked up from the south warmed the day and returned moisture back into the air. Ted Larson sat at the bow of Peter Lea's skiff, the gentle breeze at his face, the salt air filling his lungs. He watched in amazement as Peter, standing on the stern, poled the boat along. It was a smooth and fluid movement, and the strokes from the short man seemed long and lean. The boat sliced through the water as straight as an arrow, and moved faster than Ted thought possible. Mira and Sherry sat together on a middle bench, while Bess rested near Peter's feet.

The bay sparkled, the clear blue water beckoning the kinship between man and sea. It was undeniable. The sensation and joy of being connected to the world was never so prominent, so significant, and Ted became overwhelmed. He sighed as he breathed in the smell of salt and heard the call of seagulls overhead. And the day itself, all the fragmented pieces that came together, conjured thoughts of a life he no longer had. He shook his head as he tried to clear the cobwebs that filled it.

Peter the tour guide pointed out various places and small spits of land and marshes. Some of the noted locations were dotted with hundreds of pelicans, others littered with oysters and conchs, while many were white sandy beaches. Peter stoked the imagination as he talked about the islands that cluttered the bay, and the deep passes that had been carved by tides and hurricanes. And he talked of Dauphin Island and the area's rich and long history. The stories rose up and gave life and purpose to all that surrounded them. Land and sea and south Alabama were as beautiful and amazing as they were meant to be.

"Peter, you mind if I give it a try?" Ted asked as he motioned to the pole.

Peter, like most Islanders, was relaxed and deliberate and easy going. He also recognized opportunity, and if he had the chance to sit and rest while someone else did the work, then he wouldn't object. "Sure can, besides it's easier than it looks," he offered as added enticement.

"I would think so," Ted replied with confidence.

Bess moved to the bow as Ted stumbled toward Peter. The skiff rocked as the large man lumbered from bow to stern, took the rod from Peter, and stepped onto the flat decked stern as Peter stepped down.

"Need any pointers?" Peter asked.

"No, I've been studying you and I think I got it." And with that, he thrust the pole into the sand and pushed. The boat jerked forward and Ted nearly stumbled overboard as everyone else fell backwards.

"A little strong there," Peter mused.

"I'll get it, just give me a minute."

The boat started moving forward, quite nicely, but soon turned to the east. It continued turning further as Ted labored to correct the direction. But he over-corrected and made it worse. They were now headed back, toward the Bayou, as other boats in the armada skirted past them.

"Ya'll leave something in the Bayou?" Toke yelled as his skiff slipped past.

Ted gritted his teeth. He reasserted his focus and used brute strength in an attempt to manipulate the tiny craft. But the skiff didn't respond as he had hoped, and a moment later the boat was circling, like buzzards. Ted said nothing as he fought with a boat that had a mind of its own. After a few more dizzying circles, he started making progress. And finally the boat headed in the general direction of the Island. They zigzagged for a short distance, Ted panting and sweating profusely. But he continued, his skill increasing, and the boat begin to cut smoothly through the light chop of waves. He figured he now had the hang of it as he caught up with the rest of the boats.

As the skiff moved forward, Ted jabbed the pole into the bottom. And he realized it felt different from the sand he'd been dealing with. The pole stuck, in the mud, and Ted's body jerked backwards. He clung to the lodged pole as the boat continued on, without him. He danced on his toes like a ballerina that had pranced onto stage. The boat slowed and finally stopped, though Ted remained terribly out of position. Like a clamp, his hands held the rod with a death grip, the tips of his toes needling along the edge of the wooden stern. He balanced for a while, afraid that if he took a single breath he'd go into the water. After hanging on for what seemed like forever, he worked the skiff back beneath his feet and pulled the pole from the mud. He regained his firm stance, but not his composure.

Peter, as well as men from the boats that surrounded them, enjoyed the spectacle and laughed boisterously.

Miraculously Ted remained dry as he paused for a long breath. "You could have helped me," he panted.

"You looked like you were doing ok," Peter said with a friendly smile.

"Ok?" Ted said as he wiped sweat from his brow. "You know I wasn't ok!"

"Yea," Peter said as he shrugged his shoulders and chuckled.

"And how come you didn't tell me about that mud stuff?"

"I offered to give you pointers. Anyway, you're good for a first timer. Twice you almost went in, but you hung on. You'll be a local in no time!"

Ted's tussle with the pole had been amusing, but the time for joking was over. Peter had been watching a distant ship in the channel ahead and gestured to Ted. "How 'bout I spell you for a second?" Ted gave no argument, and the men swapped places. A huge ocean going barge moved through the channel, which was still a fair distance from them. Ted and Sherry gawked at the size of the vessel that moved rapidly, and with quiet grace. It was hundreds of feet long and very tall.

"That's the reason we don't cross at night," Mira said to Sherry.

"I'm glad we didn't. Something like that could crush you!"

"Ted, you may want to sit down," Peter said from the flat decked stern, the pole balancing in his hands like a tightrope walker. All of the skiffs had gathered, and all of them nudged their bows to the southwest. They waited.

"The ship's past us, what are we waiting for?" Ted asked.

"Ted, you may want to sit down," Peter said again.

Ted didn't sit, and almost immediately a wave from the massive ship's wake rolled across the boat's bottom. The bow went up and then down, as the stern followed suit. Ted stumbled back, then forward, reaching for anything to hold onto but only finding air. He'd almost recovered when another wave of about the same size followed. It was no use fighting the inevitable. He staggered and again reached for whatever was close. He found Peter's shirt and clung to it.

"Not me!" Peter shouted as the boat rocked and he dropped the pole onto the deck.

Ted, the much larger man, gripped Peter's cotton shirt and flung him around like a toy doll that had no choice but to obey. Ted's motions dictated their movement and it was only a question of when. Both went over the side and into the depths.

"Dad!" Sherry screamed as she jumped to her feet.

"They'll be fine" Mira said calmly.

And before Sherry could respond, her Dad popped up.

Ted stood in water up to his chin, and wiped the wetness from his face.

Peter popped up next to him, like a cork bobbing in a creek. He stared at the man with contempt, refusing to wipe away the soaked hair that hung like a curtain across his eyes. "You know, there was no reason to take me in with you," Peter said. He spit salt water with each word. "You could have been a man about it and just went over the side by yourself."

The men in the other skiffs laughed. It was a funny moment, but also inviting, and Jake sailed from the side of his Dad's boat. Jimmy Clark and his Dad did the same, and the water filled with men swimming about.

"They aren't going to have all the fun," Mira said. She too jumped in as Sherry and girls from the other boats followed. The wives were all that were left aboard.

"Give me a beer and get in," Toke said with a bright smile as he swam next to their skiff and held on to the side. Laura didn't hesitate.

The swim was nice as the water remained seasonably warm. The group frolicked for almost an hour, before deciding to meet on a small island just north of Dauphin Island. After climbing into their skiffs, they all joined in and sang lively songs as they traveled to Little Dauphin. They beached their boats and set out to prepare a meal. The men immediately scattered and soon returned with washtubs filled with oysters, crabs, and fish. And Ted was amazed that they could accumulate food so quickly. Fires were made and skillets and pots began cooking. It was a nice place for lunch and the conversation was fun and friendly.

Sherry looked across the bay that separated them and Dauphin Island, and was awestruck. "It's beautiful," she said to Mira. "I see why you love it so much."

"There's plenty more to see," Mira commented with enormous pride.

"I'm sure there is… but this is breathtaking." Sherry reached out and took hold of Mira's hand, and squeezed.

There was no disguising the island's beauty, or the islanders' poverty. No one made excuses or attempted to mask their lack of wealth; as it would be impossible to do. And both Ted and Sherry were taken aback has they made their way into the village. They could easily see how much poorer they were than the Bayou, or for that matter most any other place either had ever seen. Houses couldn't even be consider average, nor well built. There were no cars, no pavements, no sidewalks; nothing that could be considered modern. And it could have easily been 1841 instead of 1941. But it was okay. In fact, it was better than okay. Ted felt a spiritual ease, a connection to an unspoiled, untainted world. It was inviting and quiet and filled with love. He paused along one of the many paths that crisscrossed through the village and watched those ahead of him. Everyone carried something; pots, bags, a blanket… perhaps everything they owned was being toted home. It left him overwhelmed, and his eyes welled up with tears. He didn't know why, he couldn't put a finger on what tugged at his emotions. And he didn't know if he was happy or sad. "They have nothing," he thought as he shook his head. "They took me and my daughter in, no questions asked. And they don't even know us." He wiped the corners of his eyes.

Ted had regained something valuable over the last few days, something he'd lost years ago. And he wished his wife were here. She would love the beauty and calmness the island places in your soul. She would have loved the dancing last night, and Laura and Bess and…… Rebecca. "No," he said to himself as he became embarrassed when he thought about Rebecca and how he allowed her to dote over him. He shook his head again, this time vowing to his wife that he'd never allow that to happen again. He had his daughter, who had turned into a lovely woman, who had made a wonderful friend in Mira, and who had brought him to know these incredible people. And that was enough. It'd have to be enough! "God knows I miss you, and I love you," he said as he looked to the bright blue sky. "I'll always love you."

Chapter 29

For the center of the universe, Mr. Willy's bar was as
unassuming a place as there ever could be. And Mr. Willy,
William Burton Senior, wanted it that way. He wanted
something that reflected the island, the lifestyle, the…. who
am I kidding; he simply didn't have the money to do any
better. And so, the bar was open, in an uncluttered and
unrestrained way, serving as a refuge for the locals. It also
functioned as the cultural center of the entertainment and
business district. For that matter, the bar, and a small general
store owned by Henry Cullen, summed up the extent of said
business district, and in a way it was Main Street, or in the
Island's case; Main Path.

Willy's bar was airy and rustic, and comfortable and
inviting, as well as all the other idioms used to describe a local
hole in the wall. The inside walls were planked with cypress
that had aged and turned white over the years. Fishing
equipment, from generations of collecting, hung as trophies on
the walls. And solid oak flooring, cut from local trees, was
heavily scuffed and in need of refinishing. But rustic or not, it
did have some nice and solely unique qualities. It had a
beautiful bar made of laminated cedar that showed every grain
and hue of the colorful wood. And outside, a covered deck
draped the water's edge, a place where the beauty of the bay

and the unimaginable sunsets and ecology of south Alabama came to life in stunning fashion.

Willy's was nicely open and airy, with screened windows and doors. And though it just so happened to be resting in a magnificent setting, Mr. Willy is what made the place wonderful. Every night, every single night at closing time, there was always a plea of "wanting to stay and drink another round!" And Mr. Willy was the one doing the begging! He always drank a beer with the regulars and tolerated those who could only pay a little at a time or "next week." He was a good man who truly loved people.

Ted Larson began his first and only night on the Island, sitting with Peter Lea on Mr. Willy's back deck. The moon was but a sliver of itself as stars scattered with sparkling delight. The breeze was relaxed and offered little more than a few unorganized puffs. Faint waves lapped against the deck's pilings. It was a spot that on a clear night you could look out across the bay and watch ships move effortlessly by, peaceful and silent. The night was soft and easy, and would have been perfect if not for the mosquitos that had ventured from the surrounding marshes. Apparently they had worked up an appetite, and were thick enough to walk across. After a short time of swatting and scratching, Ted and Peter decided to move inside and take up residence behind the protective screens.

The two had just sat at one of the tables scattered about the room, when Julius Carter swung the front door open, and he and his son Pate marched through. The elder Carter demonstrated an angry disposition, and took a growling look around the room. Julius rarely came to the bar, and his appearance caused a stir. "We need to get Jim Cowl!" Julius was in a huff and directed at anyone who would listen.

"What you need the Sheriff for?" Mr. Willy asked.

"Some bastard stole parts from my engine and took nearly half my fuel. We know who they are and I ain't gonna stand for it!" Muscles in his jaw flexed while veins bulged from his neck.

Julius Carter owned a 6 cylinder Caterpillar diesel engine, and it was important not only to him but the rest of the island as well. The engine operated a sawmill, and if you wanted to build or repair a house or skiff on the Island, Julius was the man to see. He and his son made a good living with the backyard mill, and it showed in the things they owned. Among their possessions was the only motor boat and generator on the island, as well as a 1939 Plymouth that they kept across the bay at Cedar Point. And although it wasn't unusual to see him riled up, he also had a good side that was, if nothing else, decent. He treated people fairly for his products and even allowed the generator to be used during special occasions, such as the movie showings at the church.

"How do you know who it was?" Mr. Willy asked.

"It was those damn Gorman's," Julius replied.

"You saw em'?"

"Didn't have to, they were the only ones here when my things went missing. I cut some boards for Saul's skiff the evening before the ball game, and when we returned today, the stuff was gone. Besides, I've known the rest of you my entire life. Hell, we're kin."

"Someone could have come to the Island, took the things and left," Ted Larson intervened from his seat.

There were two mistakes with his statement. First, he clearly didn't understand the difficulties that would exclude anyone from going to so much trouble for a few parts. And secondly, he was an outsider, and his opinion, in the eyes of the Julius Carter's of the Island, didn't matter a hill of sand.

Julius turned his head and tilted it to one side as he looked at Ted, who sat at the table with Peter. He stared peculiarly. His eyes nearly crossed from the long, fixed, angry glare. He turned back to Mr. Willy and pointed a thumb in Ted's direction. "Who the hell is that," he asked.

"He was at the game yesterday. Knocked Nolan clean out," Peter said rather loudly from his seat next to Ted. "Didn't you see the fight?"

"We're thinking about making him a local tomorrow," Toke added from the lone barstool at the bar. The bar sported only one stool, which Mr. Willy reserved for his favorite customer. As for the rest of the patrons that wished to belly up, they had to literally belly.

Julius shook his head as if they were crazy. He started again. "We need to get Jim and arrest those bastards!"

"I'm just saying it could have been someone from off the Island. When I met the Gorman's they didn't seem like thieves. Loners maybe, and without question dirty; but not thieves. Besides, what would they do with that kind of stuff? Do they have a diesel engine also?" Ted was incredulous as he spoke.

Julius turned and stared again, this time his eyes did cross as his anger moved beyond control. He replied. "Seriously, who the hell is he?" Julius was not in a playful mood.

"He's a newcomer," Mr. Willy answered.

"I get it, he's a newcomer," Julius said with irritation.

"He's going to be a local…." Toke began but was halted by the hand that Julius held up.

"Yea!" Julius said gruffly, his hand remaining in the air. He paused and thought about that. "Yea… a newcomer… now that makes sense! Maybe I should be looking at an outsider." He placed emphases on the word "outsider."

Ted smiled at the accusation being leveled.

"Might want to be careful there Jules," Toke said with a rhythm that sounded a lot like a wedding toast. He raised his glass as he rested on his stool, his hat tilting somewhat left of center. "The initiation process is about halfway over and soon enough he'll have all the local perks. God bless 'em." And with that, everyone lifted a glass and muttered "here, here."

Julius looked at the locals as if they were loco. "A local? Ha! And be careful of what?" Julius' head nodded in Ted's direction, "Him? I'm as mad as a hornet and he'd better stay out of my way! It's gonna take a mighty big man to whip my ass!" He was clearly flustered and looking for a fight.

Ted stood and extended his broad and hulking frame.

Julius blinked and his body contracted from the sight of such a large human being. "Yea, a mighty big man…… but it won't take him long," he said under his breath as Ted started toward him.

Julius bowed his chest and pushed the sleeves of his shirt up; readying himself for whatever the behemoth would throw at him. But Ted casually walked past, pausing and looking him in the eye. He then went and stood at the bar next to Toke, who held a rather gleeful expression.

Toke said, "Don't worry Jules; Ted was with us the entire time. So luckily you won't have to beat a confession out of him." Everyone in the room laughed.

Julius paused for a long time, before continuing. "Well someone stole my things and they didn't come all the way to the Island and then leave. They could have found that stuff a lot easier in Mobile. And Toke, quit calling me Jules."

Everyone knew Julius was right. The Gorman's were the only ones who returned home after the game, and it pointed to them. Julius went about the room, visiting with individuals as he continued with his indignation to anyone who would listen and give a sympathetic ear. But he didn't bother with the newcomer.

"Speaking of locals, how long your family been here?" Ted asked Toke as he took a sip of room temperature beer. The bar only offered room temperature beer and whiskey straight up, no ice. His face puckered as he was unaccustomed to hot beer.

"About sixty years. But that's nothing compared to Laura's bunch. One of the first Manier's to arrive in this country is buried just down the road."

"No one knows that for sure," Peter interjected after coming over from his table.

"I know," Toke said, "because Willy and I saw his coffin. Ain't that right Willy?"

Willy was wiping a glass with a rag and only blinked his eyes, never saying a word.

"So you saw Jean Batiste's grave?" Peter said with doubt.

"Yea, we ran across it when we buried," Toke stopped and thought for a moment. "Willy, was it when we buried Uncle Buddy or when we buried his leg?"

Willy shrugged and continued what he was doing.

"You're absolutely right Willy, it was his leg," Toke confirmed.

"Uncle Buddy's leg?" Ted asked with hesitation.

"Poor Uncle Buddy," Peter said as he shook his head.

"Yea, Uncle Buddy. He got hit by a stingray barb in the calf. And the infection got so bad they had to amputate just above the knee. Me and Willy were told to get rid of the leg, so we wrapped it up, made a little coffin...... You know, that was a mighty fine coffin I built. I made it out of that old cedar tree that fell on the Shell Mounds. Hey Willy, remember that coffin I made and the little handles I carved in the side so pallbearers could properly tote it?"

Willy smiled broadly, almost laughing.

Toke continued. "Then Willy scribbled, 'Here lies Uncle Buddy's Leg, the right one', across the top. We figured if someone ever dug Uncle Buddy's leg up, they'd want to know it was the right one. Then we took it to the cemetery. We buried it along the tree line so we wouldn't disturb anyone. Dead people don't like being disturbed."

"Buried his leg in a coffin?" Ted murmured with a chuckle.

"I sure miss Uncle Buddy's leg," Toke said, his eyes wondering to the ceiling. "It seems like only yesterday it was walking around this very bar. You know, I remember when we buried Uncle Buddy and we tried to get him as close as we could to his leg. That man sure loved his leg." Toke spoke as if he were talking about a man and his love for a wife, or child.

Ted laughed out loud as he pictured Uncle Buddy's leg walking around the bar.

"Quit being silly and let's hear about Jean Batiste," Peter said impatiently.

"Oh yea," Toke said, bringing his eyes back in line with the men. "But first I need another beer."

Willy quickly provided what had been asked.

"You got this one," Toke said while looking at Ted.

Ted nodded in agreement.

"Well then, let me see now. That's right. We dug a hole, and at about three feet we hit Jean Batiste's grave."

"How do you know it was his?" Ted asked.

Toke paled. He acted like the question was not only absurd, but that the answer was obvious. He looked at Willy who lifted his brows in response, and smiled. "You're always right," Toke said to Willy. He turned back to Ted. "It had 'Jean Batiste Manier' written across the wood. Looked like oak. Don't you think it was oak, Willy?"

"I don't believe this," Peter said. "I believe this is another one of those crazy concocted stories you always come up with. And if it isn't, then take us to it."

Toke considered that for a moment. "We could do that but we'd have to dig up that big oak that sits in the corner. I think the grave was under that oak, or maybe the one across from it. You know Uncle Buddy lies about halfway between the two and if Willy can't recall for sure, we may need to dig up both."

"I knew you were full of bull," Peter said.

Toke appeared hurt and took up a defense. "It's not just my story. Didn't you hear what Willy had to say?"

They all turned to Willy who wiped at the counter. As the men stared, Willy glanced over at Toke and said the only thing he could. "You heard me gentlemen. And I stand behind every word I said."

Toke looked at his friend and smiled from ear to ear.

Chapter 30

The living room of Will's home was warm and stuffy; the windows open though no measure of a breeze existed. Will sat on the couch, his injured leg propped on a pillow, Sherry resting alongside. She periodically checked the bandage on his shin and acted like the nurse she would one day be. Jake and Mira stood nearby as a kerosene lamp glowed in the corner, struggling on a night when the moon offered little assistance.

"Let's go for a walk on the beach," Sherry finally said, disturbing the sullen mood filled the room.

"I don't think I can," Will replied.

"Well, we can just go to the beach and sit, come on." Sherry wasn't accustomed to begging, she'd always gotten everything she ever wanted by simply asking. But she had few chances in life to sit on a romantic beach at night, whether by herself or in the company of a cute guy. And she wasn't about to let this opportunity pass her by.

"Come on you big sissy," Mira added.

"Why don't the three of us go and let em' rest his leg," Jake said as he tried to fend off the pack and take some of the pressure off his buddy. Mira cut her eyes at Jake. She didn't understand why he would say something like that. Jake could feel her gaze, and all of a sudden the room had gone past stuffy. It was downright suffocating.

"Sherry, why don't you and I go to the beach and leave these two here," Mira said with a matter-of-fact resolve.

Jake knew the tone all too well and decided Will would have to fend for himself.

"No... if Will can't go, then I'll stay here too. I really don't mind. Besides, the two of you need some time together." Sherry acted magnanimous although she was clearly not happy with the outcome of tonight's events. But she had done this before, realizing long ago that small pacifying concessions often paid bigger dividends. It was a form of negotiating without having to beg.

The room was quiet and motionless as the flicker of the lamp's wick morphed shadows on the walls. Five minutes passed before Will relented. "You're not gonna see much, it's so dark out." He paused and then added, "But I'll go and sit on the beach."

Sherry and Mira were both excited, and Mira's excitement excited Jake.

A squall drifted to the east, miles out in the gulf, as the four made their way to the cool sand of the beach and took up residence, only a few feet from the water. Lightning flashed furiously, streaking across the sky like an ever changing spider web. There were no sounds, no thunder, only beauty. In brief moments, as each flash erupted, one could see the outlines, the silhouettes of the large billowing clouds.

"It's magnificent," Sherry said as her eyes glistened, reflecting each stroke that raced across the sky. She knelt next to Will who had plopped down on the beach, while Jake and Mira scurried about, gathering dried driftwood. Jake dug a hole in the sand, and made a fire. The four sat around it. There were a few mosquitoes out, but with the gulf side of the Island void of marshes, it was bearable.

Mira sat between Jake's legs, her body leaning to his. She used the nail of her right index finger to draw imaginary hearts and write words of love on Jake's pant leg. Sherry edged next to Will and took hold of his hand. She waited for the return acknowledgement, but it never came. She didn't know what had happened, but Will had been distant since they arrived on the Island. He wasn't the same as last night, the night of the dance, and it was obvious something wasn't right. They may just as well been brother and sister; judging by the way he cupped her hand. "Maybe he's just terribly shy and the alcohol last night made him braver than he really is?" It was all Sherry could think to comfort herself.

"I really hate to go back to school tomorrow," Sherry said.

Jake didn't want to hear anything about school, about leaving. He wanted to tell Sherry to just shut up and mind her own business. He wanted to tell her that he was the one who loved Mira, that he was her best friend, and that the episode last night with the kiss was completely across the line. In truth he wanted Sherry to leave. But he said nothing as he slid an arm around Mira's waist and pulled her even closer.

"You're awful quiet Will," Mira asked as she rubbed Jake's legs with her hands.

"Just enjoying the night air, relaxing... you know."

"Y'all don't realize how good you have it. This night, on this beach..." Sherry couldn't find any other words to describe what she felt. She took a huge breath that was followed by a long sigh.

"It's so dark you can't see a thing other than that dang squall." Will's tone confirmed the self-pitying role he'd established.

"God, just listen to those waves; its music, beautiful sweet music. Have y'all heard it so much that you take it for granted?" Sherry looked at the three for a response, the fire crackling in rhythm with the lonesome night, and lighting their stunned faces.

"Your right, you're absolutely right," Mira finally said as she too accepted the night and the wonderment they'd been given. "We are lucky!"

The fire faded, just as the evening seemed to be doing. And Jake reluctantly moved from Mira so he could throw more wood on the fire. The air was warm for October, a perfect night for those in love, if you were in love.

"Let's go for a walk," Mira said as she rose to her feet. She took Jake's hand and the two sauntered into the enveloping dark, the blackness making them invisible. Soon, distant giggles were all that remained of the two.

"They're good together," Sherry said to Will.

"He loves her more than his own breaths. He's loved her since they were kids and everyone knew it except her. Well, if she did know she didn't let on about it. I really don't think he could live without her." Will stared in the direction the two had headed even though he could no longer see them.

"That kind of love must be a great comfort."

"I guess," Will said halfheartedly.

"What about you Mr. Burton, ever been in love?"

Will didn't say anything. He just shook his head as he turned to the gulf and the mesmerizing display of lights.

Jake and Mira were finally alone, though no more than a few hundred feet from the others. But they might as well have been the only two on the planet, as they held each other with a longing, their passion for each other building. Jake had never touched Mira in any way other than as a gentleman, but as they kissed and their bodies melded, his hands found their way to her rear. He squeezed with both hands and Mira pulled her lips away from his. Her eyebrows arched as she stared into his eyes. She smiled devilishly, her breaths coming rapidly.

Jake was about to remove his hands when Mira moved even closer, pressing hard against his body. Her hips moved seductively, beautifully. She kissed his neck and her hands roamed, searching and caressing his body. Jake felt as if he would explode! Groans from deep down began to rise in a continuous and mounting rhythm. Hands frantically searched, exploring and caressing places that neither had ever known. And delight, beautiful and sweet delight swept through the air as desire shared a brief moment with love.

"What was that," Jake asked in a startled tone as his lips jerked away from Mira's.

Mira cupped her hands around his face and pulled his mouth back to hers. "Just a cow or goat or something," she said in between tiny pleasurable kisses.

"No, there ain't no animals on the beach this time of night. I think someone's watching us."

The fact that someone may be watching them garnered Mira's attention. Tiny hairs stood on the back of her neck as they both looked back at the fire that lit Will and Sherry's forms. It wasn't them; they were still sitting next to each other, though no longer holding hands. Another sound, something like a snapping branch came from behind Jake and Mira. The two spun, both becoming rigid and frozen. It was definitely something out there. They squinted into the black and Jake thought, with the help of a flash of lightning, that he saw someone move near a small sand dune. "See that," he asked Mira as he pointed. His voice was but a whisper as he stepped forward.

Mira moved to Jake's backside as if she knew he would protect her, no matter what. "I didn't see anything, but I don't like it. Come on Jake, let's go back to the others." She tugged at the back of his shirt as she spoke.

"I want to see who it is. Probably Pate," he said with disgust. "That perverted little bastard!"

"Don't Jake, it's not important," she pleaded. "Let's go back to the fire with the others."

Jake turned and looked at Mira. He could feel her fear as much as he could see it on her face. Relenting, he nodded in approval and they headed back. Jake wasn't happy about the retreat, and kept a constant vigil into the darkness they'd just left behind.

"You two have a good time?" Sherry asked coyly.

"We did, until we heard something," Mira responded.

"What'd you hear?" Will asked as he struggled to his feet and began scanning the vast darkness.

"I believe I heard someone, and I think I saw them moving about," Jake added.

"Pate?" Will asked hopefully.

"Maybe, probably," Jake said.

"We don't know that it was Pate or anyone else. It could have been a cow that got loose or something," Mira said in an attempt to keep the two boys near.

"Wanna go find who it was?" Will asked as he moved several feet from the group so the light from the fire would no longer blind him.

"If your leg was better we would," Jake said as he glanced at Mira. He decided to let it go.

Will stood for a while, searching the night for any signs. He couldn't believe his luck and what was happening. He prayed it was Pate, although he knew it wasn't. He had his own idea of who was out there, and it made him cringe.

The rest of the night was uneasy as the four sat and chatted before making their way home in the early morning hours. Jake was distracted for the rest of the night as he struggled with the fact that someone was out there watching them. It pissed him off that he and Mira were disturbed, especially at the time they were disturbed, and he wasn't going to let it slide.

Chapter 31

Early Monday morning, Julius hadn't yet cooled off and eagerly awaited the Sheriff. He had asked his son Pate, and Jimmy Clark to head to the Bayou and fetch Jim Cowl. The boys set out before daylight and were able to convince Jim to come to the Island. Now, Julius stood at the shore as the white motor boat puttered toward the beach. The boat nosed itself onto the sand and Jimmy threw an anchor onto shore. Jim jumped off and shook hands with Julius. Julius spoke quickly, filling Jim in on what had happened. The two started inland as a crowd was coming towards them. Peter Lea, Mira, Jake, and the Larson's were walking toward the beach.

"Headed back," Jim asked Ted politely.

"Yea, the girls have class and I need to get back to the farm." Ted reached out and shook Jim's hand. He then nodded politely at Julius. In the short time Ted had known Jim, he'd grown to respect him. You could tell when a man was a standup guy, and there was little doubt that Jim fit the bill.

Jake wasn't into pleasantries this morning and didn't waste time. He made a beeline for Pate who jumped from the skiff and was dragging the anchor further onto shore.

"Think your cute, don't you," spewed from Jake's mouth as he reached for and grabbed Pate's collar.

Pate let the anchor rope go and jerked away, ripping the seams of his shirt. His collar hung to the side as he in turn grabbed at Jake's shirt. Neither boy minded a brawl, especially when the other was the opponent. "Who the hell are you to grab my shirt," Pate muttered in anger as the two drew in tightly, their noses nearly touching.

"I'm the guy that's going to beat the shit out of your perverted ass. Then we'll see how much of a kick you get out of spying on people." Jake was fuming.

It was an ugly scene and Jimmy tried his best to break the two up, but couldn't.

"What the hell you talking about, you ignorant bastard," Pate asked angrily.

"Get off it! We know you were watching us last night. You came to the beach for no other reason," Jake said as a flicker of spit landed on Pate's cheek.

"That's the thing about you Cullen. You always think you're this perfect person in your own perfect little world, who knows everything. Well I'm here to tell you you're not. And you're not always right! You're pathetic and stupid and you need to get over yourself. I wasn't anywhere near the beach last night, Mr. Smartass." Pate was now mad for a reason other than it just being the normal feud with Jake. Jake's accusations ripped at his manhood, and in front of his Dad and others.

Jake glared eye to eye with Pate as he dismissed the thought that he may be wrong. He knew Pate was lying. He just needed to get it out of him, which he'd be glad to do.

Ted grabbed the two boys, and with little effort plucked them up and pulled them apart, one in each hand. "He's right Jake. Pate was at the bar last night. There's no way he could have been on the beach." Ted's tone was solemn. In truth, he liked Jake and wanted him to be right. But the boy wasn't.

Jake was speechless. He looked around and everyone was staring in disapproval. Even Mira held an expression he'd never before seen, and he didn't like it. And truth be told, he liked himself even less at this point. Jake's face reddened and then grimaced with embarrassment and shame. He took in a deep breath before turning to walk away.

"Jake," Mira called after him.

Jake stopped halfway up the path, turned and raised his hand in a half-wave to say goodbye. He then continued on, toward home.

"Take care, and let me know when you get back this way. We'll go have a beer with Nolan," Jim said with a chuckle to Ted.

The groups parted and Jim and Julius began walking toward the village. Ted offered a slight laugh before continuing to the skiff with the rest of his party.

Will Burton stood at what amounted to an intersection on the Island. Jake walked up the palmetto lined sandy path from the beach, stopped in front of Will and said, "It wasn't Pate." He then turned right and continued on, heading down the path that led home.

Will heard what Jake said, but didn't offer a reply. As early as last night he was sure it wasn't Pate. He retrained his focus as the Sheriff came into sight, and wondered why he had come to the Island. Julius and Jim continued toward him, all the while talking, and then turned left at the spot he stood. He decided to follow along.

Chapter 32

Will trailed Jim and Julius, and struggled to keep pace on a road that seemed equal parts oyster shells, dirt, sand, and tree roots. When the men finally stopped, Will leaned against a fence post that had no fencing attached. But the break was welcomed as he rested his sore leg.

Jim and Julius made their way to the Gorman's front door, and it wasn't a casual approach. Jim had come a long way on this morning, and he meant business. Will took in the view of the scanty dwelling, the two men, and... Mary. He spotted her at the back of the house, hanging clothes on a line. His interest peaked when Mary dropped a clean shirt onto the ground just as she saw the men approaching. And from her reaction there was never any doubt that she was mixed up in whatever was going on.

Mary felt dizzy. She knew Jim was the Sheriff, and panic ran throughout her body. Breathing became difficult as she searched for cover. The wall of the house was her only protection, the only thing blocking them from her. Yard hens pecked and scratched at the ground around her feet as she flattened her back to the wall. She peeked around the corner as the men made their way to the front door and knocked.

Mary's mind raced and her heart pounded as she struggled to keep her composure. She dropped the remaining shirts onto the dirt. They'd to be washed again, but she didn't care. She was too terrified to move, to even breathe. Her thoughts turned to running away. She could never face the Sheriff, or anyone, and explain all that's happened.

Will watched Mary move next to the wall. His eyes switched back and forth between her and the two at the front door. "Why is the Sheriff at their house and why is she hiding?" He shook his head as he tried to piece it together.

The front door opened and Leo Gorman stepped out. He never offered a hand or any kind of warm reception. But he did give them the Gorman stare. "Sheriff," Leo said in his ruff voice as he wiped his hands with a rag. The unshaven man with disheveled hair appeared to be wearing clothes that hadn't been taken off in days. He was unreasonably dirty and didn't seem to care.

"Leo, there's something I need to ask you. Julius had some things stolen and I was wondering if you knew anything about them?" Jim spoke in a tone that left no doubt he was in charge and that he wanted straight answers from the start. He wasn't a man to mince words and his directness was often mistaken as rude and cocky.

"It sounds to me like he needs to take better care of his things." Leo didn't say it in a tone that sounded like a smartass; he said it as if Julius was at fault for his own things being stolen.

Not amused, Jim added, "Let's cut through it then. Julius had some things taken and you and your family were the only ones on the island when they went missing. He's looking for his things and I want answers so I can get back to my job."

"What kind of things," Leo asked as if he'd stolen plenty during his days and wanted to know what he needed to confess to.

"Engine parts and fuel. They were taken sometime after the game on Saturday night or early Sunday morning," Jim explained. "Now I'm not accusing you of anything, but everyone knows you and your family were the only ones to head home after the game."

Mary was silent, the rear of the house separating her and the verdict she so feared. She struggled to hear the men talking, and could only make out muffled voices. It didn't really matter though as she was positive they were talking about her. She just knew it! And it was only a matter of time before they came for her. Anxiety spread through her as if an earthquake rattled every bone in her body. Frightened, she only wanted to find a dark place that she could crawl into and never be seen again. She sensed her life draining from her body with each passing second, and there was nothing she could do to stop it.

"Why are you hiding?" Will's voice startled Mary as she spun to look at him.

"You need to leave Will," she said with nervousness in her voice and fear etched upon her face.

"Why are you hiding?" he questioned again.

Mary again peeked around the edge of the house to make sure no one was coming for her, at least not yet. "Please Will, just go. I don't want my Paw to see you. It'd be terrible if he sees you talking to me."

"Well, he's busy and looks like he will be for a while." Will was irritated and wanted an answer. "So you might as well tell me."

Mary stared at him as her eyes swelled with tears. She didn't cry, but a person couldn't have come any closer without doing so. Her head shook in silent thought, imagining all the possibilities and consequences of her actions. She covered both eyes with the palms of her hands, and turned away from Will and toward the gray planks of the house. Disgust pushed her to the point of being ill, and she didn't want Will to see the putrid her life had become. She leaned her forehead against the wood while still holding tightly to her eyes. For now, this was the only dark place she could find.

There wasn't much to think about, Mary finally realized. Even though it was Will, the only person in her entire life she'd ever trusted, she felt it'd be impossible to tell him. She didn't think she could bear it. She had promised herself too many times that she would never utter the heinous things she had done. And so, in the end, she said the only thing she could. "I can't. And you need to leave." Her voice was faint, unconvincing.

Will stared at the back of Mary's head. He wanted answers… well, he did want answers, but more importantly he wanted to help. Ever since the day Mary beat the hell out of Jake, the two had been stealing small moments together; a kiss here and there, a brief afternoon together when her brother and father were off fishing. And for whatever crazy reason, he liked her. Perhaps he loved her. He didn't know for sure the answer to the question about love, but he could think of nothing other than helping her, of protecting her. "Whatever it is, just let me know and I'll help you. Just be honest with me."

"Just leave." Her voice had transcended from meek, to cold and void of emotion.

Will relented to the fact that he wouldn't get an answer to his question, so he tried a different approach. "Why were you watching us on the beach last night," he asked.

"Us?"

"Yea, me and Jake and ...."

"And who?" She asked as she moved her hands from her eyes and stared at the wall.

Will hesitated.

"Who?"

"Mira and Sherry."

Mary couldn't believe what she was hearing. And it caused her as much alarm as the Sheriff coming after her. Of all the hurt she'd ever known and the agony her life had absorbed, this caused the greatest pain. "You have a girl...." She moved her trembling fingers to her lips and again buried her head against the wall. Her body shook as tears fell to the ground.

With that one sentence from the girl everyone mocked from behind her back, Will's heart broke. He couldn't believe how stupid he was or how callous his accusation had been. He could hear Mary laboring to breathe and there was no denying her loneliness, her inescapable prison. Shame rose up inside of him, and he turned his head while collecting his thoughts. When he finally gathered himself enough to look back at Mary, she no longer hid her face. And the expression she held was of a person who no longer cared for anything.

"Leave Will!"

"But Mary?"

"Now!" She wasn't going to be swayed by anything or anyone, and her condemning tone made that all too clear. She stared at Will, unfazed, unyielding, and determined.

Will wanted to stay, but realized it was over. He shook his head in disbelief as he turned and walked away.

Will walked slowly, with his limp, out of the yard and down the trail toward his Dad's house. Mary watched him go and the sadness that filled her heart was overwhelming. Will had been the only person in her life she'd ever loved, but the years of hate and disgust and filth were too much to overcome. And her heart became dark and lonely once again.

Leo took a long look at the two men standing outside his front door. "I didn't take anything. My family didn't take anything. We've been here for years and nothing has ever come up missing that I heard of. And all of a sudden we're the only ones who could have done it. We may be poor and not kin folks like the rest of you, but we ain't thieves. I'm just a man who's always tried his best to do what's right for his family. If you want, you can search my house. I have nothing to hide." His tone was rigid, but sincere. And if he was lying, well…he was good at it. "Besides, what would I do with that stuff?"

Julius had wondered what Leo would do with the stolen items ever since Ted Larson first mentioned it at the bar. "Could I have been wrong about this man? He never did anything bad to anyone that I knew of." The thoughts ran through Julius' mind, scrambling into an answer he didn't like. Confused about his convictions, he only wanted to walk away with his humiliation.

Jim glanced at Julius, who appeared considerably less of a man than when he first arrived. "What you want to do Julius?" Jim asked as the three stood there.

"I'm not sure," Julius said in a humbled tone as he ran his hands through his hair. It should have been an easy decision. But for Julius it was an admission that he was wrong. So he said nothing.

"Sorry we bothered you Leo and I hope you have a good day," Jim said as he and Julius turned and walked away.

Leo watched the men venture off with Julius explaining something while animating his arms profusely. He couldn't hear what the men were saying but felt sure Julius was clarifying his mistake. The two were out of sight before Leo headed back in the house. Leo's boy, Jeff, had listened to the entire episode from behind the open door but decided to stay out of view.

"What ya think Paw," he asked as the older Gorman sat down at the table and took up his coffee, which was now cold.

"I think they're crazy. We've done a lot of things, but we ain't no thieves," Leo said with conviction. His son looked at him and frowned. A moment later the boy headed out of the house.

Jeff looked at Mary and the wet and dirty clothes that lay at her feet. "Something wrong?" he asked.

Mary was dazed and in no particular mood to talk to Jeff, or anyone else for that matter. "No," she softly murmured as she scrambled to pick up the clothes and continue her chores.

Jeff looked away from his sister and noticed a slow moving Will heading down a trail and away from their home. When he turned back to Mary, she stared him dead in the eyes.

Chapter 33

Will kicked the screen door open and walked onto the back deck of his Dad's bar. He had a beer in each hand and brought one to his mouth and chugged with the gusto of a dejected man. He then flipped the emptied bottle into the water and threw himself into a chair next to Jake.

Will sighed, and it was loud enough that it should have gotten the attention of anyone within a hundred feet. But Jake was impassive. He just sat there, set in stone, his gaze fixed on the gathering clouds that hazed over and mostly obscured what should have been a beautiful sunset. And for the two of them, it had been the longest day either had ever known.

"You gonna ask me what's wrong," Will finally asked.

Jake sipped at his beer, thinking, his mind tightly wound and fixated on his own issues and truths. He was attempting to sort through everything he'd ever believed to be right. "Let me ask you Will. Do you think I'm self-centered?" He spoke, but never offered a glance in Will's direction.

Will flicked his eyes over at Jake and raised one brow before resigning to a miniscule smile. "I've got my own problems that I need help with," he said as his paltry smile turned to a glossy frown.

"Maybe I am," Jake said in response to his own question and as if Will had vanished. "There's times I get aggravated with people for no reason. Maybe I expect too much? What do you think? Do you think I expect too much?" Jake rested the cheek of his face on one hand and tapped against his teeth with his fingernail. He pondered who he was and what his life had become. He picked up his beer and put it to his mouth.

"Man I sure messed up today. I know I've told you this before, but I got woman problems," Will said. "And I need help!"

"Yea," Jake said while bobbing his head.

Will smiled as he awaited his friend's support. But it never came.

"I think I can change. I know I can. I just need to be honest and confess to those I've wronged that a lot of these things are my fault. Well, at least a few are my fault."

"It's entirely my fault!" Will said. "She is so upset with me, and rightfully so… I just don't know. But I do know there's something else that bothers her and I'm afraid it's really bad. But she won't let me help. She won't let me in!"

"Yea, I can see some of it being your fault," Jake said as he squinted with his right eye and took another drink. "But never mind that for now. Do you think it would be best if I apologized to everyone, starting with Pate?"

"I need to apologize," Will said, "but do you know she won't even tell her Dad that she's seeing me. And now she's so mad that she won't see me long enough to apologize. And she absolutely refuses to let me talk to anyone else about us."

"Why would I let you apologize?" Jake asked as he turned briefly from the strokes of lightning that raced across the sky. "I appreciate the offer and I see that you're mostly right, but I need to do this on my own." He paused. "I need to find Pate, that's where I need to start!" Jake's tone was righteous as he snapped his fingers.

"I need to talk to her. She has to be reasonable!" Will fidgeted with the beer bottle as he tried to think of a way to make her see his side.

"Have you seen Pate?" Jake asked as his eyes flickered with every bolt of lightning that fought the approaching darkness. "No, I guess not. But I appreciate you listening to me. And you're a good friend. I needed that." Jake turned to find Will staring distantly. "Will, are you even listening to me?"

"What?"

"I can't believe this! I just poured my soul out about how I've been selfish and self-centered, and how I've changed. And you're not even listening!" Jake stared at Will with disbelief. In a huff, he stood and walked into the bar.

"Sorry, Jake!" Will hollered as Jake paced away and vanished through the screen door.

"How insensitive," Jake said under his breath. "I'm always having to listen to his petty problems and give him advice; and he damn well knows it. But when I need a little help of my own, it's still all about Will."

Jake walked to the end of the bar and put an arm around his Dad, who was in his all too familiar place. Jake hugged him tightly. "Have I told you recently that I love you?" Jake asked with sincerity as he squeezed his Dad's shoulders.

"No, but it's good to hear. And I love you too." Toke was accustomed to his son being open about how he felt toward him, but this had a different ring to it than normal. "Is everything ok?"

"Everything's great. Just setting a new course for myself and I wanted to start with you. I tried to start with Will but he's too into himself. I used to be that way, but not anymore! And Dad, for all the grief I've ever caused you, I'm truly sorry."

"Thanks son, that's a load off my mind," Toke replied evenly and with a straight face. "You're a good boy."

"Thanks Dad."

Jake continued to drink his beer as he stood next to his father. Their conversation was no longer about Jake's problems, but fishing, baseball and another beer. The two were Cullen's and talking was not only one of their strong points, it was their defining point.

Pate Carter and Jimmy Clark strolled into Mr. Willy's. They stopped at the bar, said a few words to Willy, and then headed to a table with a drink in their hands. Jake took notice and felt it was fate that had brought Pate here tonight.

"Well Dad, I've got other people to right, and I see the main one sitting at that table." Jake pointed to Pate. As soon as Jake finished his beer, he was determined to fix all the wrong in his life.

Chapter 34

"Look at that smartass," Pate said to Jimmy as both eased into chairs at a corner table and sat their drinks down. Jimmy didn't have to see who Pate was talking about, but twisted in his chair to confirm that it was in fact Jake.

"He's not so bad," Jimmy offered, knowing Pate would take exception.

"Not so bad! All the things he's done to us over the years. How can you say that?" Pate's voice got louder as the sentence carried itself out.

"Honestly, he's never done anything to me or anyone else I know. It's always been between you two."

Pate's brows narrowed as he reflected on the past.

Jimmy waited.

"Can't be," Pate finally said as he shook his head. "He's too spiteful for it to be just between the two of us."

"I'm sorry to inform you, but it is just between you two. So tell me, do you even know why you don't get along?"

Pate relaxed, his body finally easing into the chair, the drink soothing his distress. He spoke softly. "Yea, I know."

"Wanna talk about it. Because I've lived here my entire life, and I don't have a clue."

"It's really not that much to tell. We were just kids when he started all this."

Jimmy nodded just to be agreeable. "If you tell me, then I might dislike him as much as you do."

That was a darn good thought, and it cheered Pate up. "Ok, I'll tell you."

Pate inched his chair closer to Jimmy and reseated himself. "We were about seven or eight, and were playing on the Shell Mounds. I remember it as clear as yesterday. Back then me and Jake were best friends, even though he was a bit of a bully. But see, I wouldn't allow him to push me around and fought back when needed. And because of that, I think he saw us as equals or something."

"He was the bully?" Jimmy asked quizzically.

"I said he was, didn't I?" Pate said with a hint of ire. "Well anyway, we'd been digging on the mounds, looking for Indian teeth and any other valuables we could find."

"Yea, I have a peace-pipe and about a dozen teeth I found up there. They sit on my dresser."

"I know, I've seen them a thousand times," Pate said coarsely. He shook his head. "As I was saying, we'd been digging for quite some time and had holes scattered everywhere, when we ran across something, some type of hide. But not like a pig's or goat's; maybe deer or buffalo. Yea, deer or buffalo," he said with confidence although he'd never seen either. "But anyway, the leather was brown and folded over so that it was closed. And it had a leather string wrapped around it a few times and tied." Pate paused, thinking it a good time to flex his control and get Jimmy to buy the next round. So he lifted his empty glass and dangled it before Jimmy, who had been enthralled with the story. Jimmy sighed as he pushed his chair away from the table, took the glass, and went to the bar for a refill.

Jimmy set Pate's drink on the table and nudged his chair back in. "Tell me something."

"What?

"How long's this story?"

"You got somewhere to go?"

"Nope, just trying to figure if I have enough money to see it through."

Pate wasn't amused. "Do you want to hear the story or not? Because it makes no mind to me if you hear the story."

"Yes I want to hear it," Jimmy offered reluctantly. He hated that Pate ruled the conversation, but he desperately wanted to hear the story. He resigned to the fact that it would likely cost him more.

"Then I shall continue." Pate clearly held the upper hand. But as he continued, he leaned in and whispered. "We both knew this bag was the mother lode we'd been looking for. Indian teeth were nothing compared to this! So we untied the string and rolled it open, right there on the ground. I still remember how I felt at that moment. Just thinking about it makes my body tingle." Pate's eyes looked to the ceiling as his glare wandered far away.

"For God's sake, what was in it?" Jimmy asked. His excitement had built to the point of exploding, and he could hardly contain himself.

"I'm getting to that. Just calm down, will ya?" Pate again lowered his voice as he moved his chair even closer to his friend. He then glanced around the room as if he were on a secret mission and would have to eat a coded message if captured by the enemy.

Jimmy's eyes glanced about also, although he didn't know what he was supposed to be looking for.

"There were two items inside," Pate whispered. "When we unfolded the sack, the first thing we saw was this piece of pottery. It was like nothing either of us had ever seen. It was a statue, about six inches tall." Pate used his hands to show roughly the size of the object. "It had the body of a bear and the head of a bird. The nose on it came to a long point, about an inch or so, and looked like a bird's beak. It was perfectly smooth with delicate lines that showed the face as well as the hands and feet... or maybe paws. It could have been paws now that I think about it. Anyway, etched on the back of its head was the sun, with rays shooting from it. We've all seen tons of pottery, but nothing like this. It was perfect in every detail and not a piece missing; not even a chip."

Jimmy turned his head sideways and cut his eyes at Pate. "Do you think it was a toy or something?"

Pate glanced around the room again to make sure no one was listening. He spoke even lower, almost inaudibly. "No, I think it was an idol of their God."

"Their God!" Jimmy said loudly as he jumped from his seat.

"Shhhh," Pate hastened as his face grimaced and his hands motioned downward as if he were doing imaginary pushups. "Sit down and shut up," he hissed.

"Wow!" Jimmy said. He was taken aback by the notion. He reseated himself. "Wow" he kept saying in disbelief. For now, he had forgotten to ask about the other item in the bag as he pictured the idol being held by Indians, who danced around a fire and chanted spiritual and mystical words. "Wow!" he managed again.

"That's not all. That's not even the best part," Pate said as the story built.

"Not the best part? What could be better than that?"

"Well, beneath the idol, tucked into a crease in the hide," Pate took in a deep breath, "there was a gold doubloon."

"A gold doubloon!" Jimmy blurted as he again leapt from the chair.

"Crominy sakes Jimmy, will you please hush. And sit the hell down." Pate's face contorted, showing more anguish than the first time he had quieted his friend.

"You're kidding. Why haven't I heard this stuff before? And where is it?"

"I'm getting to that. And that's also the cause of the rift between us to this day. Now you have to promise not to repeat this to anyone. It's been a secret all these years and neither Jake nor I have spoken a word to anyone."

"Fine, fine, whatever... just continue," Jimmy said with enthusiasm.

"Right about that time I was a lot bigger than Jake. Remember when he got so sick that he nearly died?"

"Yea, I remember," Jimmy said, recalling the time.

"Well, since I was bigger and he was, well, sickly; and the fact that I'd started digging on this particular hole first. Which I did! I felt these things should be mine."

"No Pate. Don't tell me you took it all?"

"Well kind of, but not exactly."

"How does that 'kind of' thing work... exactly?" Jimmy said with a spin on words.

"First off, you have to remember we were kids. And secondly... well, we were kids."

"I think I can remember that," Jimmy added cynically.

"Well, when I saw the idol, I snatched it up and took off in a run. I had no idea there was a gold coin in there because it was tucked in the fold. I was hauling tail across a large pile of green oyster shells and," Pate stopped his story. He wasn't proud of what happened next and needed a moment to assess the embarrassment he was about to expose himself to. "I tripped. I tripped and the idol flew from my hands as I landed on the shells. I cut myself pretty good I might add. Anyway... the idol hit hard and the nose broke off and the body split in half." He again shook his head. "It was worthless at that point," he added, trying his best to salvage something from the debacle. "I still have it in a shoe box if you wanna see it?"

"Maybe another time. But for now I'd like to know what happened next," Jimmy asked with guarded reservation and lessening excitement.

Pate was fraught with anguish as he spoke. "I was crying when I got to my feet. And blood was all over me! I turned and saw Jake laughing, and of course, holding a gold coin in his raised hand. He might as well have spit in my face! So, I went over and beat 'em up. He put up a good fight for a sick kid, but I finally took 'em. Then, well, then I took the coin." Pate's head was facing downward, at the table, as he concluded. It was obviously not one of his proudest moments.

Jimmy looked at him for a long while. He studied Pate and for the first time in his life, saw him differently. "I can't believe

anyone would do that. I can't believe even you would do that."
Jimmy shook his head in disgust.

"I told you we were kids. Besides that was a long time ago.
I've changed since then."

"Yea, we all change," Jimmy offered, wanting Pate to
understand that their friendship was about to change.

"So, where's the coin?" Jimmy needed to hear the rest of
the story, even though he wasn't very happy with his best
friend at the moment.

Pate was really uncomfortable now and arched his shoulders to
stretch. "I don't have it anymore." His voice faded with the
words.

"Why don't you have it? Did you lose it?"

"Not exactly," he uttered.

"Here we go again. You might as well spit it out and get it
over with. This is already a catastrophe of biblical
proportions."

"Remember, I was just a kid."

"Mmm mmm," Jimmy said with closed lips while nodding.

"Well, we went to the Bayou for the ball game a few months
later. Mom told me not to take the coin, but I did anyway."

"This ain't good." Jimmy shook his head at what was coming.

"And I sold it."

"You did what!"

"Shhhh," Pate hissed again while emphatically using the same
hand motions as before.

"Please do tell. How much did you sell it for?" Jimmy's tone
was anything but subdued.

Pate turned his head and said something so quietly that he himself couldn't have heard it.

"How much was that? I didn't hear."

"A quarter and two pieces of bubble gum! I sold the damn thing for a quarter and gum. I hope you're happy now!" Pate's embarrassment had turned to anger.

"A quarter! A piece of gum!" Jimmy yelled in astonishment.

"Two pieces of gum," Pate said as if another piece of gum made all the difference in the world.

"Well then," Jimmy said, his tone filled with mockery, "I think you should have asked for a soda pop with that. That would seem to be a fairer rate for gold." Jimmy was now loud enough to get the entire room's attention.

This time, Pate didn't even bother with a "Shish." He just looked around the room at all the faces staring back. "Yes, I sold it for a quarter and gum! I sold a gold coin for a quarter and gum," he shouted. "Now everyone knows and I don't have to deal with this damn secret any longer. It was stupid, but I was a kid! There, I've said it and it's over! So all of you can laugh and joke, or whatever the hell you want!"

Not a soul laughed, and after a moment Mr. Willy calmly interjected. "Pate, the entire Island has known about that since it happened. Well, everything but the second piece of gum. We thought you only got a quarter and one piece."

Pate was furious, his face glowing as red as a beacon. He glanced at the floor and breathed a heavy breath. Belittled, he stood from his chair and looked at the faces that were trained on him. He threw up his arms as if he surrendered, and walked out to the back deck.

Chapter 35

The screen door to the back deck opened and Jake walked coolly out. Pate sat in a chair, his eyes bloodshot and his feet propped on the railing that ran the length of the deck. His back was to the door. "Go away," Pate said with a toneless manner. Sullen, to the point of bursting, he wasn't in the mood for company. But Jake was on a mission to clear his own conscience, no matter who was in the way. And he had decided before he walked out, that now was the time.

The rain cloud that had been gathering in the west now ruffled the bay to a light chop, the winds no longer content with simply providing an evening breeze. The wind joined with the approaching rain and cooled the air to the point of leaving a chill. And it felt good as the ever present humidity vanished.

"It's gonna rain," Jake said as he stepped to the side of the surly Pate. He listened to the distant thunder. He liked the thunder and rain, and believed it to be a good omen.

"I don't feel like it Jake. If you're looking for a fight, just go away and we'll do it tomorrow." Flashes of lightning were closing in.

"I'm not looking for a fight, just the opposite." Jake's voice was mellow and in control.

Pate cocked his head to one side, and glared at the water as he rubbed his forehead with his left hand. His fingers gripped at the stress that ballooned from behind his eyes. He tried to sooth his anguish. "Fine, we won't fight. Still, just leave me alone."

"You may not believe it, but I'm here to help," Jake said. Jake was being genuine, and wanted to share the bliss. "Pate, I never told anyone about the idol or the coin." Jake's voice had become friendly, soft, and conciliatory.

"It doesn't matter who told. I don't really care anymore. Truth be told, you had a right to tell." Pate's voice had ebbed from the anger induced state of earlier, and became entrenched in self-pity.

"Maybe I did, but I promised you I wouldn't, and I didn't. But you're right, it doesn't matter. And actually, the reason I'm out here is to apologize for all the strife we've had through the years. What you said to me yesterday, about the way I act sometimes, was true. I can be self-centered and self-absorbed. Well, I use to be those things. But I've changed."

Although Jake sounded sincere, Pate struggled to trust him. He decided it wasn't time to let his defenses down. "You've lost it! I always knew you were nuts, but you've finally lost it."

"No, I've found it. And you pointed me in the right direction. I want us to be friends again. More than ten years is a long time to carry a grudge, and I'm tired. So I'd like for you to accept my apology. So we can be friends again."

Pate turned his head and focused on Jake, who had propped his butt on a rail and was staring straight at him. Pate stared back, and saw something he hadn't seen in many years. His head slowly nodded as if he approved. "How do I know this ain't some type of joke? And as soon as I let my guard down, you'll be there to take advantage?" Pate had an honest concern.

"I didn't tell anyone about what we found on the mounds that day because I gave you my word. And I'm giving you my word now. I truly want us to be friends again."

The evening had since turned to night and the thunder and lightning moved closer all the while. The air had cooled considerably and Jake crossed his arms and cupped his hands on the bare skin just below his sleeves, in an attempt to keep warm.

"Let's say we become friends, then what? I don't want it to be like you and Will and all that emotional stuff." Pate was hesitant with his words, but a part of him wouldn't mind having Jake back as a friend. The island was a small place, and eligible friends were limited.

"We become friends I guess. Maybe go floundering or hunting… and no more fighting."

"No more fighting?" Pate said with alarm. "Couldn't we fight a little? Nothing big, just enough that it feels like old times." Pate's disposition seemed to have finally been uplifted by Jake's revelation to unite again, and his tone reflected as much.

Jake nodded his head as a smile broadened across his face in approval. "I'd like that. We don't want everyone thinking we went completely soft."

Chapter 36

Jake moved to sit in a chair near Pate. As soon as he settled in, a raucous from inside caused both to jump to their feet and rush through the door. Pate's dad, Julius, and Jimmy's dad, Saul, were standing near the bar, surrounded by everyone in the room.

Pate moved to his dad. "What's going on," he asked.

"We've been robbed again. Someone took most of the diesel we had left and loosened the cowling on the engine. I guess they got interrupted before they could take whatever else they wanted." Julius rubbed the back of his neck.

Saul Clark then spoke up. "I went to west point today to herd my cattle back, and two were missing. I thought they may have swum to Pelican Island so I took my skiff over and found them. Both had been butchered. And someone knew what they were doing because they carved 'em to the bone."

A drizzle began to patter against the tin roof and it sounded like a heavier rain than it really was. The men stood around the bar and discussed the possibilities. Some ideas were crazy, while others were filled with conspiracies that involved the Bayou folks. But no one could fully explain what was going on or how the theft of engine parts and butchered cattle were related, if they in fact were.

The conversation eventually exhausted itself as the steady rain, which drummed melodically on the roof, increased in intensity. The thunderstorm burgeoned across the island, and with every crackle of lightning more and more headed for home. By the time eight o'clock rolled around they had all retired for the night except Toke and Mr. Willy.

Weathering a storm was something Toke and Willy did quite well, and in their usual style. They continued to consume beer, lots of beer, and talked about the old days. They always talked about the old days, and they always laughed with silliness once they'd had too much to drink. And tonight, well tonight Toke's hat was well left of center.

"What do you think about all this stuff with Julius and his engine? It doesn't add up," Willy said as his body draped over the bar, propped up by his elbows.

Toke thought for a while. "Remember how much Julius lied when he was a kid?"

"Yea, he was quite a shit back then. But he seems to have grown out of the lying part." Willy took a long swig of beer. "But he's still a shit." He chuckled. "Hey, remember that time he was walking back from the west end and we were riding in the back of Old Man Clark's wagon?"

Toke had already begun laughing, his eyes starting to water. "I don't remember that." Toke said he didn't remember, only because he liked to hear Willy tell the story.

"Oh you remember," Willy said with a smile that grew into a chuckle.

Toke's entire body was shaking as he shook his head no, signifying that he didn't recall the time.

"Ohhhh, you remember." Willy had to stop, he was laughing so hard he found it nearly impossible to breathe. Willy contorted his face as he tried to keep the laughter in. "Remember," he put his hand to his mouth, "old Man Clark pulled the wagon alongside Julius, who was walking along and swatting mosquitos, and said..." Willy wiped the tears from the corners of his eyes. "He said; Julius, tell me a lie and I'll give you a ride up with the rest of us." Willy burst into laughter, and as he laughed he continued talking. "And Julius looked up at the old man with this pitiful expression and said... Mr. Clark, I don't lie anymore." Willy could barely control himself now, his eyes watering and his entire body shaking. "And Old Man Clark said...that's the best one you told yet, hop on!"

Both men burst with laughter, uncontrollably, and Toke had to put a hand to his side. Toke had nudged Willy into telling this story hundreds of times, and the response was always the same.

Toke and Willy's conversations meandered along, like a boat lost in the fog. They touched on many topics, from serious to outlandish and from absurd to hilarious, till the rain had stopped. It was fast approaching ten o'clock and Toke's hat rested to the side while Willy's face had turned red from the mixture of alcohol and high blood pressure.

The night of drinking had led them to the exact reason for everything that was happening on the island, although neither could recall what the conclusion was. But they had solved the mystery, and by tomorrow they would fill the entire island in on the details. It was just too late to do it tonight.

"I gotta go, Laura's probably put dinner away by now and I'm starving. I'm so hungry I could eat my own appetite." Toke's speech slurred a little. But in his own mind he thought he managed rather well.

"Come on Toke. You can stay a little longer," Willy pleaded.

"Nope, can't do it. I want to come back some day." Toke rose from the stool.

"Come back? You can always come back. You're my best fellow." Willy was sincere and looked somewhat pitiful as he stood with his arms spread, his palms turned outward to Toke.

"Well Willy, if a fellow don't leave, how can he come back?"

Willy blinked several times as he scratched his head and thought intently about what Toke said. After deciding he couldn't muster a response to the question, he relented. "Toke, put the lamp out and pull the front door shut when you leave." He then walked to the side door and exited. He staggered down the steps and into his house only a few feet away.

Toke blew out the lamp and closed the door behind him. He stepped into the crisp night air.

As Toke started home, he looked at the soft glow of light coming from Willy's house. And as Willy's shadow crossed the curtained window, he reflected on his good friend. His thoughts about Willy led his mind to each of their sons who were also best friends. It was good to have someone like Willy, like Will. And he realized how lucky he and his son were, and that he wouldn't want it any other way.

Chapter 37

The rain fell in sheets across the open gulf. The wind was out of the north and the island served as a breaker for the waters to its south. Waves formed in the gulf but remained small rollers that capped onto the beach with a consistent rapidity of gentle determination. Darkness drenched the Gulf's landscape as much as the rains, and in the midst of the open waters, a sleek black object rose quietly and without fanfare from its depths. As the battery powered engine whirled, with an almost silent yet monotonous hum, the German U-boat, U-70, closed within 500 feet of the shoreline. The submarine lay low in the water and even if it had been a clear night and full moon, it would still be nearly invisible.

Kapitanleutnant Ernst Mettler and two officers made their way to the subs conning tower as the rain and lightning spurred thunderous roars. Water ran from their black rain suits as they stood atop the matte finished, black hull of the sub. They surveyed the landscape with binoculars, looking for movement and lights along the beach. It was the same routine as the previous two nights, just before sailors made their way to the beach and then to a diesel engine for spare parts. And again, a crew would soon do the same.

U-70 and its 33 crew members successfully completed their mission four days ago, when one of the submarine's two

Krupp Germaniawerft built 6 cylinder diesel engines failed. Since then, the sub had been slowed, resigned to its lone remaining diesel and auxiliary power engines. The U-boat had been running low on supplies and fuel as well, and repairing the faltered engine while gathering supplies was critical for its safe return home. Before the sub could make a run through the Straits of Florida and rendezvous with a supply ship in the much safer open Atlantic Ocean, it needed both engines at full strength, as well as enough fuel and supplies.

The war in Europe was more than two years old now, and the United States, weary of German intentions, had quietly ramped up the construction of bases, including many for anti-submarine defense. And these bases, all along the US seacoast, included the central Gulf coast. In particular, the American's had grown suspicious of German infiltration and covert operations that threatened US autonomy, and sub hunters and reconnaissance balloons searched the gulf and oceans at length. And the Straits of Florida were particularly prone to search and destroy practices, making it the most dangerous strait in the entire western hemisphere. So, U-70 would need its full allotment of engines and power if it had any intentions of returning to its homeland.

Months before, in early June, U-70 concluded its first mission, dubbed NAS 4, and successfully infiltrated the gulf coast's coastline. It was early morning, hours before daylight, when the sub made its way up the deep channel of Mobile Bay and deposited a man and woman along a foggy stretch of beach on the Bay's eastern shore, near Fairhope Alabama. The couple that exited the U-Boat soon made contact with sympathizers and were given a vehicle, keys to an apartment, cash and credentials. They immediately headed for Pensacola Florida. The two would pose as husband and wife, and conduct their business of spying and sabotage for the betterment of

Germany. Both spoke perfect English and were given the mission of infiltrating Pensacola Naval Air Station, which was the training facility for nearly all American naval airmen. Once in position, the couple, like all those loyal to the ring of Nazi spies that swelled within the US, would relay information back to Germany. They were ordered to described troop movements and training post and weaponry numbers, all the while causing setbacks in military base installations and operations.

Mission NAS 4 was proving exceptionally successful, and the current extension of that mission, up until four days ago, had been the same. The U-70 had deposited a lone man, a man with falsified engineering credentials from Duke University, to nearly the same drop off point as before. The spy had effectively slipped ashore, met with sympathizers, and then headed toward the construction site of Naval Station Biloxi.

The German tactics and planning were sound, meticulous in fact, but as the sub exited the bay an engine failed. A piston rod snapped and was damaged beyond repair. It had to be replaced. Starting with the furthest points from cities, sailors were sent ashore in the least inhabited regions. This was a keen approach as it greatly reduced their chances of being detected. And as fortune would have it, Dauphin Island and Julius Carter's engine fit the bill perfectly. U-70 would soon have what they needed, and one more successful night on the island would see them to the end.

Chapter 38

Two sailors and one officer boarded an inflatable raft and pushed away from the sub. They rowed the small craft to the beach and dragged it into the bushes behind a small dune. The rain continued, and they hoped it would not subside until they completed their mission. One sailor stayed with the raft while the officer and other man, a mechanic, headed to Julius Carter's house for the final parts.

Like shadowy ghosts the sailors moved imperceptibly through the dark. No words were spoken as they snaked through the dim crevices of peoples' yards, darting from object to object, making their way to the engine. Efficiently and in unison, they pulled a heavy canvas tarp from a bag and draped it over themselves and the engine. They were all but invisible. With the officer holding a small flashlight, the mechanic began stripping the parts needed.

The Germans worked continuously for more than two hours and finally had the piston rod. It had taken longer than anticipated, and by the time they finished, the rain had halted. The sailor began wrapping each wrench in individual cloths so they wouldn't clang together, while the officer began folding the canvas tarp. The officer paused, putting a hand to the sailor's shoulder. It was a warning that someone was coming. The officer doused his light and quickly stuffed the tarp in the bag as the sailor hastened the process of collecting the individual tools.

Using his index finger the officer made a circling motion, signaling that he wanted to quickly wrap things up. The sailor responded by rapidly putting the unwrapped wrenches and piston rod in the black bag and closing it. They rushed from the engine, slipped into the brush, and stood motionless and silent. They were hiding only a few feet from the engine when the officer spotted a single wrench faintly glistening on the motor's cowling. He pointed to it. The sailor was about to move when the officer made a fist and held it to his chest. The man knew to hold steady and wait. They would let whoever was approaching pass, and then retrieve the wrench before heading to the raft.

Chapter 39

The rain may have stopped, but the clouds remained. The wind blew hard from the north and Toke shook a chill as he brushed against wet leaves and limbs that outlined the path home. He held a flashlight in his right hand, which he used sparingly so as to save the life of the batteries. He flipped the light on and spotted Maynard's Pass. Maynard's Pass was a narrow wooden bridge that crossed over a bayou that cut into the island. The bridge had no railing, and Toke used the light to see himself safely across. Once on the other side, he didn't really need the light since he knew where most of the roots and holes were, having walked the route countless times. As he strolled along he hummed a tune while staggering every now and then.

The trip home wasn't all that far as the entire distance from the two furthest houses was less than a mile, with Mr. Willy's bar resting nearly midway. Toke moved along the winding path, at times through the yards of neighbors since the road was formed from the necessity of people getting home. It was shortly past ten and not a light shone in any of the houses he passed.

The hefty breeze rustled every tree limb on the island, and Toke liked it when the wind blew. He liked the way it bowed trees and limbs and moved stagnant air. But especially, he liked it when northerners blew through, cooling the air and leaving little doubt the next morning would be chilly. And that was particularly noteworthy, since snuggling next to Laura was one of his favorite things. This brought a smile to his face, and left him upbeat. In fact, his humming soon echoed into a song. Toke could sing, and much like his story telling he often shared his talent with anyone that would listen. And tonight, well tonight the trees were his audience.

Toke was passing through Julius' yard when nature called. As he stepped to the side of the trail he heard a clinking noise and what might have been footsteps. He looked up at the limbs that continued to clash together as he tried to decide which direction the noises had come from. His singing quieted to a murmur as his eyes darted about. He flipped the flashlight on and scanned the area around him. Having decided it was just some of the junk in Julius' yard banging together, he flipped the light off. He finished his business and started to move on when he heard the sound again. The hair on his neck stood, the cold wind adding to the goose bumps that formed on his arms. He had a bearing on where the noise came from, and it wasn't in the direction of Julius' junk pile.

The German officer cut his eyes at the sailor while keeping his head straight and steady. The sailor had allowed the unwrapped tools to bump against each other, drawing the attention of the man who stood before them. Both sailors watched the man, only a few feet away, stare in their general direction. The officer again cut his eyes to the sailor who nodded ever so slightly. The sailor eased the bag of tools to the ground and the tools again clinked.

Toke became leery as he now knew exactly where the noise was coming from. He reluctantly eased in its direction.

The sailor slipped his hand to his side and drew his Knights head naval dagger from the sheath on his belt. He brought the nine inch blade up to his chest and gripped it firmly in his right hand, the point of the blade jutting to the sky.

The officer slid his pistol from its holster and held it at his belt line, pointing it at the man that slowly approached. He would use the gun if he had to, but as a last resort because of the sound it would make.

The clouds were thinning and faint beams from the moon slipped into the night sky, allowing the rain soaked leaves to glisten like a million stars. But the glistening leaves only made things worse as everything appeared, at least to Toke, to be moving. He thought he saw someone hiding behind every tree. Toke didn't like how this was playing out, and an eerie sensation overtook him. He became afraid. But still, he inched closer to the brush and couldn't believe he was walking toward the noises. It seemed awful stupid at the moment. He tried to convince himself it was nothing, just some old junk. It was the only way he could make his feet move forward. His mind rattled with every step he took. And as of right now, not even Houdini himself could have hidden the fact that Toke was scared of the dark and terrified of being alone!

Chapter 40

The sailor began to sweat. Anxiety pressed hard against his chest as if it would crush him. The young man had trained at the naval base in Kiel Germany and learned how to quietly and efficiently kill, though he had never been called upon to do so. His training had been extensive, every eventuality calculated. His instructions dictated that once the individual was close enough, he needed to grab the back of the victim's head with his left hand and run the blade of the dagger up and through the neck, just above the Adam's apple. The thrust of the blade would continue through the back of the man's throat and nasal cavity and into the base of the brain. The target would make little more than a gargling sound and it would be over in seconds.

The sailor had been on the U-boat for nine months and the submarine had sunk four freighters and undoubtedly killed many men during this time. Above this, dying was a part of war, he knew and understood that. But this was different. His own hands would be doing the killing, and it would be personal, and bloody, and irreversible. He fought with what was about to play out, and became nauseated and unsteady. His body swayed and he thought he may faint. He didn't know if he could look into the eyes of a dying man, a man he had slaughtered like a pig. He didn't know if the blood that would surely gush from the man's throat would cause him to panic, to run. And he didn't know if his mind could win the struggle with sanity once he felt the victim's last breath leave his body. The only comfort he could find to calm himself, was the fact that death would come swiftly, although painfully.

Toke was at the edge of the bushes and stared in. The sailor gripped the knife even tighter, his knuckles becoming white. Sweat poured from his brow line and mixed with the water droplets that fell from the limbs. The mixture of sweat and water rushed down his face and neck. Toke was also beginning to sweat as fear rose to the top and poured from his pores.

Toke's hand started upward, with the light in it, the beam clearing a swath of the night and turning it into near daylight.

The sailor's hand shook nervously as he struggled with what he was about to do. Finally, the seaman's nerves hardened, like the steel of his dagger, and he moved forward to make the kill. He knew he had to do it before the light came to rest upon them, and the man yelled, or ran.

 The officer stood fast, ready to help drag the body in the brush... or shoot if necessary.

Chapter 41

"Who the hell's out there?" A deep voice yelled. Toke spun to look, his startled body shaking from the unexpected interruption. A beam of light shown about, searching for its purpose. Julius stood on his porch, a shotgun nestled in one arm, a flashlight in the opposite hand. "I said who the hell's out there?" The light flicked around and soon landed on Toke.

The two sailors faded further into the shadows.

"Just me," Toke hollered back. "And get that damn light out of my eyes."

"What you doing out there?"

Toke shook his head, the light still focused on his face. He then turned in the opposite direction and pointed a finger at the faint glint of light coming from Willy's house. "That's where I was," he said with sarcasm. He then turned toward his own house, a few doors down from Julius', and pointed again. "That's where I need to be." Once again his tone revealed nothing but sarcasm. Then pointing to his feet, he said. "And this is where I be. Now turn the damn light off!"

"You could get shot out there. You know people been stealing and I got a hair trigger these days," Julius called back as a dog barked in the distance and a light came on in the house next door.

Toke had had enough and turned his own light toward Julius and shined it in his face. The two stood as if they were old west gunfighters waiting on the other to make the first move.

"Turn that damn light off, your blinding me," Julius said.

"You turn yours off first because you've been blinding me longer," Toke replied.

They stood for a little longer and finally Julius turned the light off, followed by Toke.

After his eyes adjusted to the darkness, Julius made his way down the steps and over to Toke. "Why you over here by my engine?"

It sounded like an accusation, but Toke figured the man had been robbed enough to ask such questions. "I was on my way home and heard something. I stopped to see what it was." Toke's voice trembled as the adrenalin in his body slowed.

Julius flashed the light on the engine and noticed the cowling had again been removed and the engine disassembled. He looked back at Toke in a condemning manner and stared.

It took Toke only a second to understand and not appreciate the glare. "Yep, you caught me. Next week is me and Laura's anniversary and I wanted to get her something special. So I said to myself, what is it that Laura don't have? And it came to me, something off Julius' engine. She ain't got nothing like that. So don't you go spoiling the surprise, Jules."

"Fine Toke, you can stop with the sarcasm. I get it." Julius was simply aggravated and upset at the fact he was being robbed, yet again.

"What's that?" Toke asked, pointing at the engine.

"What's what?"

"Right there." Toke aimed the beam of his light directly at the object, and Julius walked over to it.

The sailor had since put his knife away and now pointed a machine pistol at the men's heads. He looked down the barrel and aimed as he awaited orders. He flicked the safety off and eased his finger to the trigger. The incursion wasn't turning out as the Germans had hoped, and things could get considerably worse if shots were fired. If that happened, the entire Gulf would be put on high alert. The officer knew they'd either have to kill them both, which would make considerable noise at this point, or they could just slip off and return to the sub. The officer was no fool, and having the final parts for the engine made the decision easier. He put his hand on the sailor's arm and had him lower the weapon. He then nodded in a direction to their rear and the Germans silently eased away.

Julius studied the wrench and then showed it to Toke. And neither was able to make out the strange word written on its side. Julius' body jerked, suddenly aware that someone may still be close by. The motion startled Toke, but he soon realized Julius' reasoning for the high anxiety. Both men swept the tree line with their lights, and Toke made a closer inspection of the area from where he had heard the noises.

"I heard em' Jules. I must have walked up on them while I was headed home."

"I think your right," Julius added. "It's too bad you didn't get hold of 'em. We would have showed 'em they can't come to Dauphin Island and rob people blind."

Toke winced at the thought. "Yea, it's good that I didn't get my hands on 'em." His voice was hesitant and unconvincing. He also felt uneasy, standing in the open. After a short time of scanning the surrounding woods, Julius headed back in his house and Toke headed home.

Toke climbed in bed and put an arm around his wife.

"Is everything ok?" Laura whispered. "It's awful late."

Toke told her about the night's events and it frightened her. But Toke made it okay as he pulled her close, in a reassuring manner. They lay and talked for a long time, discussing what it all meant. Finally, in the early morning hours, they both fell asleep as Toke snuggled close.

The next day was clear and cold and word had spread by mid-morning about what Toke and Julius encountered. Everyone agreed that they needed to take the wrench to the authorities, which meant Jim Cowl. Jim had the wrench by late that day and Julius and Toke and Saul relayed the entire story. Jim said he'd get back with them, soon. He didn't say a lot after studying the object, but knew what it was and who it belonged to. And to him, it all made perfect sense.

Two weeks passed and Jim and three Government men showed up on the Island. They asked for everyone to gather at the church. Two of the men never said who they were. They only asked questions and took notes. The other, in an Air Force uniform, gave a speech to the entire group after all the questions had abated.

In the end, the Air Force officer said nothing about Germans as he explained that the military had decided to place a garrison on the island. He further explained that the presence of soldiers wouldn't mean a lot to the locals and that they could, and in fact should, go about their business as usual. But what he added next was monumental. He said that an actual military base would be forthcoming and that that meant electricity. "Soon," he said, "work will begin on a transmission line from the mainland to the island".

To most of the islanders this was all very exciting. But to others it marked the beginning of the end. The Island was changing, and for better or worse there was nothing anyone could do to stop it.

Chapter 42

All of November proved unseasonably warm except for the last week of the month, which was miserably cold. And for the most part that's the way winter worked on the island. It was an ebb and flow relationship, where a front would come barreling through and for a week to ten days it would be cold, sometimes bitterly cold. Eventually though, the winds would shift and blow from the south, across the warmer Gulf. Temperatures would then return to more seasonal averages, until the next front marched through.

It was two days before Thanksgiving and the days had grown shorter as the afternoon sun distanced itself over the gulf. And Dauphin Island was dealing with temperatures it rarely faced during its coldest months of January and February. The old-timers always yakked about how cold it was when they were young, but when they wrapped up in every garment they owned while still in their homes and next to their stoves, you realized they were just gabbing like old-timers do. Temperatures hovered in the teens during the day and plummeted into single digits at night. Parts of the bay iced over, as did the two fresh water lakes that rested in the center of the island.

Toke, Laura, and Jake sat at their kitchen table. They drank coffee, ate galettes, and talked. The fire in the cast-iron potbelly stove battled the frigid air that seeped through cracks in the aged house. A half-empty coffee pot rested in a momentary state of dormancy next to the stove's stack. It was late in the afternoon and the three had been cooped up for two full days. Above that, Toke hadn't been to the bar in three days and was itching to head to his favorite spot.

Toke's mind drifted to his friend Willy and a few afternoon beers, which seemed unlikely. You see, they were talking, as a family. And he would never say he wanted to go to the bar while the three sat and talked... as a family. Toke had long since realized how much these quiet moments meant to Laura and how she clung to every second, every word with her husband and son like it were the last time she'd see either. So even though the urge to leave tugged mercilessly, he decided to bide his time. He'd wait until the conversation completely exhausted itself, or Jake went to visit Will... or something!

The conversation was quick and witty and fun, and they were laughing at something crazy Toke had said, when a knock came at the door. The three glanced at each other in a moment of confusion, then turned their heads and stared at the door, waiting for it to open. Toke cut his eyes at Laura, as if she somehow knew who it was. The door never budged and they returned to their coffee and conversation.

There came another rap and once again they all turned to look. Toke twisted in his seat, rested his elbow on the back of the chair, and scratched his jaw.

"Must be the law," Jake said with utmost certainty.

Toke nodded his head as another knock interrupted his thoughts. Finally, he rose and walked to the door.

Pate Carter stood in the cold, waiting patiently for someone to answer the door. Toke, taken aback for a moment, eventually found his manners and asked him in. Pate nodded appreciatively as he passed by and walked to the table and said hello.

"Good to see you Pate," Jake said. It was odd to have Pate in his house after so many years, but this is exactly the type of thing he'd intended when he decided to mend fences between the two. And as a small acknowledgement of his newly found benevolence, Jake realized it felt really good to say "good to see you Pate."

"Just came by to ask you something," Pate replied.

Laura quietly stood and fixed Pate a cup of coffee as the boy sat at the end of the table.

"Thanks Ms. Laura," he said as he sipped the brew. "You know, this place looked a lot bigger when I was a kid. I guess I haven't been here in over ten years."

Jake nodded in agreement as the front door opened and Will strolled in with his usual carefree demeanor. He never looked at anyone seated at the table as he strolled to the stove and fixed himself a cup of coffee.

Will turned from the stove and imparted a smile to everyone seated. If it shocked Will that Pate was in the Cullen home, which it should have, then he disguised it well. Everyone stared at Will for an awkward minute. He felt as if he were expected to entertain the group with some sort of song and dance routine. "Coffee's good," he finally said. He raised both his eyebrows and cup in approval, as if that was what everyone had been waiting for.

Laura nodded politely and gave a thankful smile as another knock came at the front door. Everyone but Pate turned to see if someone was going to enter. Will wrinkled his brow as another knock soon followed and the four glared at each other for a moment longer.

Pate obliviously buttered a galette.

"Must be the law," Will said as he set his empty cup on the counter.

Toke tilted his head and his face gave a look of weariness and show of apathy. He was becoming more irritated by the second, and tiring of all the intruding. He stood again, but as he made his way to answer the door the irritation turned to an inner smile and his thoughts lifted with an idea.

Toke pulled the front door inward and before he could react, a figure, completely covered from head to toe, sprinted past and over to the glowing stove. A frigid Sherry Larson didn't say a word as she shoved Will aside, using both hands, and desperately tried to warm herself.

Laura poured another cup of coffee and handed it to the shivering girl. Her hands shook as she drank from the small mug.

Sherry's appearance was unexpected, but Jake quickly realized that if Sherry was here then Mira would be here. He made a hasty dash to the door. He stepped outside and onto the porch, which was nothing more than three narrow steps that landed on the ground, and looked in both directions. His eyes immediately watered from the cold wind. He scanned the area for as long as he could stand it without a coat, before heading back to his chair.

"Keep your britches on, she's coming," Sherry said as she finally started to thaw. "How in the hell do ya'll cross the bay when it's so cold? That wind is awful!"

As soon as Jake sat, another rap came at the front door. He leapt back to his feet in excitement. But before he made a step his Dad scrambled from his chair and erupted in a tirade. Jake froze in his tracks.

"That's it! I've had it with all this knocking," Toke said with a plan and the best acting skills he could muster. "All I wanted was a little peace and quiet with my family, that's all a man can ask for. But I guess that ain't gonna happen!" His hands moved just a little for affect, but not too much as to draw suspicion. He never looked at Laura, mostly because she could always tell when he was trying to pull something. Instead, he focused on the kids as he ranted. He angrily made his way around the table and put on a coat. He commenced with what everyone in the room already knew he was going to say. "I'm going to Willy's and don't any of you come looking for me 'til I cool off." Toke gave everyone a heated glare and pointed a threatening finger as he put his hat on and headed for the side door.

"Toke?" It was the first word Laura had spoken since the kids started arriving.

Toke stopped, his hand short of the door knob. And like a lion tamer, he was now attempting to put his head in the animal's mouth. He felt all eyes were deeply ingrained upon him, and how he was going to handle his lion.

"Would you mind if I join you?" Laura's voice was soft, almost pleading.

A broad smile crossed Toke's face as he turned to look at his girl. Laura knew before he turned what the answer would be, but the smile was what she really wanted to see. She needed that assurance and it made her feel wanted once again. Toke didn't say a word as he reached for Laura's coat and helped her put it on. The two slipped into the cold, holding hands and talking like school kids as they headed down the path.

"What was that about?" Pate asked. "That was a little weird."

"Weird?" Will said. "What's so weird about two people loving each other? Weird my ass! You just don't have a clue what love really means." Will rarely got upset, but either the thought of having to deal with Sherry for a few days, or the fact he couldn't be with the girl he loved, raised and directed his ire at the first person to speak.

"I think it's sweet," Sherry said as she moved close to Will and traced a finger down his arm.

A loud banging came at the front door and it jarred the entire house. It startled everyone as they'd forgotten someone else was outside. Jake raced to the door, full of hope. Instead of the joyous face he wanted to see, he glared headlong at an angry Ted Larson who pushed him aside and marched to the stove.

"What kind of people are you? Do ya'll not know to let someone in when they knock?" His tone was clearly angry as he briskly rubbed his hands together and stood as close as he could to the heat.

"I do apologize," Jake said with honesty though there was a lack of assertiveness.

"Behave Daddy," Sherry said as she put her arms around him and tried to warm his body. "No one left you out there on purpose. It was an honest oversight." Everyone knew she was probably the only person on the planet that could talk to him with any measurable discord and get away with it.

"Well, the next time be a little more respectful of visitors will ya," Ted said to everyone as his body warmed and his temper cooled.

Jake nodded understandably but didn't say a word. He then ducked back outside and looked wistfully for anyone else that may be approaching. But he saw no one. He walked back in and plopped down at the table once again.

"Hang in there kid, she's coming," Ted said with reassurance before adding, "Where's Toke?"

"He left for the bar. You just missed him," Pate said.

"Thanks." The large man said as he kissed his daughter's cheek and headed out the side door.

"Let's go shoot some ducks tomorrow," Pate said to anyone interested, but mostly aimed at Jake. "Jimmy said he'd go. And we can take Dad's boat. Maybe we'll head to Cat Island. I bet our moms would love some ducks for Thanksgiving dinner."

He was right about the dinner thing, Jake thought. "I'll go," he said. "What about it Will, you in?"

Will thought for a while, weighing the decision to spend a frigid day with Pate or stay on the island and dodge Sherry the entire time. "Yea, I'll go," he said gladly.

Sherry moved a few feet from Will and looked somewhat dismayed.

Jake took notice of this but offered nothing. He realized he was still the only person that knew about Will and Mary.

"I think I'm gonna head down to the Lea's," Jake said with rising impatience.

"She's coming!" Sherry said with her own sense of aggravation. "I swear, you two are just alike. Love and needy and you're both always talking about it. Ohhh I love you, no I love you, yea but I love you more. You know, people get tired of hearing about it all the time."

"Amen," Will said as his brows rose.

Jake stood awkwardly silent while Pate buttered yet another galette.

"Want a galette?" Pate asked Sherry.

"What!" At first Sherry's voice was harsh, but then softened. "Actually I would love a, a…. what did you say that was?" Sherry sat next to Pate and inched her chair close to his.

"It's a galette, a bread of sorts. Ms. Laura's are very good," Pate said as he buttered one and put it on a plate for Sherry. He then drizzled honey over it.

"You're so sweet." Sherry's hand ran through Pate's hair, and goose bumps rose up as his body tingled from the touch of such a beautiful girl. Sherry watched for a reaction from Will, but it never came. Will simply poured and then drank another cup of coffee, like it was just another plain ole ordinary day. Sherry was to the point of rebelling. She was an inch away from completely giving up on Will, and was about to tell him how she felt, when Mira came through the side door.

Mira walked in from the cold and immediately looked at Sherry, nestled against Pate. She wrinkled her nose in confusion. Sherry gave Mira a look of contempt and leaned her head on Pate's shoulder. Mira shook her head and glanced at Will, who stood alone and looked as happy as a lark. She shook her head again while trying to make sense of it all. Finally she saw Jake, and the other stuff didn't matter. They stared at each other as Jake walked over, took her hands and leaned in for a kiss. Mira was excited, her body tingling. But before their lips touched, Jake pulled back and cut his eyes toward Sherry. Her tirade, moments earlier, made him pause before he pecked Mira on the forehead, like a father would his daughter. Mira's lips had been ready, hungry, and this confused her.

"A kiss on the forehead? I haven't seen you in over a month and all I get is a kiss on the forehead?" Mira was embarrassed, and it made her angry. Sherry though, sat in scornful delight as Will whistled a rather happy tune. "And you," Mira said with a finger pointing at Sherry. "What the hell are you doing with Pate Carter of all people?"

"Hey!" Pate said in his defense.

"Let's face it Pate, you've always been an ass." Mira was fired up and didn't stop there. "And as for the boyishly innocent, smile flashing Will Burton; this girl has been throwing herself at you and you could care less. She is the prettiest girl in school, has a great personality and is more beautiful inside and out than anyone you'll ever meet. And all you can do is act like you're in love with someone else. You act as if…," Mira paused to think about what she said, reflecting on past events. Her body and mind slowed as she pieced things together. "You're…"

Jake suddenly pulled Mira close and planted his lips on hers. He kept pressing his mouth to hers as she mumbled words that no one understood.

With their mouths pressed tightly she looked into Jake's eyes, and she knew. She knew it all. She released herself from Jake and looked at Will, who'd reddened and now gave the appearance of a haggard old man. Will looked at the floor and waited for whatever Mira had to say. A long pause filled the room.

"Do you mean all those things?" Sherry interrupted. She had not grasped the full gravity of the conversation.

Mira had been in deep thought before Sherry's words broke the trance. She turned to her friend. "Yea, I meant every word," she said with soft sympathy, her eyes filled with compassion and understanding.

Sherry pushed away from Pate, who was incredibly disappointed by her departure, and walked over to Mira. She wrapped her arms around her. "You know I love you," she said.

"And I love you too," Mira added.

Jake, annoyed by Sherry's exploits, turned away. He didn't know if he could stand any more of this.

Pate was confused, and could only imagine what Sherry and Mira meant. He'd never heard two girls of their age say "I love you," to each other.

"And I'm sorry," Mira added with a whisper.

"Why?" Sherry asked as she clung to her friend.

After a short pause Mira shook her head. "I'm just sorry for everything."

Chapter 43

Ted Larson walked into Mr. Willy's bar. He shook off his coat, and the cold. The room was warm and filled with smiling faces. And he was mildly shocked to see Laura sitting on Toke's stool and talking to Rachael, Willy's wife and Toke's eldest sister. Ted had never seen anyone but Toke seated on the stool, but figured Laura outranked him in many ways.

Toke walked toward Ted with an extended hand. "How you been you old son of a gun?" Toke asked with a big grin.

"Good, except I'm freezing. I don't see how ya'll stand this wind." The two wandered to the bar as they spoke.

"Get my friend a cold beer, will ya Willy?" Toke said.

Willy gave an affirmative wink and stepped through the side door and onto the porch. A moment later he returned with a beer. "Here you go, fresh from the icebox," Willy joked as he placed the beer on the bar.

Ted took an enthusiastic drink. "Thanks." He then strolled over to Laura and Rachael and gave both a long hug.

"You look good," Ted said with an honest appraisal. He stared at Laura and thought she exuded a youthful and energetic glow.

Laura had never considered herself beautiful, her personality wouldn't allow it. But she realized she had something, something she saw as a "spark" of sorts. And she believed that "spark" was what others saw when describing her as attractive. Now Toke had told her countless times that she was the most beautiful person in the world and that he loved, adored, and downright found her perfect in every way. And to some extent the years of his affectionate regards had made her believe that she was perhaps prettier than she really was. But it was Toke saying it, her husband, a man who was good at talking and the only person that could make her believe almost anything. Besides, since the day they'd wed, she felt he was somewhat required to dote over her and say those wonderful things. But this… this wasn't Toke. And the remark made her blush.

Ted smiled, accepting the blush as the innocent gesture it was.

"Thank you kind sir," Laura said bashfully. "And you look quite handsome yourself."

"Thanks." Ted wanted to offer a different reply but the words wouldn't form. He needed to unburden himself while hearing the compassion of a woman's voice and the kindness that goes with it. He figured he was like most men, needing the honest warmth of conversation that only a woman could give. His wife had always listened, always responded with gentleness. And he'd never forgotten the moments they shared and the many talks they'd had. They had been good memories, delicate thoughts.

"You ok?" Laura asked as she took notice of Ted's slumping features.

"I'm fine." He paused as he tried to find the words.

Laura watched him agonize with what he wanted to say.

"I don't know where to begin."

"It's ok. I'll be around anytime you feel like talking. I'm a good listener." She pointed a finger at Toke who was telling Peter Lea a story. "I have to be."

Ted chuckled at Laura's keen observation of her own life. She was a wonderful person that without doubt he could count on. And truthfully it wasn't just Laura. It was everyone here that had so extraordinarily entered his life. It was all very remarkable, and it was what made Dauphin Island special. The island and its long stretches of white beaches, its towering sand dunes that faced the gulf, and the plush green sanctum of the inner woods were all rare and exotic and beautiful. But the people made it whole and trustful. And as Ted looked around the room, he saw people he'd only known a short time. But it felt right. He took in each of the smiling faces, many looking back at him, and they weren't just dear friends. They were now his family. He felt he may cry.

Peter and Toke bordered Ted, and Willy stood across the bar from him. Laura slid from the stool and she and Rachael set out to visit with Bess, who sat at a table against the wall.

"You know we're gettin electricity," Peter said with fidgety excitement.

"Yea, were getting electricity," Toke added with apathy.

"You got something against electricity?" Ted asked with puzzlement.

"It's not that I don't like it, I just don't want it." Toke said.

Ted shook his head and looked at Peter with bewilderment. He then turned back to Toke. "So let me get this straight. You like it, but don't want it? Is that correct?"

"Yep, that's it." Toke took a long swig of beer soon after answering.

"That doesn't make sense," Ted replied.

"That's what I've been telling him," Peter added.

"Well it makes perfect sense to me," Toke said with self-assurance. "It's like this. You've been to the island twice now, right?" Toke held up two fingers.

"Yea," Ted said.

"And you may come back again," Toke added.

"Yea, I'd like to," Ted confirmed, then paused. "Honestly... I been thinking about building here, about maybe living here half the year."

Willy and Toke smiled as Peter patted Ted on the back. "We'd love to have ya," Peter said.

And once again Ted's beliefs in the community were reinforced.

After Peter bought another round and they raised their glasses for a toast, Toke picked up where he left off. "So Ted, you want to live here someday, become a part of the island. Is it because we might have electricity?"

"No, I just like it here. I like the people. I like everything about it."

Toke nodded, believing the point was delivered. "Yea, well I love it here and I love the people. And electricity means people you don't know or don't like, showing up. The lack of electricity is the only thing that keeps all the unwanted types out, like this Air Force Base, and the ones that use and manipulate people and are driven by greed. Once this place has electricity a bridge will follow and land grabbers will take whatever they want. The newcomers will want a mayor that don't know his ass from a hole in the ground but will make stupid rules all the same. And people will have their hands out, wanting something for nothing. And the locals, well, we'll be left with nothing once their done. By then it'll be too late and neither you nor I will like this place very much." Toke was passionate in his speech and they all took notice of what he had to say.

Ted furled his brow. He knew Toke was right. He'd never thought of it that way. But as he reflected, he recognized that every community in the world changed once electricity was available. And he wasn't too sure it'd always been for the best. Even Peter, a staunch supporter of electricity coming to the island, seemed to have doubts about the benefits and changes that will surely come. But for now, whether Toke was right or not wasn't important. It was something else he said that garnered Ted's attention.

"Air Force Base?" Ted asked.

"Yea, they're gonna put a base here. That's why we're getting electricity," Peter said.

"Why do ya'll need a base?" Ted asked.

Toke, Peter and Willy told Ted the entire story about the thefts and the tool they found on Julius' engine, and the visit from the Government men.

"So you had Germans on the Island?" Ted said.

Peter wrinkled his face and shook his head as he replied. "No! Didn't you listen to the story?"

"Yea, and it sounds like you had Germans here," Ted reiterated.

The three studied the large man as if he were off his rocker.

"Germans," Toke said while contemplating the idea.

Willy's face looked strained as he tried to put it into context.

And Ted, well he just stood there, waiting for the coin to drop.

"Mmm, Germans," Toke said again. "Yea, it all makes sense… it was Germans!" he shouted.

Chapter 44

When Jake stepped outside, he nearly backed out of the hunting trip. Heavy clouds blanketed the sky, the breath of winter an intolerable acquaintance. Frost lay heavy on the ground and trees, and the grass crackled beneath each step he took. The wind blew out of the north, though inconsistent and swirling at times. And Jake, well he didn't like the world he'd stepped into.

Before heading out this morning Jake pulled his long-johns on, slid into two pair of pants, added three sweaters on top of a long sleeved shirt, and then pulled his heavy coat over top of it all. He then warmed himself by the stove and drank two cups of coffee. But as he scurried outside, the cold invaded his clothing and the warmth quickly vanished. As he walked down the path to the Shell Banks, where he was to meet the others, he reflected on the chain of events leading up to this point and the stupidity he'd displayed.

This was not Jake's idea of fun, and there was only one thing he could do; pray. He prayed for a miracle, and that by the time he reached the beach his eyes would stop watering from the cold and behold a vacant strip of land. He prayed the rest of them had backed out.

As Jake rounded the last oak tree that led to the beach, his eyes continued to water as his spirit and shoulders slumped. "Stupid miracles," he said to himself. Sadly, none of the others had backed out for fear of being labeled a wimp. And now, they were in it 'til the end.

The boys piled themselves and their guns into the boat, shoved off, and headed north to Cat Island. The teeth of the wind gnawed at their faces as the boat raced through choppy seas. And Jake realized he'd have gladly accepted the label of wimp had he done the smart thing and stayed home. Hell, he'd still be in his warm bed.

Will and Jake looked at each other and decided this wasn't the time for bravado. Will threw his arms around Jake, no sign of shame whatsoever, and clung to his friend. Jake didn't push him away as the two huddled for warmth while sitting on a bench in the middle of the skiff. After a few minutes, Jimmy joined the group and buried his frozen face into Will's shoulder, like a child afraid of the dark and seeking out a parent's protection. But for Pate, there seemed to be no problems. He stood at the wheel, like a defiant captain about to face pirates. And he never flinched at the frigid swords that sliced the air around him.

At seven in the morning they arrived at the small island, two miles north of Dauphin Island. Captain Pate turned the boat toward a small landing area and awaited his crews' response. His crew, however, remained a hugging mass of shivering regret.

The small island was mostly barren, and for good reason. Unimaginably it was even flatter than Dauphin Island, and the tide, when at its peak, ran like dozens of small rivers, crisscrossing the spit of land. And the salt water that rose daily killed all vegetation except marsh grass. There were no trees, no shrubs, no sandy beaches, and no solid ground. The snip of land was a mud hole with a slew of small ponds that attracted ducks and alligators as if there were an endless supply of each.

Pate nosed the skiff onto the muddy beach as Will and Jake and Jimmy pried their bodies apart. Jake and Will jumped off first. It wasn't their first mistake of the day, but it was a big one. They should have gingerly stepped off since both buried to their knees in the muck. They instantly found themselves sucked into the quagmire and struggling to get out. And boy, this mud stunk!

"This day is getting better and better," Jake rued.

"Could be worse, I could be back there fighting Sherry off," Will said with his usual smile and upbeat enthusiasm.

"Better for you, but not me! Besides, there could be worse things than fighting off a beautiful girl." As soon as Jake said it, he regretted it. He knew exactly how Will felt, and understood the cruel facts of life. Will wanted Mary like he wanted Mira. And he understood that a man couldn't just decide who he loved, because you either loved someone or you didn't. The comment was stupid, and Jake was even stupider. "Sorry," Jake said as his right foot released from the suction the mud had created. Jake vowed, as the smelly mud continued the death grip on his left leg, that he would never again parade what he and Mira had in front of Will. He would never again make his best friend feel bad about being in love.

Jake and Will finally freed themselves of the mud, with the help of Jimmy and Pate, and the four plodded inland, through more mud. The island was a haven for many animals, as evidenced by all the holes that alligators used for den entrances, as well as raccoon, bird, and crab tracks that snaked in every direction. And although there were a lot of animals here, gators were the only ones to fear. They'd all seen gators, lived around and even killed a few. And a person had to be cautious when in their environment. But with the weather as frigid as it was, there would be no gators out today.

As the boys struggled through the endless muck, a renewed friendship beckoned. It was just the guys, doing manly things, and they found they enjoyed each other's company.

"What's the deal with you and Sherry?" Pate asked Will.

"Nothing really, just friends," Will said. He shook a chill and used his fingers to turn up the collar of his coat and pull it in tight around his neck.

"I don't get it. She's the prettiest girl I've ever seen and you treat her like she's got the measles!" Pate was fishing for his own catch.

"There's nothing to tell. If you want her, go get her."

Pate followed the same line of questioning for a bit longer, his eagerness apparent. Will eventually tired of anything to do with Sherry, and all other questions about the girl were met with a simple shrug of the shoulders. Pate soon got the message and moved on to other subjects.

A light drizzle, nothing more than a mist began to fall. It was already miserable, but that wasn't good enough for this day from Hell. The mist soon turned to rain, and moments later into sleet. Jake looked to Jimmy, and both looked to the heavens. Jake shook his head. They were here, miles from home, freezing and ankle deep in mud. There was nothing that could change the moment. They realized the sooner they got what they came for, the sooner they could return home. So the four loaded their shotguns and crept to an opening where three Red Heads had just settled down.

"Let's make this quick guys, I can't feel my fingers or toes," Jake whispered. Will and Jimmy nodded in agreement.

The shallow pond of rainwater, in the center of the island, was a refuge for several types of ducks. And of particular note, two geese also enjoyed the temporary layover. Light brown marsh grass whipped in the wind as each boy pointed a finger at the ducks they would each shoot. This was done so they could kill as many as possible on the opening salvo. There would be no second attempts.

Their eyes watered from the bitter day, and Jake hoped he would hit what he aimed at. But there were no guarantees since he couldn't see the birds through the large droplets that formed in the corners of his eyes. Jake wished for quick success, as he figured the others were doing, when they opened fire in unison. It didn't take long, just one volley and no more than five seconds. And once the smoke cleared they had all the birds they needed. There were even enough for a few other families. They sloshed into the pond, also a mud hole, and gathered the birds. Having got what they came for they quickly headed out and back toward the skiff.

As the boys made their way to the boat the rain increased, as did Pate's pace. By the time the group arrived at the beach, Pate had raced more than fifty feet ahead. The idiot jumped into the skiff and pushed away from shore. He began wrapping the cord around the flywheel of the motor, so as to crank it, as the boat drifted with the tide.

"What the hell you doing?" Jimmy hollered to Pate, who was now well offshore. Jimmy turned to the others. "What the hell is he doing?" They were shaking, the mixture of freezing rain and sleet bouncing off their hats and dripping down the back of their necks.

"Doesn't he know we're freezing to death," Jake said. Jake shook as the wind whipped hard and the rain came in at an angle. He pressed his body next to Will's.

"He knows, he just don't care," Will chattered. Faint puffs of smoke were produced with each word.

The three boys sat the birds on the ground and huddled together. The wind seemed to strike from every angle. There was nowhere to turn and nothing to hide behind. The engine on the boat came to life and Pate hastily turned the bow away from shore and raced away.

"If I don't die out here," Jake said, "I'm gonna kill that son of a bitch. I should have known better than trusting him!" He looked at his fingers that had curled from the cold. He couldn't feel or straighten them as he blew his breath across them. It was a vain attempt.

"No, you're not gonna kill him," Jimmy injected. "I am!"

The three shivered, helplessly, on the muddy beach, wet and cold, their shotguns draped across bent elbows. They didn't know what they were going to do when all at once the tiny boat raced from around the other side of the island, its engine singing sweet, sweet music to their ears.

"Thank God," Jimmy said in relief, although the pain was unbearable.

Pate slowed and made a motion as if he were coming to the beach, when he suddenly gunned the engine and headed offshore again. They heard him laughing over the roar of the motor as he moved away and again disappeared. A moment later he returned and headed back to the beach. Relief filled the boys, only to be extinguished by Pate's torture. He came close to the beach and then sped off once more.

The three could no longer stand it as Pate headed toward them. Jake looked at his distorted and immovable fingers. "Will, when he gets close enough, you shoot that bastard. I'll take the blame!" He shivered uncontrollably, his teeth chattering.

"I can't move my hands, Jake. I think I got frost bite!" Will glared at his gnarled purplish fingers.

"I'll get him," Jimmy snarled. He needed help from Jake to move his gun from his bent elbows to his hands. "That son of a bitch is as good as dead!" Jimmy struggled to raise the barrel of the gun and keep it level.

Jake knelt to the ground. He faced the water and boat that was approaching. "Put the gun on my shoulder," he muttered to Jimmy. "I don't want you to miss!"

Pate was moving toward shore, like he had several times before, when he noticed Jimmy pump a round into the shotgun and lay it across Jake's shoulder. Pate started waving his arms and hollering for him to stop. Jimmy didn't heed Pate's request and sighted the weapon. Pate wasn't close enough for the bird shot to kill, but he was close enough that it might maim him for life, or blind him.

Jimmy shook, just as the gun and Jake did. He held the aim on Pate for a long time and thought about the consequences of shooting. "The other two would back me. And if I shot him so we don't freeze to death, it would be considered self-defense," he thought.

Will glared at Jimmy, his anger rising to the top. If his hands weren't so distorted, he'd have snatched the gun from Jimmy's grip and fired already.

"If he don't stop, shoot the bastard!" Jake hollered.

"Shoot him!" Will yelled, "Shoot him... shoot him now!"

"Shoot damn it!" Jake raged.

"Damn it," Jimmy said with self-disgust and as the skiff slid onto shore.

"Calm down fellows, I was just having a little fun," Pate said as he helped them onto the boat and then threw the ducks and geese in.

Chapter 45

Coal and wood fired stoves bellowed smoke, forming a haze over the island. The aroma of gumbo, roasted ducks and baked pies permeated from busy kitchens. Women worked, most men slept, and it was the morning of Thanksgiving Day. The community prepared, as it always had, for the celebration. Soon, the fires would settle to ash, and eating and fun and a special treat would claim the day. The afternoon had been cast, the Arch Diocese of Mobile having provided a movie for showing at the church.

"Where you going?" Laura asked.

Jake slipped on his coat and moved toward the side door. "I'm going to see Mira. See if she needs anything."

Toke lay on the couch. He shook his head in disbelief. "That's not even close to the right answer," he thought. He skulked as far into the cushions as possible.

Laura nodded slowly, her dark hair pulled back and pinned, one spiral dangling down her cheek. Her apron, tied around her waist, was covered in flour from the pies she'd just slid in the oven. "You gonna help Mira so she can get done with her work? What a thoughtful boy I've raised."

Jake smiled appreciatively, nearly coming to a blush.

Leaving the house crossed Toke's mind. But he decided not to, believing he'd draw too much attention. So he continued to lie on the sofa, pretending to be asleep.

Laura moved next to her son, smiling all the while. She then popped him in the back of the head with an open hand.

"Hey, that hurt," Jake yelled.

"Well I didn't mean for it to feel good," she said. "Toke!" Laura raised her voice so Toke would know she wasn't playing. She had been working since before daylight, and was tired and aggravated. When Toke didn't respond, she offered another way of saying how she felt. "Toke, you better get your ass off that couch and get in here!"

Toke jumped to his feet, blinked repeatedly, and then nervously pressed the wrinkles in his shirt outward with his hands. He walked over to Jake whom he quickly popped in the back of the head.

"Hey, what's going on? Isn't this supposed to be a day of thanks?" Jake rubbed his head with both hands, now that he had two knots.

Laura's glare burned through Jake, although he wasn't sure what he'd done wrong. He decided it best to just play along and be quiet.

"Take this duck and go to Rachael's and Bess', they'll have something else for you. Then take it to the Gorman's and give 'em our regards." Laura was resolute in her speech.

Jake nodded his head but said nothing, although he hated going to the Gorman's.

Toke had been in this type of situation before, and decided an evasive tactic was his best option. "Boy, you do as your Mom said and take that stuff over. And don't be playing around." He pointed a finger at his son.

Laura looked at Toke.

Toke tilted his head and smiled sweetly. He then winked as if they were on the same page and that he understood her plight.

"Thank you," she said.

He breathed in a deep breath. "You're welcome my love."

"Mom, you know Dad's just fooling you. Shouldn't he have to go too," Jake yapped, and to his father's dismay.

Toke bit his lip. He then shook his head at his son, the traitor.

"That's a good idea. Toke, you go with him. It'd be good for you to say hello to Leo. Besides, it's not like you're helping around here."

Toke's lips drew tight, his face twisting with aggravation. He again popped Jake in back of the head.

Jake and Toke walked toward Willy and Rachael's, Jake toting a Dutch oven that held the duck. "I didn't mean to make Mom mad," he exclaimed.

"You didn't, she's just aggravated."

"Well she popped me like she's mad."

Toke thought for a second. "Maybe she was mad. I don't know. That's something you'll learn about women. You never know what they're thinking. And once you think you've got 'em figured out, they change just for the hell of it. I'm not gonna lie to you son, it's tough dealing women."

"Well you do ok with mom."

Toke gave half a laugh before answering. "Well… I keep my mouth shut for starters. I also act like I'm asleep on the couch. Do you think a man could sleep as much as I do?"

This set Jake back. "You're not asleep when you're on the couch?"

"Sometimes… I'm sure your mom knows. Besides, it keeps me out of her way. And that's what this little trip is about, keeping us out of her way." Toke was genuine and Jake knew it. "And just in case your Mom don't know, don't tell her about the couch thing."

The two arrived at Willy's and walked through the side door without knocking. Rachael had made an oyster stew and handed it to Will, who was eager to get going. The boys started out and Jake turned to his Dad. "You coming?"

"Nah, I'd better stay here with Willy. Besides, the moment we walked out of the house your Mom knew I wasn't going to Leo's. And I never aim to disappoint her." Toke shrugged his shoulders as he spoke.

"Fine," Jake said as he rolled his eyes and they left.

Jake and Will strolled along the short path to Bess and Peter Lea's house. The day was overcast and cold, and the warm pans in their arms felt good. "I complained about having to go to the Gorman's, but not you," Jake said as they walked along.

"So? I'm just trying to be neighborly," Will stated with a smile.

Jake snickered and nodded. He was happy for his friend.

As the two walked up the steps to the Lea's, Sherry came rushing out. Mira lagged behind, her arms full of bowls.

"We're going with you," the empty handed Sherry blurted.

Mira never said a word.

Will glared at Jake. He became quiet, no longer interested in the trip.

Jake didn't like Sherry coming along either, but for other reasons. "Great," he said awkwardly. Jake looked at Mira but never moved to kiss her, though it was all he could think of.

The party of four walked briskly, and quietly, towards the Gorman's. The mood, as drab as the day, never felt right. Jake had a sinking feeling in his gut, like something terrible was on the horizon. And it was obvious, from the moment the girls joined them, that Will was the dark cloud, the storm that was brewing, the sinking feeling. Jake firmly believed Will's wrath would soon be unleashed, and there was nothing anyone could do to stop it.

"How much further," Sherry asked.

A scowl crossed Will's face. His arms were tiring from the weight of the bowl he carried. And he couldn't believe the empty handed Sherry was complaining. Well, she may or may not have been complaining, but either way, an empty handed person needs to keep their big flap shut!

"We're almost there," Mira said wearily.

Moments later the broken down house of the Gorman's came into view. Will's mood lifted. Jake and Mira remained apprehensive. And Sherry was Sherry.

"It seems they could fix that place up. It looks like a sty," Sherry said with a bit of repulsion.

Will's face fell.

Jake gave him a glance, and it was obvious he was reaching his end. He wanted to say something to calm his friend, to ease the distress. But instead, he pushed his own loathing aside and directed his attention to Sherry. He tried, quite pleasantly, to explain how some people suffer no matter how hard they try. "They're very poor you know," he said. "They may prefer to eat instead of fixing up the place." Jake had made a solid point, and hoped the discussion over a lack of wealth was complete.

But Sherry was Sherry, and responded in Sherry fashion. "Well, all of you are poor, but at least you give it an effort."

"Yes, but…" Jake began, but was cut off.

"You make it sound like a bad thing?" Will said. "I'd take being poor and having the friends and family that I do, over all the money in the world and being a snob."

"You calling me a snob?" Sherry asked, her voice wrought with anger.

"No he's not, and the two of you behave." Mira intervened. She wanted to calm the situation before it turned ugly.

"No Mira, you're wrong. I am calling her a snob," Will replied.

"What's your problem?" Sherry shot back.

"My problem…? My problem…? I don't believe you!" Will had long since passed annoyance. His face reddened as he shook his head in disbelief.

"Stop it!" Jake growled. "Mira, you take Sherry back and let me and Will finish this." His head nodded in the direction they'd just come.

Mira nodded. She then heaped the food onto the boys.

As the girls walked away, Will added, "thank God she's finally gone!" He made sure it was loud enough for the girls to hear.

Sherry stopped and turned. "Kiss my ass, Will Burton!"

Will was going to reply when Jake jumped in. "Calm down. She don't know anything about how you really feel."

"That don't give her the right to talk about how poor we are."

Jake looked at the bowls in his arms and did a quick move to keep them from falling. "Will, I hate to be the one to tell you this, but we are poor."

"Well damn it… no one has to point it out!"

Jake said nothing else as he tapped the Gorman's front door with the toe of his shoe.

Chapter 46

Mary Gorman spent the morning like she did all others. And her life had become a black and inescapable abyss. Secrets turned dreams to nightmares, extinguishing a belief that happiness was out there. Like all little girls, she once dreamed of Prince Charming and the fairy tale ending. She dreamed of being rescued by her true love. But somewhere along the way the fairytales and happy endings vanished. Her nightmares screamed endlessly. She had one final chance to walk away from the disgust that attacked her life. And it was up to Will, her prince, to save her.

Breakfast was over, though it didn't really matter. The next chore would now begin, followed by the next and then the next. Leo and his son sat at the table, drinking coffee, as Mary cleared the plates from around them. For Mary it was just another day, and didn't even realize it was Thanksgiving. Perhaps none of the Gorman's knew what day it was. But that wasn't the point, had she known she still wouldn't have cared.

A tap came at the door and Mary spun. Leo gave her a quick stare as he stood from his chair, headed to the door and opened it. Jake Cullen stood there, his arms full of covered dishes, a smile on his face. And next to him was a grinning Will Burton.

Leo didn't offer a hello. He just looked at the two and waited.

"Mr. Gorman, our Moms sent this over with their regards," Jake said as he fumbled and nearly lost a pie that rested on top.

Mary moved close to the door and could see Will through a crack, where the door's hinges were mounted. Her brother Jeff remained seated and looked on, focusing on his sister. Mary watched with eager fascination. She longed to just run out, grab Will's hand, and…and…and it didn't matter what happened next. It would be over, whether they ran away together and were never to be seen again, or whether her Father took things into his own hands and delivered his own justice. It just didn't matter. She felt her body jerk, as if she were about to follow through on her thoughts. She steeled her nerves and took a step towards the door. Jeff had quietly approached from behind and placed a hand on her shoulder. Her eyes went to the floor, tears forming in the corners.

"We don't want what you got. We ain't no charity case," the older Gorman said. He was abrupt and started closing the door.

"Mr. Gorman," Jake said pleasantly. "We didn't mean any disrespect. Our moms wanted to send you something since ya'll never come to the Thanksgiving dinner with everyone else."

Leo looked the two boys over and shut the door, vanishing from view.

For Mary, it might as well been the slamming door of a prison cell. She watched in horror as the thin strip of light that had shone through the door's opening, disappeared. And one more of her dreams followed.

"Let's go" Jake said as he turned to walk away.

"No, to hell with that!" Will said. And before Jake could stop him, Will pounded on the door.

"Damn it Will," Jake implored.

The door immediately opened, as if Leo knew they were going to knock again. "I told ya'll to leave, and I told you nicely," he said. "Don't make me tell you again."

"We're gonna leave... after I speak," Will said. "You think we're looking down on you, but we're not. Look around you, we're all poor. But that don't mean a hill of beans. And it don't mean you can act like an ass to someone who is trying to be nice. You may think we believe we're better than you... well we don't. And if you don't want to come to the dinner, don't. But take the damn food and be thankful!"

Leo looked the boy up and down. His eyes narrowed as he appraised the lad. "Who are you boy?"

"Will Burton," Will replied with a bit of a bristle.

"Well Will Burton, take the food back to your moms and thank them nicely. Tell them we don't want it," Leo said.

Will shook his head.

"Tell them we ain't no charity case." But this time, when Leo Gorman spoke, it was different. Something had happened to the burly man who blocked the doorway. Both his voice and body language changed. "But also tell them that we'll be there for dinner and that we'll also be bringing our share."

Will smiled brightly. And although he couldn't see Mary, she did too.

Chapter 47

A procession of islander's filled the church rectory, all of them eager to get out of the cold. The entire island turned out and within moments the building burst at the seams. And with so many people in such a small place, kerosene heaters were doused, followed by the opening of windows.

It took only ten minutes for the ladies to spread the food out, and Thanksgiving dinner was ready to be served. The Gorman's arrived last, and strode in amongst hushed voices and blank stares. And Leo obligingly returned the gaze, though it wasn't in typical Gorman style. He did so with a smile on his face. The Gorman's had always believed they were targeted as outsiders, because they had no family here. And the glares seemed to prove as much. But Leo had decided he'd endure the day, whatever the islanders decided to throw at them. And it was all thanks to Will. The boy had left a permanent impression on him, and the man was determined to give it a try.

Each one of the Gorman's sat a bowl of food on the table, including a platter of smoked mullet, and people quit staring, no longer fascinated with their arrival. And again, conversation swelled in the room.

Will moved through the crowd, closing in on the table. He wanted to be near Mary. He eyed her, but she didn't return in kind. Instead, she was listening to Laura, who talked about how lovely she was and how she'd turned into a beautiful young woman. Mary's eyes never left the woman in front of her, nor did she smile or nod appreciatively at the kind remarks.

Will was entranced, Mary so beautiful and…. close. "Just look at me," Will thought.

Leo, after shaking hands and saying a few words to a man in the crowd, turned to Will, catching the boy's eye. He gave an appreciative nod. Will smiled, believing this to be a very good sign.

Leo moved to his left, temporarily blocking Will's view of Mary, and shook hands with even more men. Will thought it good that Leo Gorman was socializing, but wanted him to move, just a little. He did, and when he did, Mary was no longer speaking with Laura. She was staring straight at him. Will's heart raced. Leo took his daughter by the arm and the two moved away from the table. Will's eyes followed the girl of his dreams, his trance overwhelming. Jeff stepped between Will's gaze and his sister, and stared Will in the eye. He shook his head to make sure Will understood that none of this was acceptable.

Will had had all he could stand of the rude and obnoxious Jeff. He rolled up his cuffs and started in the boy's direction.

Sherry tapped Will on the shoulder. "Will," she said candidly.

Will turned. The air left his body. "What Sherry?" His voice was cold and distant, his eyes looking past her.

"Will." She struggled to keep her temper under control. "I wanted to apologize for the things I said earlier. I didn't mean to offend anyone, especially you. I care too much for you." As she finished, she felt better about herself and hoped the rift between them could be repaired.

"Good, you should be sorry," Will said. He wasn't happy about anything and everything, and wanted everyone to sense his displeasure.

Sherry gave a huffing sound, as if she were a child about to throw a temper tantrum. But instead of making a scene, her eyes watered and she walked away. Will watched her leave. And what just happened was unbelievable. He couldn't understand how he'd become this callous monster. Realizing this thing with Mary was an ever tightening noose, he needed to resolve it. One way or another it was going to end, or the noose was going to strangle him to death.

Mira tried to comfort Sherry, her sympathy gathering momentum with every sniffle and tear the girl shed. She decided to tell the entire story of Will and Mary, hoping it would ease her friend's misery. She was about to speak, when Father Malone called everyone to the table. After a short word of thanks, a prayer and sign of the cross, a line was formed.

Jake fixed himself a large plate of food and strolled to the corner, where Will stood. "You ok?" He asked.

Will didn't feel like eating. He held a cup of coffee in his left hand and sipped at it every now and then. "This is driving me nuts," he exclaimed. "I must be off my rocker to put up with this. And what's bad is she's hiding something. And whatever it is, it's got to be horrible. It's making me sad, and I can't do anything about it." He constantly scanned the room as he spoke. "The craziest part is, the less she lets me in the more I want to be in." His frustration was clear and it began to boil out of him. "I have to do this, today." Will wrapped his hand around the cup like a vise.

"No you don't. Let it go for today and do it at a more private time. Don't let everyone see it. It's none of their business."

"I don't care Jake. I don't care who sees it. I need it resolved, today."

Jake knew there was nothing he could say. He knew because he had been in the same place a few months earlier. And it finally raged from him with uncontrollable abandon. "Whatever happens, I understand. And when it's all done, good or bad, I'll be there."

Will nodded as he scratched the dry chaffed skin on his cheek that the cold weather had caused.

Chapter 48

Children ran in all directions. The large Thanksgiving Day meal slowed the older folks, but inspired the young to run faster and scream louder. Jake sat next to Mira and held her hand with gentlemanly affection. Sherry sat next to Mira and rubbed her palms together with distinct loneliness and frustration. And the seat they had reserved for Will, next to Sherry, was empty. This day hadn't started out like Jake planned, and it was evident, from the earlier conversation with Will, that it would end even worse.

The rows of pews were packed, with many more standing along the outside aisles. Father Malone thanked the Arch Bishop of Mobile for the movie, and concluded with another prayer and another sign of the cross. And as if on cue, Julius' diesel engine came to life and could be heard in the distance, followed by the glow of a single light bulb that hung from a cord next to the projector. Adults murmured in approval as children scurried to their seats. Moments later the projector flickered on the white wall of the church, and "The Freshman" starring Harold Lloyd, became larger than life.

The crowd's laughter rose and fell in a perfectly timed chorus as Harold Lloyd didn't disappoint. The clicking of the projector moved steadily for more than thirty minutes, and Will still hadn't come to his seat. Jake craned his neck, searched the entire room, and found Leo and Jeff sitting with a vacant spot between them. They were however, laughing.

***

Will and Mary walked to the school house and slipped inside. Mary was as quiet as usual, and Will did most of the talking.

"We have to resolve what's going on," Will stated. "I can't deal with this much longer."

Mary's brow furled. She tilted her head as if Will's dilemma was a minor thing. "You can't deal with what?" She asked.

"I can't deal with all the hiding and secrecy. It's not right. It's not…. normal."

Mary never hesitated. "Then let's leave."

"So you don't even want to talk about it?" Will stammered. His frustration began to churn again.

"No. Let's leave the Island and never come back. We can go where no one will ever find us. I don't want us to be apart but we can't be here." Mary's eyes never left Will's as she spoke. Her voice was even and meaningful, and she meant it.

It took only a split second for Will to respond. "I can't do that. We can't do that. All of our family and friends are here, everything I know is here." Will's voice was tinctured with pleading.

"The only way we'll be together, is if we aren't here," Mary said with the same evenness as before.

Will gave a deep sigh and asked the question he'd always wanted to ask. "Mary," his pitch was low and soft, "when I look at you, when I talk to you, I see something… something sad. I don't want you to be sad and it bothers me. You deserve more than that."

"Please don't."

Will glared at her for a moment. "I have to. But I promise I'll never ask again." He paused. "What's wrong? What makes you so afraid that you won't allow anyone to get close? Not even me."

Mary's eyes moved to the blank chalkboard behind Will. A frown, larger than usual, appeared. She bit her bottom lip. "Please Will…." She shook her head.

Will continued to stare, waiting.

Mary's lips trembled, her voice but a whisper. "I'm not… I'm not whole."

**

Jake continued to scan the room for Will. He was a no-show, and Jake hoped that would be the worst of it. But things soon changed. "Damn it," he thought as he watched Leo lean to his son and whisper in his ear. Jeff stood and headed for the door. Jake patted Mira on the leg and nodded his head toward Jeff. He stood and followed the man out.

"Didn't like the movie?" Jake asked as he stepped quickly so as to catch up with the younger Gorman.

"Leave it be!" Jeff responded.

"Leave what be? I just needed a break and happened to step out the same time you did."

Jeff shot him a glance and then headed in the direction of Mr. Willy's bar. Jake followed at a close distance. He knew what Jeff was looking for, and if he found them, then he was gonna damn well be there.

***

"You're not what?" Will asked, quite confused. "What does that even mean?"

Mary's head nodded with the faintest of movement. She looked at Will, her lips continuing to quiver. She was trying to speak, trying to form the words she'd always needed to say, but couldn't. She rubbed beneath both eyes with her fingers while fighting back tears. Once again she tried to speak.

***

Jake continued to follow Jeff, who still headed toward the bar.

Jeff stopped. He looked to his left, at the school house, and then back at Jake. He took on a look of superiority. And with a snide smile he headed in the direction of the red building. Jake picked up speed and moved steadily closer as they both closed in on the little red school.

***

Mary covered her face with her hands and spoke with a muffled sound. "Will, there's something you should know." Her voice was faint.

Now that she was going to tell him what he'd asked for, he wasn't sure he wanted to hear it. It made his heart race.

Mary's life, her entire existence had spiraled beyond reason, and in her mind it wasn't worth living. But she needed for someone to know the truth. She needed for someone to hear all the terrible things that existed. And she was now finding the strength to talk about her secrets. She moved her hands from her face. "Will," she said as her voice and body trembled. "My…"

The door to the school burst open and Jeff came rushing in, Jake on his heels. "Let's go Mary!" Jeff hollered.

"She's not leaving, so get out!" Will demanded.

Jeff raced close and grabbed Mary by the arm.

Will stepped forward and was immediately in Jeff's face, their chest bumping together.

"Get away, boy," Jeff seethed through clinched teeth.

Will grabbed Mary's other arm and pulled at her. "I said she's not going! And I'll do whatever it takes for you to understand that!"

Jeff paused. He looked at Will and then glanced over his shoulder at Jake, who had balled his fist. Jeff thought briefly about taking the two on but decided otherwise. He knew a fight would raise too many questions. While relaxing his grip on Mary's arm, Jeff grinned and said what would give his sister no options. "Mary," he said as his hand moved away from her arm, "it's your choice. You can stay and I'll let Dad know what's happened. In fact I'll tell him everything." He placed an emphases on the word "everything." "Or you can go with me and I won't say a word. It'll be our secret. I'll tell him you went home feeling ill and that's where I found you." His eyes were dark and narrow, his face as unforgiving as his words.

Mary's face paled, as if she really were about to be ill, and her body became limp. She nearly collapsed. But Will held tightly to her arm, holding her upright. Tears streamed down her cheeks. She knew what her dad would do if Jeff followed through on his promise. Things would be different if Will was willing to leave the island. But he wasn't, and it left her with no options. "I'll go."

Will released his grip. His face demonstrated the shock that rattled throughout his body. "Don't listen to him! You don't have to go! They can't make you do what you don't want to," he yelled.

Mary pushed past Jake, Jeff once again clutching her arm. They headed to the door. "Don't ever give up on me," Mary said to Will as she and her brother exited the room.

Chapter 49

Six days after Thanksgiving, the heavy winds from the north subsided. The breeze changed directions, and the waters of the bay calmed. For Ted and Sherry Larson it proved to be a long seven days. They had been stranded, for a week, and the lack of control over comings and goings was not something Ted had considered when planning a future life on the island. It gave him reason to pause. Again he'd have to mull his decision. But they were finally able to make it across the bay and to the mainland.

Ted had only planned to be gone from his farm for three days and was eager to get home. For Sherry, school remained in recess, and she too made the trip to Morgan. And it was an unusually quiet ride. Ted had guessed what happened, but struggled to connect. He wished his wife were here. She'd know exactly what to say to comfort their daughter.

The Larson's exodus from the island had come none too soon as the next cold front soon barreled through. And for four straight days the wind howled out of the north. Temperatures dipped to near zero, killing most of the fruit trees on the island and again freezing parts of the bay over. And once more, people huddled in their homes and close to their stoves.

The latest bout of bad weather was like most others, swift, forceful and soon over. As the days slowly warmed, routines were reestablished. Men began to fish, women washed laundry and hung it out to dry, and Toke took the mail to Cedar Point. But Toke returned to the island early, and empty handed. He never waited for the mail truck and was now pulling his skiff ashore at seven-fifteen in the morning. After anchoring his boat, he made his way along a narrow path to his best friend's house. He gave one quick rap on Willy's door and before anyone could reply "come in," he swung it open and led Jim Cowl in. Rachael dutifully fixed everyone a cup of coffee as the men removed their hats and sat at the table with Willy. Toke and Jim struggled to get warm, their faces somber and muted.

"I figured it was the law when someone knocked," Willy said with amusement.

"Thanks for the coffee, Ms. Rachael," Jim said.

"So what brought you here?" Willy asked, knowing this wasn't a social visit. "Has someone done something?"

"I wish it were that easy," Jim said as his body began to warm. "I met Toke at Cedar Point this morning. Something's happened and I thought it best that I come to the Island and tell everyone." Jim's voice was as serious as the expression on his face.

"Tell us what?" Willy asked. He sat up straight in his chair.

Jim paused, both hands gripping the mug. "We're at war."

Willy scratched the side of his head. He leaned back in his chair. "We're at war with the Bayou?" he asked with a grave tone.

Toke's face took on a comical pose as he glanced at Jim, who was not in any mood for humor. Toke quickly decided that now wasn't the time to make a wise crack.

"The United States is at war!" Jim said with irritation.

"Sorry, you weren't clear. Besides, I was kinda looking forward to that Bayou thing," Willy mused.

Toke chuckled, and stopped almost instantly as Jim shot him a glance.

"I don't think you grasp how serious this is?" Jim countered with.

Willy's face reddened. "You think I don't understand war?" he said with his own sense of anger.

"Well you don't seem to be taking this seriously!"

"Well, let me tell you what I know about war. Me and Julius fought in the First War and we walked through trenches full of dead. And when the sight and smell became unbearable, we puked on their bodies because there was no place a dead bloated man wasn't laying. We then hurled ourselves over the banks and into a barren wasteland of meat shredding gun fire, barbed wire, and more God damned death! I held friends in my arms as their last breaths left them, and I killed more than I care to remember. So I've seen plenty enough to understand war!"

"I certainly understand and appreciate every man's service to our country," Jim said in an effort to calm the situation. "And I didn't come here to argue."

"That's the other thing I don't understand; is how whatever has happened, affects us? It sounds like you're coming for our boys and I ain't gonna have that. I've done my part and you ain't gonna get my boys." Willy knew how the world worked, and having seen all the death and manipulation that a war could bring, he didn't want his or any of the other boys of the village involved.

Jim took another sip of coffee and decided not to get into it with Willy. Willy clearly knew the score and Jim had dealt with enough veterans in the Bayou to know that you didn't challenge their beliefs. He recognized that they always meant what they said. "I didn't come to get any of your boys today. Everyone needs to know what's happened and I need help getting them to the church. I'd like to do this once and get home. I have a lot to do in my own community." He ran his left hand through his hair as he spoke.

Will had caught the tail end of the conversation, as he entered the room, but said nothing as he moved next to the stove. "War," he thought, "didn't scare him." And "death," he believed, would be a relief from the agony he was enduring.

After finishing their coffee, the four men set out to corral the islanders.

Many of the people were upset when they arrived at the rectory. They had been rustled out of their warm beds on a frigid day and told nothing. Some didn't even have a chance to fix a cup of coffee or brush their teeth.

It was the morning of December 9th, 1941 and the Island had effectively stood still as the United States plunged itself into worldwide conflict.

Jim stood by the altar, the backdrop of Christian beliefs a peculiar setting for talk of war. He held newspapers that talked about and showed pictures of Pearl Harbor. People gasped in horror as the papers were passed around the room. He then held up a paper that had a photo of Franklin Roosevelt and Congress making the declaration of war. He said that the US would not stand idly by after the naval fleet in Pearl was destroyed, killing thousands of sailors. And that those responsible, would pay! The crowd gave an approving cheer as Jim rallied national pride. But things soon changed, temperaments changed and the room fell silent when Jim talked about the real reason for him being here. He purposely kept his glare from Willy as he held an article that spoke of the draft and the duty of every man to his country. He talked about all that would be asked of every man in the room and he clearly expected all of them to abide by the law.

As Jim made his way through the events leading up to today, anger and shouting broke out. Men pumped their fist in the air and shoved one another. And it was all Father Malone could do to keep a brawl from erupting. Some relished the thoughts and glory of fighting a war, while others cried or just sat in stunned silence. And some, unable to cope with the magnitude of the event and how it affected their family, scoffed at the notion of war and drafts, trying their best to comfort themselves and their loved ones. It seemed no two people garnered the same emotions. The enormity of such a moment shocked the senses and instilled fear of the unknowing. It was as if the world were about to crash into the sun.

By the time Jim finished, most had an idea of what was expected. Every man from the ages of 18 to 65 would have to either register for service, openly volunteer for military duty, or face prison. And every man from 18 to 45, as Jim said, could expect to see action. After answering what seemed like the same questions over and over, Jim said he'd be back in a few weeks to register abled bodies for the draft. As he concluded, Father Malone quieted the crowd and followed with a lengthy prayer. After the prayer, no one immediately moved. They weren't sure what they should do with themselves.

Chapter 50

Mira was eerily silent. She clung to Jake's arm, both of them standing in a circle with the other teenagers. The morning had been a blur and she couldn't believe, or even realize, what was happening. "What had gone so wrong," she thought. She had moved quickly through college and was less than three months from graduating. And the decision to become a nurse had been a conscionable choice. She wanted to help the sick and injured, heal suffering and pain, and show compassion in the face of hate. It was the embodiment of her existence. And the thought of war made her nauseous. She had known men, Rebecca's husband and two cousins, who'd been to war. And it wasn't only the loss of life or limbs or eyes and such that raised her concern. It was how they changed. It seemed that once in battle you were never the same, injured or not. She shook her head. The belief that Jake may one day be involved in everything that's wrong and evil in this world, was pure agony.

Like most girls, Mira dreamed of life after school, of her and Jake's future. And all of her plans included Jake. They would marry, soon she hoped. Have a family and live out their years together. She loved him. She needed him. And if he left her... if he ever had to leave her, she felt the pain would be insurmountable.

***

Most of the fathers gathered just outside the front doors of the church. The ones with daughters didn't say much as they listened to those with sons. In a time like this, it didn't seem right for a man with daughters to speak out.

"I'm not gonna allow it," Willy said to the group, reiterating what he said to Jim earlier.

Julius Carter, the only other veteran among them, never said a word.

"Whatcha gonna do?" Peter Lea asked Willy.

"My boys won't be here when they come to get 'em. I'll take 'em to another island for a few days. Weeks if need be." Willy had seen enough of war, the carnage and scars, both physical and mental. And he never wanted to see it again, especially on the faces of his sons. He'd never spoken openly about his time overseas, and Toke may have been the only one he'd ever spoken to with any measure. But even with his best friend, nearly all the horrific parts were omitted; because if you weren't there, then you couldn't possibly understand. The War had forever damaged Willy, and he had done his best to forget what he'd gone through. But if he needed to remember all the pain so he'd have the strength to keep his boys safe, then he'd relive it every single day.

"What about you Toke?" Peter asked.

"I'm not sure. The Sheriff knows us all, he knows about how many kids we have. If they don't sign 'em up this time, I guess they'll either arrest 'em or take 'em later." Toke spoke with one long sustained tone. Jake was his only child, and although he and Laura had tried to have more, it just never happened. And now in their forties, it was likely that Jake would be all they'd ever know. The realization of the outside world was becoming too invading for Toke's liking, and he felt the same impulses as Willy. It would be simple to hideout for a while. To let things come to pass. But he couldn't. He thought about the other fathers and sons! About the sacrifices they'd be asked to make! And the answer was no, he wouldn't hide out! He couldn't allow the cost to others to rise above his own, not while he enjoyed the same freedoms, the same rights and privileges, and the same wonderful country. His decision was made. He and Jake would sign up for the draft, and gladly do so. Whatever a man could do for his country, he'd do it.

Leo Gorman wasn't included in the circle of men, but was close enough to hear the chatter. He interrupted, offering his own view. "If they come get my boy," he said as everyone turned in stunned silence, "I'm gonna let him go. I don't wanna, he's still my little boy, but he's also a man. And if that day comes, I'll tell everyone how proud I am and that he's my son, my child!" Leo's eyes were glassy, and he looked much older than anyone remembered.

Willy and Julius stared at each other after Leo had spoken. Julius didn't say anything before walking away. Willy watched him go and then turned to look at Leo. He didn't know if Leo had ever been to war, but thought he may have misjudged the man. He also realized that Leo was right. Willy shook his head before also turning and walking away from the church.

✻✻✻

"I'm gonna enlist in the Marines," Pate Carter said with bravado.

"Don't be stupid, you ain't gonna enlist in the Marines. You wouldn't last a day," Jimmy Clark said in an attempt to take Pate down a notch.

Pate glared at Jimmy, no longer recognizing his "friend".

Jimmy's eyes showed something deep, and different. Jimmy had finally outgrown Pate's reach and it left a bad taste in Pate's mouth.

"My Dad was in the war and I've heard enough to know. If I said I'm going in the Marines, then you can bet your ass I'll be a Marine!" There was anger in his voice and Jimmy let it be. "What about you Jake, wanna join with me? I bet the two of us could whip 'em all."

Jake mustered a smile and looked at Mira, who continued to cling to him. "I'll tell you what. Y'all take care of the war, and I'll stay here with the pretty girls."

Mira smiled and held even tighter, as if Jake's words made it all go away.

***

"Whatcha think?" Laura asked Toke. They were beneath the covers, their bodies pressed together for added warmth. It was a cold night, and the room was filled with a blackness that neither had ever known. It was as if light would never again come to this room. The two had been in bed for hours, talking and making the small room complete.

"I don't know," Toke said, "but it'll work out. I'm sure everything will be fine."

Laura could hear the worry in his voice, just as she could feel it in her bones. Toke's words were an attempt to make himself feel better, and she hoped it was working. At least one of them needed to be strong.

Chapter 51

Tis' the season! The holidays and Christmas spirits were alive and well on Dauphin Island. It was two days before Christmas and the weather was mild, though muggy. Up until now, neither Jim Cowl nor anyone else from the government had shown up to enlist men for the draft. Everyone had expected Jim to come along, but for whatever reason, he hadn't. And it proved to be a blessing. The time had allowed the shock to wear off, allowed men to search their souls and come to terms with what needed to be done. This was their country, the American flag was waving in the afternoon sun, and they were all going to protect it. National pride became the rallying call, bringing everyone together like never before. And what had begun as skepticism, turned into thoughts of a quick end to the war. They believed they only needed to ban together for it happen.

This Christmas had a different sense, a foreboding urgency in the waning days of 1941. And families strived to make this a time to remember. With a war ongoing and uncertainty a part of daily life, folks were kinder, gentler, and more forgiving. And events, the small traditions that all families partake in, seemed to garner the most attention. Like a summertime breeze off the gulf, the joy of Christmas spread across the island with endearing warmth.

There was no need for coats as Toke and Jake left the house. In fact, Jake wore cut off britches. Jake picked up an ax as he exited the side door. They burned little wood in their stove, coal being their first choice. But an ax's purpose wasn't only for chopping fire wood, though it would chop down a tree today. Instead of heading down a path, they walked a short distance into the thicket of trees that surrounded their house. And they quickly eyed what they wanted.

Pine saplings dotted the island with their perpetual green needles, and the sight of this year's Christmas tree glistened in the morning sun. Every year it was father and son, a special, almost magical moment that the two had always shared. And for as long as Jake could remember, this was Christmas. Jake looked at the tree and smiled, his mind wandering back to the early days, when his Dad would lift him onto his shoulders, which seemed ten feet high, and set out in search of that perfect tree. To Jake it seemed a much further distance back then, and maybe it was, but it meant the same thing as today. He turned to look at his Dad… he loved his Dad.

Every year Jake and Toke alternated, and this year Jake got to choose the tree. And he picked out what he thought was a dandy. Armed with the ax, he chopped a small pine tree down, inches above the ground. After trimming the bottom, he nailed two slats of wood, in the shape of an x, to the base. He then dragged it to the yard and into the house. Jake and Toke stood the tree in the corner as Laura marveled at its beauty. "You boys really out did your-selves this year," she said with a smile.

***

Pate Carter kept true to his words and enlisted in the Marine Corp. And come January 17, 1942, he'd be in basic training in North Carolina. His dad never said anything, for or against what his son had done, he simply accepted the decision. But for now he had his boy, his only child, and was determined to make the best of their remaining days together. So Julius pushed the worry from his mind and repressed his apprehensions. He decided the world was a better place with him and his son in it, and he knew God only wanted what was best for his world. He believed everything would be okay.

Julius and Pate put in a full day's work, the day before, cutting trees and sawing them into planks. When they had finished, there were thirty-one planks total. And all were six inches wide and seven feet long. Having cut the planks the day before, the two now loaded them onto a narrow wagon and hitched one of their goats to it. Julius' wife, Alice, walked out of the house, stopping on the porch. Julius knew what she wanted and walked over to her. He smiled as she handed him a box with a beautiful red ribbon tied around it.

"Mary" she said as she looked at Julius.

He knew what to do.

Pate grabbed the rope around the goat's neck, and he, his father, and the goat headed down a path and toward the other end of the village.

Julius and Pate stopped in front of the Cullen house and watched as Jake dragged a tree through the side door, his father encouraging him along the way. They smiled at each other. Pate tied the rope to a tree and the two went through the front door of the Cullen home. And with a "Merry Christmas," the men shook hands and hugged Laura.

"Nice tree," Pate said sincerely.

"I picked it out!" Jake beamed. "It's a beauty." The tree was four feet tall with a significant bowing that extended from the floor to its tip. It leaned so terribly to the right that Toke had to tie it to the wall with fishing twine just so it would stand up. But it was beautifully… crooked! Extending from the tree's center were eight limbs that jetted out and downward. And the scent of pine gum filled the room. But to everyone standing there, the tree wasn't littered with imperfections. Instead, it was a beautiful and wonderful symbol of the holidays.

As the custom, Toke, Laura and Jake spent a few minutes decorating the tree, which didn't take long. There wasn't much to decorate with. But all the same, Pate and Julius watched with delight as the Cullen's moved happily about. Almost all the ornaments were hand carved by Toke and Jake, and they were of familiar things; such as redfish, ducks, and shrimp boats and skiffs of varying sizes. After the carvings came a strand of popcorn garland followed by the crowning piece… a delicate pair of interlocking doves. Toke's grandpa, Papa Jim, had whittled the doves when Toke's grandma died. And he did it as a sign that he and his wife would never be apart. The doves rested on grandma's grave for months, until one day Papa Jim decided to give them to Toke and Laura. They both understood its meaning and they understood how precious a gift it truly was.

Saul and Jimmy Clark came through the front door and the living room became pleasantly crowded. They all shook hands and patted each other's backs as Laura fixed coffee. "Nice tree," Jimmy said as Laura handed him a cup of coffee. Jake again smiled with delight.

"Here you go Laura," Saul said. He handed her a ham wrapped in paper. "And Merry Christmas!" Saul Clark did a little bit of fishing, enough to get by, but mostly raised hogs. And every year he butchered a large sow or two and made sure everyone shared in the celebration. It was what he did.

"You must have butchered a large one this year," Laura said as she struggled to hold the weight of the pork. Toke walked over, relieved her of the burden and set it on the counter.

The house was full of laughter and friends.

"Where you headed with the planks," Saul asked, having noticed the full wagon when he and his son walked up.

"To the Gorman's," Julius replied. "I've been meaning to take 'em something and thought today was the perfect day to do it."

"Good," Saul said, "I have some pork chops you can bring 'em."

Julius smiled and gave an affirmative nod.

"Don't take 'em the chops," Toke said as he went to the counter, picked up the ham and gave it to Julius. "We'll take the chops. Laura can work magic when it comes to cooking chops." Laura, as well as everyone else, knew that the prize meat of a hog was the hams, and everybody envied who ever received them. So she walked over and wrapped her arms around Toke's waist and kissed his cheek. They both smiled.

"We got some ribs we're gonna drop off for you later," Saul said to Julius.

"Thanks Saul, it means a lot. Well, I guess we better get moving. We've got things to do," Julius said as he hugged Laura again and left with the ham. And once again he and his son were headed down the path toward the Gorman's.

"Say what you want about Julius, but the man has a kind heart," Toke said. They all thought about that for a while and they all agreed.

"Well, what time you gonna be by tomorrow?" Saul asked Toke.

Toke's face lit up as he spoke. "We'll be there bright and early this year, bright and early."

"You coming?" Jimmy asked Jake.

"Heck yea. There's not a person in this world that could keep me away."

"Ha hem." Laura gestured as if to clear her voice and gain attention at the same time.

"Well, almost no one," Jake said respectfully.

The room went quiet for a moment as Jimmy stepped out and soon returned with the pork chops. "Here you go Ms. Laura," he said.

"Thank you Jimmy, and Merry Christmas." Laura had a great smile, and it showed.

"I ain't been to Cedar Point in a while," Saul said, breaking the moment. "How far they come with the poles?" Saul knew Toke had retrieved the mail two days ago and would have noted the progress of the electrical poles that dotted the bay.

"They just made it to the channel," Toke said. "I don't know if they thought it out or not, but it's going to take quite a pole to span it. But truth be told, they've sped things up since the war started."

"I'm sure it will be here all too soon," Saul said, though no one knew if he was talking about the war or electricity.

"I'm sure it will," Toke confirmed with quiet assent.

Saul and Jimmy left after a lengthy stay and headed to the next house. They still had people to see and plenty of pork to give away.

Chapter 52

Julius knocked and Leo Gorman answered.

"Julius," Leo said nicely enough as he opened the door.

"Merry Christmas," both Julius and Pate said with enthusiasm.

Leo nodded.

"We've got something for you," Julius said as he turned his body sideways and extended an arm in the direction of the loaded wagon. "It's Christmas and we thought you could use the planks to do some mending. We also have a nice ham that Saul sent over. It looks like some fine pork!"

Leo looked at the boards and wrapped ham and then back at Julius. "It's mighty nice of ya, but we ain't gonna take em. We ain't no charity case."

Julius looked to his son and paused, collecting his thoughts. His voice lowered as he became humble... something he wasn't akin to doing. "I know you're not a charity case. The truth is its Christmas and well... I've been waiting to apologize. Ever since I accused you of stealing my engine parts, I've done my best to figure a way to show you I'm sorry. It's just some boards, and Saul's a good man and wouldn't have it any other way. We all wish you'd accept them, as well as our friendship."

Leo scratched his nose as a smile appeared below his finger. It was a genuine smile as the Christmas spirit was now becoming contagious. "I never thought any more about the stealing thing. But I can certainly use the wood. And as for the ham and friendship, a man would be a darn fool to turn down either."

Julius' face broadened with a huge smile. It made him feel better than he could ever imagine. "Where do you want me to put 'em?" Pate asked, referring to the planks. Leo stuck his head back in the door and asked his son to come out. A moment later, Jeff appeared and directed Pate to the other side of the house. They began unloading the wagon.

Julius and Leo stood by the front door and continued talking. "Is your daughter here?" Julius asked.

Leo turned his head sideways as if he were sizing the man up for a fight. "Why you want her?" he asked with a guarded disposition.

"We have something for her as well. I think she'll like it a lot," Julius said with an even bigger smile.

"She don't need nothing," Leo said, reverting back to the same stubborn tone he always used. "She'll be fine with the ham."

"The ham's for all of you and everything doesn't have to be a struggle. It's just a gift that my wife made. It'd make her happier than you know if you let Mary have this." Julius was stern in his speech and extended the box.

Leo shook his head. "Like I said, she don't need nothing."

"Leo," Julius said with kindness, "me and my wife only have Pate. But we had a daughter, for a while at least. She died of colic at the age of three and my wife never forgave herself. We tried to have more kids, but...... well anyway. My wife loved that girl more than a man could know, and to this day she makes girly things and such all the time. And every year she makes a dress to give to some girl in the community. It's the only thing my wife's ever asked for Christmas. And giving this to your daughter is as much a gift to Alice as it is to Mary."

Leo looked to the ground and then back up. He turned his head and hollered, "Mary, come here!"

Moments later Mary stepped through the door. "Yea," she said hesitantly.

Leo gave a little hitch with his head toward Julius, telling the girl she needed to look to the other man.

"Merry Christmas," Julius said as he extended the box.

Mary's eyes watered as she staggered past her dad. She stopped in front of Julius and stared at the box in his hands, afraid to touch it. Julius pushed it in Mary's direction, beckoning her to accept. She gently took the box and glared at it for the longest. She ran her trembling fingers across its edges and lightly touched the dainty bow. "It's the prettiest thing I've ever seen," she said. "I don't know what to say, I don't know how to even thank you."

Julius felt his body become weak. He had given many dresses away over the years but had never experienced anything like this. The girl didn't even care what was inside the box, she was simply grateful someone thought of her. And like a bolt of lightning, it struck him. He realized this was the first gift she'd ever been given. It tore at him. He struggled to hold back tears as Mary continued to marvel at the box. "Open it!" Julius said, his voice cracking.

Mary shook her head. "I don't want to. I…" she paused, "I just want this moment to last forever."

"Open it so you can get back to your chores," Leo said with something close to anger.

What Leo said, and how he said it, disturbed Julius. Julius' smile vanished. He wanted to punch Leo in the face. Julius would have gladly stood there all day and watched Mary, the lovely smile upon her face. He could easily see it was one of the happiest moments the girl had ever known. And he could see that Leo, her father, was taking that away. Julius fumed but said nothing. He knew if he did then Leo would take the dress away just for spite.

"Mr. Carter… would it be ok if I open it later, on Christmas morning?" Mary asked.

Julius nodded as the joy came back and he again pushed back tears with a smile. "I think that would be perfect."

"Thank you," she said, "it's the prettiest thing I've ever seen. And thank your wife for me; I'm sure she's a wonderful person." Mary turned, with the box carefully extended in front of her as if she were carrying a tray of delicate wine glasses. She disappeared into the house.

Moments later Pate returned with the wagon and the four men shook hands and said their goodbyes.

Pate and Julius headed toward home, Julius keeping to his self.

"That was nice Dad," Pate said.

Julius nodded. His thoughts were deep. It bothered him the way Leo treated Mary. "It didn't appear he treated his boy like that," he thought.

"Dad?" Pate said as if to ask if his father was ok.

"I'm ok son, just thinking." The two walked a little further before Julius put a hand on the goat's rope and they stopped. He looked at his son. He could see the little boy of yesteryears hiding in a man's body. "I know I don't say it enough, but I love you. And I'm proud of everything you've done and are about to do."

Pate rubbed his bottom lip with his free hand. "Thanks Dad," he said softly, "I love you too, and merry Christmas."

Chapter 53

For more than half a century, the men of the island "walked" on Christmas Eve. No one remembered exactly how it started, but most believed it to be an Irish custom that began soon after the Cullen's arrived on the island. And it seemed like an obvious conclusion since it sounded like something the Irish would do, and like something the Cullen's would wholly endorse. But as Cullen-like as the ritual was, it wasn't only an occasion for them. It had become a tradition, like Mardi Gras and its surrounding revelries, complete with its tableau of kings and queens, jokers and jesters.

Toke and Jake arrived at the Clark's house by nine in the morning, and Toke had already begun the "walk." As he strolled in his neighbor's house, he held a cup of coffee laced with Irish whiskey.

"Merry Christmas," Toke and Jake announced with enthusiasm. Everyone hugged like the old and dear friends they were. "The chops were great," Toke added. "And thanks for all you do." Toke gave Saul another hug.

Saul's wife Elizabeth, Toke's niece though one year older than him, had everything in place. The kitchen table was arrayed with several dishes, including deserts. And everyone began to eat. After the meal, in which no one sat, the men fixed themselves a cocktail. They stood around the living room, laughing and talking and telling stories they'd heard many times. And Toke in particular, had a way of telling the same stories over and over while still making them interesting and funny. It was the way he told them, reliving the moment and acting it out, while adding new bits and pieces each time. But Toke didn't want to tell all his stories, not just yet, and paced himself. It would be a long day. So he and Jake and Saul and Jimmy again filled their glasses with the spirit of their choosing, and exited the house.

The four walked from the Clark's house, the furthest house to the west, and into the next one, no more than thirty feet away. Henry Cullen and his family had a very nice spread, and the smell of chicken and oyster gumbo drifted through the open windows and doors. For an hour the men visited. And they again ate and drank. Henry's father-in-law, born and raised in the Bayou, now lived with his daughter and Henry. The man didn't like the island much when he first came here, but now transplanted several years, he seemed happy and content. He sat at the table and told story after story of when he was a child. And everyone listened, everyone laughed, and everyone was glad he was still with them. "Wish I was able to walk with ya'," the old man, now in his late eighties, said. And although his legs could no longer carry him along, he did his part at keeping the ritual going. He sipped at a glass of bourbon and ate when everyone else ate.

"I could carry ya," Toke said.

The old man chuckled. "That's alright, just promise you'll come back later."

"Don't worry, it's our next to last stop and I ain't not made it to the end yet," Toke said with a bit of pride and half a laugh.

Henry was the oldest of the Cullen boys. And he didn't have any sons, just two daughters, one of which wed Saul Clark and lived next door. So it was just Henry and the four other men that left for the next home.

The walk continued throughout the day with every home offering food, spirits, and joy. And with each stop the group of men swelled. By midday all the men were involved, and the group staggered along like a freight train rolling along the rails of a rickety old track. Some fellows had fireworks and tossed them about, taking an opportunity to startle one another if the moment presented itself. As for the rest, they were just happy to be along for the ride.

"So you really did it," Jake said to Pate. Pate and Jake, and all those under twenty, unless married, lagged behind the veterans of the group. The older men always led and the younger ones knew their place. It was a time for their dads and granddads to relive stories and enjoy the lives they'd carved out for themselves. And the younger ones knew the day was soon coming for it to be their time, to have their chance to lead the group. It was the same cycle since the beginning, and it was how it would always be.

"Yes sir," Pate said with a zip. "You're looking at a Marine. The best the military has to offer." Pate was proud of his decision, and rightfully so.

"Are you scared?" A boy of sixteen asked. The kid was not normally with the older boys, in any such fathom of social hierarchy, but during the walk they were all on the same learning curve, equals of sorts.

"Heck no," Pate said with a keen reply. "Marines don't get scared."

Jake and Jimmy both rolled their eyes, but said nothing.

The day was nice, though still muggy, and the mood amongst the boys became more cheerful with each stop, in spite of the war. But other than Pate's enlistment, they all agreed to avoid conversation about war and drafts. For today, the walk was all that mattered.

The men moved in harmony and became drunker by the hour. The day wound through the village, in and out of yards and houses, and finally settled in at dusk. Once darkness fell, some men quit walking because their wives made them. And some quit because they realized if they continued, there would be no prayer of them making midnight Mass. And everyone made Mass.

Mira sat quietly on the couch as the men came in and out of her parent's house. Jake moved close and did his best to smooch a kiss. Mira wasn't fond of the ritual, the drunk and slobbery men, the off handed jokes and raucous play, and pushed Jake away. She may have had to tolerate the "walk" because that was how it was, but she didn't have to pretend to like it. So she did what she was obliged to do while making herself distant. She only had to endure the idiotic custom for a few more hours. Because then it'd be time for Mass, which signaled an end to all this foolishness. And she was so ready for that time to come.

"What's wrong?" A slurred worded Jake asked as he steadied his stance by placing a hand on the back of the couch.

"Nothing Jake. Just drink and do your walking thing." Mira was ready for all of them to leave, including Jake.

"But I love you," Jake said.

"I love you too, but now is not the time. We can discuss love tomorrow."

"Tomorrow! Tomorrow! There may be no tomorrow!" His voice rose when he spoke, as did his arms. "It's Christmas and Christmas is about love. And it's about today and I'm in love…" He pointed a finger at Mira.

"Christmas is not today, it's tomorrow. We'll talk tomorrow!" Mira was firm in her speech, and Jake's reaction was that of an eighteen year old who'd been drinking.

"Fine, tomorrow we talk. And when we talk, I'll still be drinking. And I don't plan on going home tonight, because I'll be drinking with all my buddies… and that Marine fella." Jake walked into the kitchen, grabbed a hand full of fried oysters and held them in the air as if he had just conquered and plundered a country. He then stormed through the side door. But before Mira could turn away, he stuck his head back in. And with a mouth full of food said, "great oysters. You did a good job on these."

Mira wanted to laugh, but more so she wanted to strangle him. Damn it irritated her how he could be so indifferent. How could he not see she was upset with all this silliness? And how could he not care? "Damn it!" she wanted to scream.

Pate and Jimmy stood next to the barren fig trees. They draped each other, both finding it difficult to keep their balance. Will stood next to them, steady as a rock. Jake staggered from the house, stuffing the last of the oysters in his mouth.

"We gonna drink or what?" Jake said. "And you two drink like girls." He pointed at the unsteady boys.

"Like girls? I ain't no girl, I'm a Marine," Pate said as let go of Jimmy and stumbled five feet to his right. "I'll drink any of you under the table, anytime! Because I'm a Marine and that's what we do!"

"Let's do it," Jake said as he raised his glass and then downed it.

"Oh shit," Pate said as he clutched his stomach and dropped his glass to the ground.

Will took a bit of pleasure in the recent turn of events, and smiled.

Pate lurched forward and fell to the ground. He was soon on his hands and knees and vomiting. Jake, Will, and Jimmy stood behind him, laughing. Pate's body convulsed from deep within, horrible sounds and horrible odors spewing from his mouth.

"Semper... something, something!" Jake yelled, having heard Pate say it a hundred times in the last few hours but too drunk to recall exactly what it was.

"Shut up, you can't say that, you're not a ...!" Pate heaved again.

The three laughed uncontrollably.

"Shut up you hyena laughing bastards, it ain't funny." Pate was in no position to enforce his anger as he continued vomiting.

The three laughed till it hurt.

The smell of vomit reached Jimmy's nose and he grimaced. His face and neck flushed, as a burning, distasteful pain swelled within his throat. He too fell to his knees and vomited a mixture of all the foods he'd eaten throughout the day.

And as for Jake and Will, it might as well have been Christmas morning; because their gifts were on the ground before them.

Chapter 54

Mary Gorman cleared the dinner table and moved about the kitchen with energy. She hummed to herself, feeling the joy of an approaching Christmas morning. She thought of the gift the Carter's had given her, and it knocked everything from her mind. Nothing could bring her down.

Mary had just finished washing the last of the dishes when she heard voices from outside. The group of walkers lurched by, and laughter, mixed with words and firecrackers, echoed in the night air. And the laughter, joy, and celebration became a temporary strain. She envied the freedom everyone else had.

Leo and Jeff sat in silence, as if it were death at the door, the two of them waiting for it to pass over.

Mary strained to listen, if for no other reason than to see if she could hear Will's voice in the crowd. She was unable to pick him out, though she pictured his face among the crowd, his smile brightening the gathering. The group soon passed and the house became quiet, yet again.

Mary walked to the front door and opened it.

"Where you going?" her Dad barked.

Mary stopped, but didn't turn to look at him. "I'm going to get firewood before bedtime." She nervously awaited the reply.

Leo didn't say anything more and Mary departed, closing the door behind her.

Mary used a small hatchet to splinter wood for kindling. She liked splintering wood. The repeated short strokes, the shredding of something once whole, eased her distress. She calmed with every blow she delivered.

"Hello Mary."

Mary was momentarily startled, until she turned to see who stood behind her. "Shhhh, my Paw will hear you," she whispered, her face beaming with a huge smile, her hopes of seeing Will coming true.

"Yea, well I don't care if he does." The booze had dulled Will's senses, as well as any fear.

"Well I do, so quiet down."

"Fine, I'll be quiet…….. if you give me a kiss."

Mary was shocked at how brazen Will had become. But she was glad for it, because she wanted to kiss him more than anything. She peeked back at the house and the front door remained closed. She turned back to Will and smiled. He was such a handsome man. She leaned in and gave him a long kiss on the lips. By the time the kiss ended she was flustered and panted openly.

"Very nice," Will said with pleasure, his voice now low.

"Yes, very nice," she agreed as their lips met again.

"So you gonna take me in and formally introduce me?" Will asked.

Mary shook her head. "Not tonight."

"Not ever, you mean," Will said with lost enthusiasm.

"Come back tomorrow night, same time, and I'll meet you right here. There's something I want to show you." A beautiful smile crossed her face.

"Really?"

She held a coy expression while trying to decide what Will meant by his reply. "It's a present. Pate's mom gave me a Christmas present, and you'll just have to wait and see what it is." Her face held an expression of teasing, her voice flirtatious. She enjoyed this game the two were playing. It made her feel alive and connected to a world she'd somehow been omitted from. She hoped there would be many more evenings just like this.

Mary was overly excited about a single present, and it didn't seem quite right. Will began to see the larger picture, and it bothered him. In the past Mary could never have been viewed as sweet, all the school children knew this. But she was sweet; beautiful and sweet and… innocent in many ways. "It sounds nice," he said with a downward expression.

"I'm so sorry. Did you not get anything for Christmas?" Mary said, believing she'd hurt his feelings.

Will thought about that. He didn't receive a gift every year, and when he did it was usually small inexpensive items. But his parents always tried. Some years were leaner than others and Will understood that. But at least he knew they wanted to give him something, and that they loved him more than anything. He was beginning to believe that Mary's dad didn't love her at all, and that perhaps no one else did either. He looked to the ground and lied. "No Mary, I've never received anything for Christmas."

Mary paused. "When it's just the two of us, I'll make sure you get something every year," she said as she put her cheek next to his and hugged him.

As the two separated, Will lifted his head and she was smiling. He liked her smile and finally felt good about their relationship. "I'd like that. And I'm happy that you got a gift this year."

"If it's a dress I'll wear it tomorrow so you can see."

"I'd like that too," Will said with tenderness. The two kissed again.

"Mary!" Leo Gorman yelled from the porch as he looked toward the wood pile and squinted. Mary squeezed Will's hand and smiled. She then gathered the splintered wood, turning up the end of her apron and placing it in its fold, before heading to the house.

Will was exuberant, and raced down the path. He soon caught up with the rest of the walkers.

"Everything ok?" Jake asked as soon as Will fell into ranks.

"Everything's great! I think things will finally be ok."

Chapter 55

The "walk" ended an hour before the church bell that signaled midnight Mass, rang. And moments later Mass began with everyone in attendance, including the intoxicated walkers. The church pews were full and everyone sat in their usual spots, except Jake. He wasn't next to Mira, which had become the custom ever since they began dating and during times she was not away at school. Instead, he sat with Will, and the two wobbled and struggled to go from seating to kneeling and back again.

"I wish he'd hurry the hell up," Will said in an attempted whisper. "All this kneeling and standing is like being on a damned boat. I think I'm getting sea sick! Look at me Jake, do I look like I'm gonna be sick?"

Aunt Irma, who sat in front of Will, turned in her seat and gave him a glare designed to tell the boy to hush. Will responded by pretending to button his lips together. Content, she turned back to the sermon. As soon as she turned, Will commenced to unbuttoning his lips.

"Whatcha think?" Will asked Jake.

Jake didn't immediately offer a response. After another episode of changing positions, Jake could clearly see what had to be done. "Let's go to the bar. Besides, there's another Mass in the morning. We'll make that one."

Will nodded in agreement.

The alcohol had made them daring and brave, as they both knew the magnitude of their decision and the fury their mothers would unleash if they were caught. But it was okay, they had been drinking long enough to become invisible. Besides, they were crafty stealthy devils and no one would suspect a single thing.

The boys eased from the pew, craning their necks as they scanned the room for any eyes that may be upon them. They took four steps, stopping momentarily as Will believed old man Lander was eyeing him. They then slipped through the church door, on tiptoes I might add.

Laura cocked a brow as she watched Jake bump into the pedestal that held the bowl of Holy Water, nearly knocking it over. "They're idiots," she thought.

Once the boys were outside and free of the long arm of the Church, they raced to the bar, whooping and hollering along the way.

Will wiped the bar with a rag, and then retrieved two beers from his Dad's stockpile. And Jake, well he watched from the lone chair next to the bar. A single kerosene lamp flickered next to them, the black smoke rising through the flute and scattering into the surrounding black. The glow lit their faces, their talk centering on girls and war. And it was quite an innate scene as the two mirrored their fathers' movements. They moved like their dads, acted and spoke like them, and drank like them. And they loved each other, just as their dads loved each other. They were best friends and no matter what, hell or high water, they would remain best friends. So they made a promise to each other. They agreed to enlist in the Navy, if the Sheriff could guarantee they'd end up in the same unit. They both knew it was their best chance, and the right thing to do.

The day had been long, many drinks consumed, and two additional hours in the bar didn't help. "Let's go to the house," a tired Jake said to his best friend. "Momma made some galettes and we got some honey. We'll go to Mass in the morning."

Will nodded approvingly and the two set off in a stumbling haze as a light drizzle began to fall.

Chapter 56

Christmas morning, for children at least, was bright and cheery. But at the Cullen house it was more like a funeral. Laura readied herself for church and now added the final touch. She slipped her on flat heeled shoes. She sighed. There was no jubilation or joy in the air, no welcoming of the Christmas cheer, no nothing. And if it weren't for the prospect of Mass on this Holiest of days, she'd have climbed back in bed. But she enjoyed church so much so that she made a habit of attending three days a week, including confession each time.

With her shoes on, Laura stood from the chair that rested at the kitchen table. She glared at the couch, the big lump. Her husband, who mounded like a clump of unfolded laundry atop the cushions, was in a peaceful slumber. Toke lay on his right side, his arm folded beneath his head and serving as a pillow. Laura thought he looked somewhat innocent. The man didn't have a care in the world, and his deep-rooted sleep proved as much. "Oh well," she said softly and with a hint of exasperation… just before all hell broke loose. She shook Toke, who mumbled something but didn't rouse. She then frowned, before grabbing his arm and pulling. Toke fell from his nest and onto the floor. He remained a lump, though now in a different spot. But there was never any question, at least in

Laura's mind, that he would be at church. And a hangover, any hangover, wasn't going to change the fact.

Toke had a throbbing in his head, an aching in eyes, and a throat so dry that he struggled to fill it with a single drop of saliva. And as for his appearance, well it was even worse. He peeked open an eye, and then closed it. Slow to react to Laura's special attention, he rolled onto his stomach and lay face down on the floor. He might as well have slapped her in the face. Laura tugged at his arm several times, but the man just wouldn't respond. The time had come to bring out the big guns, the ultimate form of persuasion; the grabbing of the ear lobe. And from there, it didn't take long as Toke finally rose to his unsteady feet.

"Even Toke has limits," she thought. She smiled for the first time today.

Toke stood there, his eyes closed, his body swaying from side to side like the pendulum of a grandfather clock. But he was upright, amazingly, and squinted with one eye at his lovely wife. He loved her, no doubt about that, but damn he wanted to sleep a bit longer! And he was about to tell her so when she put the final nail in the liquor cabinet.

"Jake, get up!" Laura hollered while standing only inches from Toke's head.

Toke grabbed his throbbing head with both hands. He staggered to the counter and took a drink of water from a pitcher. "Please Laura, no hollering," he said with a low crackling voice.

"Jake!" Laura yelled as loud as she could, followed by a polite, yet disingenuous smile.

Toke shook his head in dismay, and found that that also hurt. "Fine Laura, be that way. I know I drank too much, but you don't have to add to the misery." Toke picked up an empty coffee pot from the stove and held it out to Laura, as if to ask what was going on.

Laura shrugged her shoulders and again yelled for Jake.

Toke decided to wait outside, while Laura went to wake Jake. He knew he couldn't endure any more yelling.

Moments later Laura walked out of the house and down the steps. She grabbed Toke's hand and jerked. They started towards the Church. "Jake must have stayed at Will's last night." There was anger in her tone.

"Yea," was all Toke could get out as he stumbled alongside his wife, trying to keep up.

"He better be at Mass," Laura said with conviction. She squeezed Toke's hand. "I saw the two sneak out last night! The idiots!"

"I'm sure he'll be there," Toke said as he used his free hand to pry his other hand from Laura's grip. He then shook his hand, which hurt nearly as bad as his head. "And yea, I know you saw him. Why do you think I moved to the couch?"

"Well Toke Cullen," she halted, grabbed his arm and swung him around to face her. "You better hope he's there! Because this 'walk' thing is your idea and your ability to walk (and she didn't specify if it were "walk" or just walk) depends on him being there!"

"Don't worry, he's a Cullen, he'll be there." Toke's head pounded so badly that he'd say just about anything if he could just make it through the morning without any more yelling.

The Cullen's front door and the church front door were exactly sixty-two paces apart. And Toke shuffled as Laura stomped down the narrow path, the ground damp from the brief shower the night before. As they moved ever closer to the church, they noticed a large gathering to the right of the church door, at the Manger scene.

Laura and several other ladies had put the scene together at the beginning of the holiday season, as they do every year, and did an exceptional job. The Manger had been erected with planks that Julius cut and donated. It was nicely built and well decorated. Several feet wide, a couple of feet tall, and covered in palmetto fronds, it was heavenly, in an island way. And to add to the blissful scene was a historical first for the island; a complete Nativity scene that had been donated by the Arch Diocese. The ceramic cast consisted of Mary and Joseph and baby Jesus, as well as the Three Wise Men and several barn animals.

Folks were joyful, laughing in fact as Laura and Toke approached. And Laura was pleased to see the Christmas joy… the…….

A whisper spread through the crowd. The group abruptly ceased the snickering once the Cullen's closed in. Toke and Laura pushed their way to the Manger and realized Jake had in fact made it to Mass. He and Will both lay on the pine straw that had been strewn about, Jake firmly clutching a donkey in his arms while Will used a lamb as a pillow.

"They are idiots," Laura said.

Rachael and Willy came up a moment later and the four looked at their sons.

"Huh, they must have rewritten the Bible," Toke said wryly. "I don't recall anything about two island boys bearing gifts."

Willy chuckled. Laura elbowed Toke in the ribs.

"Toke, that's not very Christian of you! You shouldn't talk like that on Christmas day. And those boys should be ashamed of themselves." Willy shook his head as he delivered his own sermon. Willy knew two things were prudent in a moment like this. He knew to get a response in first, before Toke could turn this around and blame him, and he knew it was important to give the right response. And he played both hands correctly as Rachael and Laura nodded appreciatively. For that matter, Toke nodded appreciatively also. He realized Willy said exactly what he would have said, and admired the wit he demonstrated.

Rachael kicked hard at the bottom of Will's right foot. He only had one shoe on, and where the other was God only knows. Will's body skyrocketed, his head banging on the planks across the top of the Manger. "Son of a bitch," Will said as he rubbed his head and tried to get his bearings. Everyone laughed and Will felt sickly at the sight of the crowd.

Will squinted in the morning sun, his blurry vision finally coming to rest on the face of his mom. "Damn she looks mad," he thought. But had he truly thought about it, he'd have realized she always looked that way. But this was different, extra special in fact. So he shook Jake's body, wanting his buddy to endure this moment with him.

"Oh Mira, I love you too," Jake cooed in his sleep. He squeezed the donkey in his arms and kissed its forehead. He giggled like a child.

The crowd broke into raucous laughter that continued for quite some time. Mira was standing close enough to hear Jake's unsuitable and humiliating comment. She kicked him, hard! The aim of her pointed-toe shoe, however, was a little higher than his foot. And it landed against his shin.

Jake immediately sprang upward and banged his head, just as Will had done. "Son of a bitch," he said. But the pain in his head, both from the soon to be bruise and the liquor the night before, was nothing compared to what was coming. Soon enough he would know real pain.

Mira turned, doing her best to keep what little dignity she had left, and walked away in a huff.

"I always liked that girl," Laura said as the episode played out.

"What the hell's going on?" Jake asked with confusion, not understanding where he was.

"You'd better watch your mouth young man," Laura said. "And quit smiling Toke, you're more to blame for this than them!"

As everyone again laughed, Toke shrugged as if Laura's comments meant nothing. But he did quit smiling.

Chapter 57

Will and Mary strolled down a long narrow road like it was just an ordinary day. The two held hands, innocently enough, Mary's unopened present tucked beneath her free arm. The island and waters of the bay disappeared in the distance and the landscape changed to countryside and dirt roads. Mary didn't know where they were headed, and didn't care. It was the happiest she'd ever been and she never wanted it to end. But the dream ended and Mary awoke on Christmas morning. She was slightly disappointed when she realized it'd been just a dream, but as she looked at the sun radiating through the curtain in her window, she smiled. The curtain was an old and faded pink dress that had worn thin over the years. It was raggedy, with large holes throughout, and offered little in the way of shade. But on this day, this beautiful sun filled Christmas day, she didn't mind the holes, or the sun, or the tattered ends of a curtain that fluttered about as the draught of winter came merrily through. And it was the first time in many years that she was happy to have greeted a new day. Mary rolled over to make sure the present was still there. She sighed with delight. It was where she had left it.

Mary decided to do the chores and get breakfast out of the way before opening her gift. She was counting on Jeff and her Paw heading out to catch seafood, or shoot ducks, or whatever the hell they do. And decided she would use that time to explore the contents of the box. Above that, she remained giddy about seeing Will tonight, and believed the contents of the box would make everything perfect. The time had come to move on, and she wanted to look nice for the man who was going to take her away from this place.

The Gorman's sat at the table and dined on fried eggs and left over ham. There was no conversation that involved Mary as her dad and brother talked about where they'd go in search of food. And to Mary, it was a good conversation because it didn't involve her. She'd grown distant over the years and had no desire to speak to either man again. She almost let a smile slip out as she thought about the joy it would bring her.

After breakfast, the men stood from the table, grabbed their guns that rested by the front door, and walked out. And it was like all other days, and exactly how Mary predicted. They didn't offer any thanks for all the work she'd put in, nor did they compliment her on the food. "They're selfish bastards," she thought. And calling them bastards, made her feel even better. It was a new day, a new beginning, and the bastards were out of the house. "Yea, life is beginning to change for the better for Mary Gorman."

Mary quickly cleared the table and washed the dishes. She walked into her room and pulled the door as closed as it would go. It never shut much more than halfway, no matter how hard she pulled. She hated the door, the house, the chores, and to some degree, the island. She longed for new surroundings with new people and new hopes. And whatever was next, a pigsty or otherwise, would be better than here. Mary didn't want to dwell on all that was wrong, not on such a fine day. So she focused on the life ahead and all that was finally coming due. She immediately brightened as she glared at the gift. The box was so pretty that she still hesitated to open it. But after a long smile she said to herself, "Merry Christmas Mrs. Mary Burton."

Mary picked the box up, loosened the bow and gingerly pulled at one end. She soon held the red lace in her hand, her face gleaming. The sun's rays striped the walls of her room like a zebra's side, the beams bouncing off the red ribbon, the colors dancing before her sparkling eyes. She laid the ribbon across her bed and carefully removed the top of the box. She lost her breath for a moment. It was as she had hoped and dreamed. Inside, a neatly folded dress rested.

Mary eased the dress out, as if it were made of fine china, and unfolded it, revealing its full length. She gasped at its beauty and ran her fingers along the lace that bordered the neckline. The dress was pale blue with white trim. It was long, with the bottom hem sporting small and elegantly stitched white hearts all the way around. And she thought it would make a perfect wedding dress. She wildly flung the dress to her body, as if she were modeling it, and spun in laughter, the smile on her face big and bright.

"Put the dress on," Leo Gorman said from the doorway.

Mary's startled body immediately quit spinning. Her back was to her Paw, and she dared not turn. She shook her head slowly and closed her eyes. She clutched the dress as if the man were going to snatch it away.

"I said put it on!"

"Please, not now. I promise I'll put it on later. Just not now," Mary said with a childlike plea.

Leo's eyes became wild and his face reddened. "You're gonna put the dress on if I have to put it on you," he raged!

Mary didn't speak. She simply released the dress and let it fall to the wooden floor.

"Pick it up and put it on," Leo said as he slapped his daughter from behind, catching her on the side of her neck and ear. Mary stumbled to the side but didn't fall to the floor. She didn't cry out either. Too many years and too many tears had been shed over the beatings, and for some time now she had not allowed the monster to see her be weak. She realized a long time ago that he enjoyed that, and if she could take nothing else from him, this she would.

Mary turned, the side of her face red and swelling. She was now facing Leo. He was about to strike her again when his son enter the house and yelled for him.

"Paw, I need your help," Jeff called from the front door.

Leo looked Mary over, top to bottom. "You'll put the dress on. I'm gonna make sure of that," he said as he turned and left the room.

Mary knew what he meant. But what Leo didn't know is that this would be the last Christmas she would spend in this house. For that matter, it would be the very last day.

Chapter 58

Father Malone stepped out of the church and stared at the two lads in the Manger. "I could have guessed who it was. I knew at least one Cullen would be involved."

"Father, it's not the boys' fault," Rachael said as she glared at her brother.

"Ohhh don't you worry Ms. Rachael, I know who the sinner is here. I've known for a long time. But more importantly, God knows."

Toke didn't take too kindly to the comment, even though the priest never said his name. But then again, the man didn't have to because the entire crowd knew who he was talking about. So Toke decided he would help Jake up and the two would go home together. Good or bad and for whatever anyone thought, he didn't care. He only hated that he had disappointed Laura.

As Toke made his way to Jake and extended his hand, Laura piped up. "You know Father… I'm the most devout Catholic here and believe eternally in turning the other cheek. But I can't do that today. I love God, I love the Church, and I love you. But I don't like you right now. Priest or no Priest you don't have the right to judge my husband or my son. I know things may have gotten a little out of hand, but they didn't hurt anyone. They didn't cause any damage other than embarrassing the Cullen name. And let's face it, the Cullen name has had much worse than this done to it. I'm going to let it go this time because it's Christmas, but the next time you say something about my boys, you're gonna have to deal with me. And I can promise you, it won't be pleasant."

"Yea," Jake shouted as he stood and pumped a fist into the air.

"Shut up Jake and don't be an idiot!" Laura said coarsely. "You don't realize how much trouble you're in. Boys, let's go home." The three gathered themselves and headed down the path toward their house.

"Please Laura, I didn't mean anything by it. I'm sorry," Father Malone called out as the Cullen's strolled away.

"Maybe Laura's right," Willy said to Rachael. "Come on Will, let's get home."

"Please, not you too," the Priest pleaded.

"It's ok Father," Rachael said, "It's just best that we head home today. We've all suffered enough embarrassment for one day."

   The other parishioners stared at the Priest, and he realized he had insulted one of them. They were all kin and he'd condemned the most loveable one among them. "I want to tell everyone I'm sorry," he said as folks started heading in all directions and toward their homes. "Please everyone, let's be reasonable. We still have Mass and this isn't about me or the Cullen's! It's about worshipping God!" His words fell on deaf ears as people disappeared down different paths. The priest now stood in front of an empty Church, his hands extended outward as if he were delivering a sermon to ghosts. He finally realized the day was lost and headed in.

Later in the day, Mira walked in the front door of the Cullen's home and sat down at the kitchen table. Laura was already seated and drinking coffee. Laura made a motion with her mug, as to ask if Mira wanted some, and Mira nodded. Laura went to the stove and filled another mug and her own.

"Is Jake around?" Mira asked.

"No, he and Toke went off...... they're probably napping somewhere," Laura said with a fond smile.

"Good, I only wanted to see you."

Laura had never seen the girl so out of sorts, so unsure of herself. But she said nothing, giving Mira all the time she needed.

"Do you think Jake will always... well," she shrugged her shoulders, "act like he has over the last two days?"

Laura sighed and then smiled. "To be honest, I thought Toke would have grown out of it by now. But he hasn't and I don't think he ever will. Does it bother you that much?"

"Well, I feel myself changing and I want more in life than just fun and games. I want a future in nursing. And I want children and a home and I want it with Jake. But I don't think I can handle a husband who hasn't grown up."

Laura nodded as she knew exactly how the girl felt. "I know you love him, but do you like him? Do you like the person he is? You need to answer those questions before you get married. Men don't change, regardless of what anyone else may have told you. And the Cullen men are the most bull headed of them all."

"That's encouraging," Mira replied as she rolled her eyes and managed a smile.

"But let me say this about them. They'll love you like there's no tomorrow. They'll be your best friend and are passionate about their women. They're always happy and optimistic, which you'll come to cherish when things get tough. And you don't have to aggravate with them because they understand you need your space and opportunities in life. And I don't doubt that Jake will make a good husband and father. He has my compassion and his Dad's humor, and neither is a bad thing."

Mira's eyes were the greenest eyes Laura had ever seen, and they reflected something distant and unknowing. "I guess I have a lot to think about," Mira said.

"Well, don't worry over it. Jake's not going anywhere and he'll always love you, no matter what." Laura stood from her chair and walked close to Mira. She leaned over and gave the girl a motherly hug. The two drank coffee and chatted most of the afternoon away before Mira left and headed home for Christmas dinner with her family.

Chapter 59

Will was eager and jittery; rehearsing over and over in his head what he'd say when he greeted Mr. Gorman. Now that he was finally going to be introduced as the fella Mary loved, his nerves were unsettled. His mother and father studied every move as he wolfed down his dinner.

"Boy, you ok?" His Dad asked.

"I'm fine, just heading out for a little while."

"It's too late to go out," his Mother said. She still appeared angry.

Will's eyes darted to his mother. He didn't want to tell either parent that he was seeing Mary Gorman, not just yet anyway, but he didn't want to lie to them either. On top of that, his brothers, who had been quietly eating, now turned their attention to their older brother. "I'm gonna go to Jake's for a little bit. See if he and Mira patched things up." Will hadn't planned this stop, but the Cullen house was on the way to Mary's and if he ducked in for a few moments, then technically he wasn't lying.

"Don't be long," his Dad said, "your punishment starts at six in the morning. That bar's gonna need a good cleaning."

"I'll be back in an hour." And with that, Will wiped his mouth with a hand towel, stood from the table, and disappeared through the side door. He headed along the path toward Jake's.

A pile of dishes rested next to the sink, and Jake was up to his elbows in suds.

Will walked in and fixed himself a cup of coffee. He closed in on his friend. "Where's your dress?" Will asked with a snicker.

"Good stuff. I didn't realize you were so comical," Jake said with sarcasm. "This is my punishment for the Manger scene... scene." he shook his head as he said it. "I gotta do this for a month... every meal!"

"You have to admit, it was pretty funny," Will said with a chuckle.

"It'd been funnier if it'd been just you."

"Nah, that wouldn't have been any good. This way we'll have something to laugh about when we're old. It'll be our story to tell, like the old-timers tell theirs."

Jake liked that idea and it cheered him up a bit. "You're right. We can start telling it next Christmas and add new things every year so that by the time we have grandkids, it'll be the best story ever."

Will finished his coffee. "Here," he said as he tried to hand Jake the mug, "while you're at it." Will tilted his head, his hand extended.

"Why are you even here?" Jake asked as he snatched the mug from Will's grip.

"Just stopped in, wanted to see if you and Mira made up. I hear she's steamed."

"I know. I saw her leaving the house earlier and tried to talk to her. But she wouldn't say anything but hello and goodbye."

"She was here?"

"I guess she talked to Mom for a while. But Mom wouldn't tell me anything either."

"That can't be good," Will added as he again shook his head.

Will could feel the minutes slipping by. He didn't want to miss his rendezvous. He started to tell Jake where he was headed when Laura walked in. "Hello Ms. Laura," Will said apologetically.

"Will," Laura replied nicely before turning to her son. "Jake, once you're done with the dishes I want you to sweep the floor. And if that don't keep you busy 'til bedtime, then I can find something else for you to do." Laura made a point to add the extra work load in front of Will. She wanted no misunderstanding that what the two had done was unacceptable.

"Yes Ma'am," Jake said.

"Gotta go," Will said. "See ya Jake. Bye Ms. Laura."

"Bye," the two said as Will exited into the dark and wandered down the path toward the Gorman's.

Chapter 60

Mary Gorman finished the dishes and cleaned the kitchen. It may have looked a little odd, her cooking and then cleaning in such an exquisite gown, but she didn't care. She felt beautiful in the new dress and imagined she were a princess, about to be saved by her prince. She just needed to sneak by the bastard troll that guarded the door. And once that happened she'd walk away and never come back.

Mary's plan was in full swing, and earlier in the day stashed clothing, food, and the box her dress came in, behind the wood pile. It wasn't much, though nearly all she owned and everything she needed. Will was the final piece, and she knew he'd be along any minute.

After dinner, Leo and Jeff sat in the small living room and talked amiably about things that didn't much matter. Mary made sure she appeared busy in the kitchen. She didn't want to draw attention. And she did her best not to over act or seem too happy. There were no clocks in the house but she knew the time was near. She only needed a few more minutes and she'd be out!

***

The night was clear and a half moon nicely lit the narrow paths of the island. And Will walked merrily down one of them and toward the Gorman's. The evening was brisk, and Will hummed an almost silent tune as he strolled along. The elation was difficult to hide, a large smile of content upon his face. A cool northerly breeze filled the air, the sounds of the night alive. A lone whippoorwill called out.

Will thought about the meeting with Mary's dad. He had thought of nothing else the entire day, rehearsing the moment. First, he'd shake the man's hand, say something witty, and then become as likable to Mr. Gorman as he was to everyone else. He planned every detail and figured he had a leg up on the situation since Mr. Gorman acknowledged him during Thanksgiving. It all added up, and he just knew they'd get along and that he'd become a part of her family as she would his. The thought made him smile brighter and gave his step a little pep.

***

Mary stood at the edge, where her bedroom and the living area diverged. "I'm gonna get some firewood," she said out loud. She thought about what she said, about whether she seemed too anxious or too nervous. She then wondered if she should have just kept quiet.

Leo never turned his eyes to her. "No, you're not going out. Jeff's going to get the wood."

Jeff looked up, his eyes meeting Mary's. He felt sick. "Paw, let Mary get it," he said nervously.

"I said I want you to go, and I want you to chop more wood while you're there! It may be cold in the morning."

Jeff realized what this meant. "Please Paw, let Mary get the wood. I chopped plenty earlier today."

Leo gave his son a disgusted look. "Don't come back until you have enough for two days. So get!"

Jeff stood from the seat, paused as he looked to his sister, and then walked out of the house.

Mary was unimaginably silent, her body frozen to the floor. She couldn't believe this was happening. She had planned it all so perfectly. And now this! She could not bear one more time. She would not allow it to happen again.

**

Will heard the splitting of wood long before he reached the Gorman's house, and the sound drowned out the whippoorwill's calling that had kept him company along the way. He stopped short of the wood pile and watched as Jeff splintered piece after piece of pine logs. He started over to Jeff but decided to go to the house instead. "Why aggravate with Jeff and risk ending up in a brawl, when Leo is who I need to see."

**

Leo walked toward Mary. Mary stood at the foot of her bedroom door. She thought of making a dash for it, believing she might be able to slip past if she caught him off guard. She stepped away from the bedroom door as her dad moved ever closer. She then moved quickly, to race past him. Leo extended a hand and barely snagged the sleeve of her dress. She immediately stopped, feeling the seams give way. The dress didn't rip, but she feared it would if she continued on. Leo pulled her close, his arms clutching her body. He pinned her arms against her side. Leo's breath, foul and disgusting, whisked by Mary's face. She closed her eyes tightly and turned her face from his direction.

"Pretty dress," he said. "I said you'd be wearing it for me tonight." His sweaty body rubbed against hers. He eased his grip and slid a hand down her side. She slapped at his hand

and pushed at his heavy set body. She looked to the door for help, but only heard the repeating sound of splitting wood.

Mary looked Leo in the eye, defying all that he was. The old man nodded in approval, a terrifying grin racing across his face, his yellowing teeth showing as he latched onto Mary's arms, spun her around, and shoved her into her room.

Over the years Mary fought less and less because the beatings worsened. But tonight she didn't care. Tonight, things were going to be different.

Chapter 61

Jeff paused from chopping. The cold dry air burned his throat and lungs, although he sweated profusely. He wiped his brow and looked back at the house. He knew what was happening, and struggled to keep his emotions in check. The fact he'd allowed it to continue for so many years was an unforgiveable sin. He looked long and hard at the house and even took a few steps in its direction. But he stopped. Jeff ran his calloused hands through his sweaty hair and pulled outward at the black strands. Tears of disgust grew in the corner of his eyes. He had let this happen so many times, allowing his father to prey upon his sister. It was sickening and reviling and…. He shook his head, the tears unstoppable.

Leo left Mary's room and walked to the front door, where he looked at the silhouette of his son. "Boy, you better start chopping," he yelled.

Jeff remained a silent figure. He stared back at his dad, the ax firmly in the grasp of his right hand. He wanted to say something, he wanted to scream something, he wanted to walk over and slam the ax into his father's head! His face grew red with anger. Jeff's eyes fell upon the ax as he repositioned his hands and wrapped both of them around it. The blade was sharp and shining, an efficient machine. His eyes lifted and he glared at his father for nearly a minute. He stomped several feet to the right, talking and muttering the entire time. Leo disappeared into the home and Jeff felt deflated. He realized he wasn't a man or even a decent human being. Disgusted in himself, he turned back to the wood pile and vigorously started chopping. He only wanted to drown out any sounds that might be heard.

Will looked on as Leo yelled to his son and then disappeared into the house. Well, at least he knew he was home. And he was glad to finally have the chance to talk things out with him.

Mary was silent and motionless, standing next to her bed. She listened as her dad reentered the house and closed the front door. He returned quicker than she imagined possible, but that was okay. She had found a weapon during his absence, a long skinny board that rested on the window seal. The slat of wood was used for propping the window open in the summer, and she picked it up. She hid it behind her back, her knuckles white from the clutch it was under. It was the hardest object she could find during the brief moment, and believed if she caught him just right, if she could catch him hard enough to cause him to fall, then she could dash past him.

Leo stood in the doorway, his figure casting an ominous shadow. For a moment it appeared he would stand there all night, gauging his daughter, eyeing her form. But he didn't, and he headed toward her. He walked close and touched his daughter through the dress. Mary didn't wince, and Leo didn't like that. Her courage wasn't appreciated. He needed her to be the little girl she used to be, the one who screamed and cried and tried to scratch his face. He longed for that time.

With all the strength Mary could muster, with all the anger from all the years, and with all the hate she had ever known, she swung the board around and crashed it into Leo's face. He wasn't expecting it, and he wasn't expecting the fight she was determined to give. His nose broke and a mixture of blood and splintered wood flew in all directions. The man staggered, put both hands to his face and doubled over at the waist. Mary gave another swing. The board was considerably shorter now, having broken in half with the first impact. But she was close, close enough that she caught the corner of his right eye. The skin around his eye sliced open as the edge of the board found its mark. It looked like someone had cut the belly of a fish, blood gushing from the opening. Mary kicked once in the direction of Leo's face, catching his hands that he had placed on both sides of his nose, before racing toward the bedroom door.

Leo was angry, a madman, and as Mary made it to the opening, he reached up and grabbed the back of her hair. He dragged her back in. Leo gave a stern punch to Mary's face. She staggered and crashed into a corner table.

Will was walking alongside the house, on his way to the front door, when he heard the crashing and banging from within. He turned and looked at Jeff who labored with the wood. Another crashing noise from the house recaptured his attention and he went to a window. He searched for movement through shredded pink curtains.

Leo drew Mary up from the floor by her hair and threw her on the bed. She was dazed but continued to claw at his face. And Leo liked it! He liked it when she became a trapped animal, and it aroused him. He slapped her hard across the mouth and rolled her onto her stomach. She kicked and screamed with less and less strength, her body tiring, her breaths becoming short and labored.

Will found a fairly large hole in the curtains and peered into the dark room.

Leo punched Mary with his right hand while pressing against the back of her neck with his left. He pressed so hard that Mary thought she would pass out. He then tugged at the hem her dress, pulling it past her waist.

"Noooo," Will yelled!

Although Mary's ears were ringing, she still heard the yell. And she was able to turn her head enough to see Will looking in, the moon positioned above his head.

Leo also looked up, and into Will's eyes. And for the first time ever, he was afraid. But before he could react, a dull thump echoed through the lonely night. Jeff had dealt a blow to the back of Will's head with the ax handle, and the boy crumpled to the ground.

Chapter 62

Although aware that she'd blacked out, Mary wasn't sure how much time had passed. She rolled over and into a seating position. Her entire body hurt, especially her swelling face. But she pushed the pain aside, thinking only of Will. She tried to stand on unsteady legs, but her strength hadn't yet returned. So she sat there, crying. Will was the only person that mattered, and he now knew her secret. And just like that, it was over. Any thoughts of a life with him had vanished.

"What the hell you hit him for?" Leo yelled. Leo and Jeff were outside Mary's window, standing over Will's lifeless body.

"He saw what you was doing Paw. I had to do something!"

"What I was doing? I wasn't doing anything," Leo said as blood streamed from his eye and nose.

"I know what you were doing," Jeff said with conviction.

Leo grabbed the boy's collar and pulled him close. He stared into his son's eyes as he spoke. "I'm gonna tell you this one time. I wasn't doing anything. And you'd better remember that." Leo threw his boy backwards as he released his hold.

Jeff stumbled a few steps before regaining his balance. He shook his head. "We need to get him help. I think I may have hurt him bad!"

Mary gasped for breaths. Blood trickled from her mouth, her right eye, and from beneath her dress. She was weak, though she found the strength to push herself to a standing position. She staggered the few steps to the window. One eye had swollen shut, the other nearly as bad. The curtain hung before her and she pushed it aside. Will lay on the ground as her father and brother stood over him and argued. Mary couldn't believe it had come to this! She couldn't believe Will had been hurt!

"We ain't gettin no help," Leo replied sharply. "We're gonna take him to the fort and put him on the rocks. Everyone will think he slipped from the top of the wall and hit his head."

"He may die Paw! We can't do that to him, it ain't right!"

"Boy… you're the one that hit him so you'll be the one they lock up. And you don't want that!"

"But I hit him because of you," Jeff pleaded.

Leo backhanded the boy. His mouth began to bleed. "Like I told you, I wasn't doing anything. And if I hear it again, I'm gonna beat you to death!" The rage in Leo was unnerving, even to Jeff.

"What about when he wakes up and starts talking. What we gonna do then?" Jeff asked, now that he was onboard with the plan and doing his best to cover their bases.

"That'll be tomorrow at the earliest. We can be gone by then. We'll take 'em to the fort and come back and get what we need. By daybreak we'll be gone." Leo spoke as if the plan would work. He realized, if Jeff spoke up or got caught by the sheriff, that his son would turn on him in the blink of an eye.

So his only choice was to leave. They needed to go to a place where no one knew them and where no one would be asking questions.

Mary staggered to the front door of the house. She leaned against the door jamb, her body slumping forward. Jeff and Leo carried Will's body past. "You can't do it Jeff. Please don't listen to him. It ain't right." Her voice was weak, but they clearly heard what she had to say.

Jeff looked at his father and then to Mary. "I got to, there ain't no other way."

"Get in there and start packing," Leo roared at his daughter.

"Jeff, this is the one time you can help me. I know you always wanted too, but…….. please Jeff, don't let this monster destroy us both." Mary sobbed uncontrollably as she spoke.

Leo laid the weight of the boy on Jeff and walked over to Mary. He backhanded her across the mouth and pushed her into the house. "Jeff, you take the boy like we said and we'll be ready once you come back. I'm gonna stay with Mary so she don't go talking. Now go boy!"

Jeff looked at his Dad and did as he was told.

Chapter 63

Toke and Laura sat at the kitchen table. They were finishing they're last cup of coffee before heading to bed, when two quick taps came from the side door and Willy entered.

Toke looked at his friend, whose face was emblazoned with worry.

"I'm looking for Will. He was supposed to be home hours ago. Said he was going to see Jake when he left the house." Willy was never one to panic, but alarm resonated in the rapidity of his speech.

Jake heard the voices and moved from his room and into the hallway next to the kitchen. He listened.

"He stopped in earlier and talked to Jake for a few minutes. But he left. He's been gone well over two hours now," Laura replied with growing concern of her own.

Jake walked in the kitchen. "I bet he went to Mary Gorman's house," he said. "He didn't tell me where he was going but I know he's been seeing her for quite some time."

"What," Willy said in disbelief. "He'd have told me if he was seeing someone."

"I'm sorry Mr. Willy, but it's true. Mary made him promise not to tell. She said if he did, then her Dad would get upset and he'd have no chance of ever seeing her again."

***

"Get packing," Leo said to Mary.

Mary shook her head as she slid to the floor.

"You're going with us, or I'm gonna kill ya! Those are your choices."

Mary lay on her side, her head lying on an extended arm, her long red hair draping her blood soaked cheek. "Then kill me, because I ain't going. I should have done this long ago when you first started. It should never have happened more than once, and that's my fault." She took a moment to catch her breath. "But it won't happen again. I'd rather be dead." Mary had found the resolve she always knew was there, and she was no longer afraid. "I should've stopped you before someone else got hurt."

Leo's eyes filled with anger and he tore into Mary. His brutality was unspeakable as he did in fact try to kill the girl. And he didn't stop until Jeff grabbed him from behind and slung him away.

"Enough, you're gonna kill her!" Jeff screamed.

"Move away boy!"

"No Paw, it's over!" Jeff stood between Mary and his Dad, and looked the old man in the eye. "The beatings and rapings are over. I won't allow it anymore."

Leo's breathing slowed. "She said she ain't going with us. If she don't go, she's gonna tell the sheriff." Leo was calm in his response as he now tried to reason with his boy.

"I don't care what she does. She's had to live with you and all you've done for way too long. I've had to live with knowing and not doing anything about it, and I'm tired of it! It's over for Mary! I won't allow it to happen again if I gotta strangle you with my own two hands!" Jeff's face was tortured, his eyes burning from tears of anger. He meant what he said. And he'd kill his Paw if necessary.

"So whatta we do now?"

"We do what we said we'd do. We leave. If Mary don't go, then she don't go. If she decides to tell, then I guess we'll live with it."

Leo paused for a long while. He finally nodded in agreement.

Chapter 64

Jeff moistened a dishrag and knelt next to Mary. He placed it to her swollen lips and wiped away the blood. He then dabbed at the dried blood around her right eye, using gently strokes. Someone knocked at the front door and panic raced through the room. Jeff glanced to his father before hurriedly dragging his sister into the bedroom. Leo eased to the door.

"Who is it?" Leo shouted through the closed door.

"Willy Burton," Willy yelled back.

"We ain't taking company tonight, come back tomorrow," Leo said as calmly as he could.

"Fine, I'll be back in the morning," Willy replied.

As Leo stepped away from the door, it came crashing down. Willy had put his shoulder into it and knocked it from its hinges. Three men, Willy, Toke, and Jake, rushed in and looked around the room.

Leo had forgotten about his face and the dried blood that matted the short white whiskers on his cheeks and around his mouth. He acted incredulous by what just happened. "What the hell is this?" He questioned the three.

Willy took another look around the room, and then at Leo's face. He grabbed the man by the shirt collar and pulled him close. "Where's my boy," he seethed as if he were the devil himself.

Jeff entered from a side room. He never said a word.

Willy shook the older Gorman and fear began to show in the man's eyes.

Leo shook his head slowly, as if he had done nothing wrong.

Willy shook even harder.

"He hurt him." The voice was weak and it came from a frail and barely alive, Mary Gorman. She stood just outside her room, her arm on the wall, her head slumped forward. The intruders turned. They gasped.

Toke rushed to Mary's aide. She fell into his arms, her body becoming lifeless. He couldn't believe the sight. Her face was so disfigured that she was unrecognizable. He eased both their bodies to the floor and laid her head across his lap. Unable to look away, his eyes watered. Shock rattled his existence as he brushed the blood soaked hair from her face.

Jeff saw an opportunity and took it. "Paw hit Will with an ax!"

"Shut up boy!" Leo yelled.

"Where's my son!" Willy screamed into Leo's face.

"He said he took him to the rocks at the fort. He wanted it to look like an accident." Jeff pretended to be alarmed, pacing and pointing a finger at Leo as he spoke. "He told me where he put the boy."

"The boy's lying. He hit 'em!" Leo pointed a finger back at his son. "He dragged his body off! It's all lies I'm telling you!"

Leo was afraid. He was no longer the bully of the house, and was as scared as a child during a thunderstorm. His day had arrived and a reckoning with Jesus was upon him.

"It was all you Paw! You hit Will and you raped and beat Mary! And when Mary comes to, she'll tell ya'll the same."

Leo tried to jerk from Willy's grip and go after his son, but Willy held tight and punched the man in the stomach. It stole Leo's breath, and he fell to his knees.

"Come on boy, let's find my son," an angry and very scared Willy said to Jeff.

As Willy turned to head out the door, Leo managed to his feet.

"Behind you!" Jake yelled.

Willy spun, just in time, and blocked a punch Leo threw at him. To Willy it was obvious that Leo had never been in the war as he didn't fight with any military training. He wasn't even a brawler. But Willy did train, and delivered a jab to the man's Adam's apple. Leo grabbed his throat, gasped for breath and watched as Willy's fist slammed into his jaw. Leo's jaw snapped. He screamed in pain and fell to the floor.

"Jake, go tell Julius to get Doc Meyer and the Sheriff," Willy said. He then turned to Leo. "You need to pray to God that my son is ok. I've killed enough men in my life that I don't think God will hold it against me if I take one more!"

Jake slipped out the door but stopped as his Dad called after him, "Get Mira, your Mom, and some of the ladies to come tend to this child!"

Jake darted from the house and toward the village, as Willy and Jeff headed in the opposite direction.

Toke sat on the floor, Mary's head lying in his lap. He kept an eye on Leo who squirmed in agonizing pain from the broken jaw.

Mary came in and out of consciousness, almost lucid at times. "Is Will ok?" she whispered, unable to move her swollen lips.

"Will's fine," Toke answered. His body swayed, gently rocking her.

Mary did her best to smile, but her mouth only moved a little. "Is my new dress ok?" She asked. Her eyes were completely swollen shut.

Toke glared at the dress. It was torn to shreds and bloody. "It's a beautiful dress," he said, "not a stitch missing."

Mary again tried to smile before she passed out once more.

Chapter 65

Jake raced to Julius Carter's house, banged on the door with both fist, and woke them all. Breathlessly, he explained what had happened. Julius and Pate grabbed their coats and headed to the Shell Banks. Jake then ran to the Lea's, where he again banged at a door. Peter answered. His hair was out of sorts, his eyes puffy from where he'd been rubbing the sleep from them.

"What's going on?" Peter asked.

"We need Mira to come look after Mary Gorman. Her Dad beat her. He also hurt Will," Jake said, panting and holding his side. Peter ducked back in the house and after a few minutes reappeared with Mira and his wife.

"Bess you stop and get Rachael and Laura, and we'll take Mira," Peter said.

Bess walked at a quick pace toward Rachael's while the other three ran toward the Gorman's.

"Will's been hurt," Jake said to Mira as they rushed along.

They stopped running and Mira placed a hand on Jake's arm. "Will?" She said as she looked at the faint features of Jake's worried face.

"I'm sorry I forgot tell you," Peter said to his daughter as he caught up with the two.

"How bad?" Mira asked.

"I'm not sure. The old man hit him with something and took his body to the rocks at the fort. Mr. Willy and Jeff went to find him."

Mira glared at Jake and then grabbed his hand and squeezed. The three again took off in a sprint.

***

Willy and Jeff made it to the rocks, and Jeff put on a good show. For nearly ten minutes they searched in different directions. And of course, Jeff eventually found the body. He yelled for Willy to come over. Willy knelt down and placed his ear next to his son's mouth. There was a hint of warm breath. "Help me get 'em off these rocks," Willy said to Jeff. The two men worked together and once on sure footing, Willy snatched the boy up and headed back to the village.

***

Peter had to walk away after seeing Mary's face. The sight was more than he could stand. His daughter, however, did what she'd been training to do and tended to the girl. Mira never hesitated, and her ability was phenomenal.

Jake watched from the doorway, admiring Mira's strength and passion. "She'll be a great nurse," he said to himself. He stepped aside as other ladies began arriving.

"Let's get her to a bed somewhere," Mira said.

"Our house is the closest," Laura said. "We can put her in Jake's bed."

"As someone gone for the Doc?" Mira directed the question to everyone, anyone.

"Yea," Jake said.

Jake helped Toke lift the girl and situate her in Toke's arms. The crowd headed out the door, except for Peter. He elected to stay behind and keep an eye on Leo.

As the group flooded from the house, Willy and Jeff were approaching with Will.

"Is he ok?" Rachael asked as she went to her son.

Willy was worried and unable to reassure his wife. "I don't know," he answered honestly.

Mira moved to Will and held her fingers to his wrist. His pulse was weak. "Let's get both of them to Laura's house. It's closest to the Shell Banks." Mira was in charge and it was how it should have been. She directed and led with the will of a titan, with the will of a nurse.

Jake watched as the group hurried along the path and out of sight. He couldn't move. He didn't like seeing Will injured, and didn't know if he could bear it if it was serious.

Chapter 66

Saul Clark helped Peter guard Leo, and to some degree, Jeff. Jimmy Clark went to the boat launch and waited for Julius to return with the Doctor. Daylight drew near, perhaps an hour away, and Will's condition hadn't improved. But Mary seemed better. She came in and out of consciousness, seeming more coherent each time. And with each occurrence she asked about Will, and her dress.

Mira had done all she could. She stepped out of the house and into the night air. Clouds were forming, obscuring the stars that paraded through the night sky.

"You were great," Jake said from a shadow. He walked into view.

"Thanks," Mira said. She stretched her back, doing what she could to offset the exhaustion. "Just doing what I've been taught."

"They taught you well. I was so proud of you. I don't think I've ever been prouder of anyone in my life."

Mira nodded appreciatively. "How are you doing?"

"Worried," Jake said as he fought back tears. "I don't know if I…." He couldn't finish the sentence. "He's my only brother!"

Mira understood what he meant by "brother." "I know," she said as the two hugged.

The distant noise of a motor wailed in the distance. Jake and Mira turned to face the path that ran toward the Shell Banks. They waited, expectantly. A few minutes later Doctor Meyer and Jim Cowl walked into sight. Both men went in the house and Mira followed. And as for Jake, he again faded into the shadows.

Jim asked everyone questions and looked at the injured. He then headed to the Gorman's. Doc Meyer asked everyone to clear out, except Mira. He examined Mary first, and then Will. And it seemed to take forever.

The Doctor closed the door as he and Mira walked from Toke and Laura's bedroom. His expression was grave. "The girl will be fine. Just keep the cuts clean. It'll take her several weeks to completely heal though. Hopefully some of the ladies here can tend to her 'til she does."

"What about my boy?" Willy asked with worry.

"The boy's in bad shape." The Doc paused. "It could go either way... and there's the possibility that if he makes it through the next twenty-four hours, he'll have considerable brain damage. His brain is swollen and until it goes down, we just won't know. I suggest we get him to the Bayou. I can keep him hydrated and tend to him better in my office. But the truth is... the truth is it's up to him and God." The Doctor rubbed the back of his neck. It had been a long night for him as well.

It was daylight by the time Will was moved to the boat. Jim Cowl had heard enough inconsistencies in Jeff Gorman's story that he decided to take both men in. So, Will, his parents, and Doc Meyer piled into the boat with Julius and Pate. Jim and the Gorman men would have to wait until Julius returned, as the boat was at its limit. Jake watched from the beach as Julius cranked the engine. The motor puttered as Pate pushed the nose of the boat from the beach and hopped on.

Pate turned and looked at Jake. He knew what needed to be done. He jumped off the boat, into knee deep water, and nodded to Jake. Jake sloshed past Pate and climbed aboard. The engine revved and the boat sped off.

The Doc kept close tabs on Will as they made their way to the Bayou. It was difficult to hear over the engine's noise, so with each round of checking Will's vital signs the Doc nodded that everything was ok.

The engine continued to roar at peak speed, and they were within a mile of the docks that outlined the Bayou. And again, Doc Meyer checked Will. But his pace was different this time, his search for a pulse desperate. He continued for a couple of frantic minutes, moving his hand from Will's neck to his wrist, and back again. Finally, he gave up and shook his head.

Will didn't live long enough to make it to the Bayou. He died on the water, a day after Christmas 1941.

Jake sat next to Julius and watched as Willy and Rachael sobbed. Their oldest son lay cradled in his Dad's arms, his head against his Mother's shoulder. Rachael's tears fell onto Will's face as she brushed the hair from his eyes and kissed his cheek.

Jake began to cry for the loss of such a good person and his best friend. As tears streamed down his cheeks, he looked to Heaven for answers. And for the first time today he noticed the sun was hiding behind the thick gray clouds, and that it shared none of its warmth with the cold morning.

Chapter 67

Mary Gorman continued to recoup from her ordeal. A day after the beating she had been moved to Mira's house, making it easier for Mira to monitor her progress. Mira performed all the duties asked of her, though she was far from alone. All the ladies of the community did their part, and with everyone's help Mary improved with each passing day.

As Mary mended, the expectancy of seeing Will increased. Each time she awoke, her first thoughts were of opening her eyes and seeing his smiling face. She did not know of Will's death, how could she, it had been kept a secret. Early on, the villagers agreed it best to wait until Mary was stronger, before breaking the news.

***

Will's wake began the night before the funeral. And it was mostly Islanders. Few people ventured from the mainland because of limited places to bed down. Most would come to the island on the morning of the funeral and leave by mid-day. Everyone needed to be home by dark.

The custom, another Irish influence, had always been that a person was waked from sundown to sunup, on the evening before the funeral. And Will's wake was no exception. It may be odd to understand, but the island had always celebrated the passing of a loved one. Most shared stories of the deceased, reliving moments of beauty and love and humor. People laughed more than they cried, and reflected on all the deceased had given. For whatever reason, it instilled belief that a life hadn't been wasted. But Will's passing was different. And the tragedy forever changed the soul of the island. Men stood outside the church and mostly talked about things they could do to help ease the family's suffering, while ladies cooked and catered food. But Rachael and Willy didn't eat and rarely spoke. They just sat in chairs, next to their boy's coffin, which rested at the foot of the church's altar.

For Jake, he was in the midst of his own struggles. Devastation beat as real as the heart in his chest. And loneliness entered his mind with an understanding that it would dwell there forever. He only crossed into the church once, as it was all he could endure. He shook Willy's hand like a man and hugged Rachael like the aunt she was. Willy never responded to Jake, never even looked him in the eye. He no longer looked anyone in the eye. But when he hugged Rachael, they both held on for dear life and the tears wouldn't stop.

As the sun rose in the morning and 10 am approached, the church burgeoned with people. Mass began, and it was a full Mass. It lasted more than an hour. As soon as Father Malone made a final sign of the cross, six men lifted and then carried the coffin out. The pallbearers moved quietly, from the church to the cemetery, and Jake walked at a distance, trailing the group. He walked by himself as the procession made its way to Will's final resting place.

"You ok?" Mira asked as she slowed and waited for Jake to catch up.

Jake nodded. "Yea," he said. He felt as if he were in a fog, unable to see his way to the other side. He hadn't slept since all this occurred and exhaustion tugged at his ability to sort the last few days.

Mira labored to comprehend the strain this had placed on Jake. She barely understood what it was doing to her. So she did the only thing she could think of. She took Jake's hand and the two walked, as a couple, the rest of the way to the cemetery.

The cemetery was small, and other than two Confederate soldiers buried near its center, everyone else was family. Islanders and mainlanders stood in the chilled air as the Priest spoke. The words were the same as every other funeral and it quickly ended. The crowd remained for a long while and hugged and kissed and cried. Jake didn't partake in any of that. He seemed out of tears, and all of his hugs and kisses had been used up. So he and Mira walked back to the church, hand in hand. The mood was solemn and filled with silence, until they neared the church and stood in front of it. Neither was sure why they had returned to this spot, but they did.

Jake turned to look at Mira. "How's Mary?" he asked.

"She's getting better. She should be up and about in another week."

"Has anyone told her?"

Mira shook her head.

"How are you?" Jake asked.

Mira appreciated the thought and laid her head on Jake's shoulder. Her nose was cold as it brushed against his neck. To Jake it felt like heaven. "I want to go off and cry. I don't want to believe any of this has happened," she whispered.

"Me neither," Jake said. "But we need to think of Willy and Rachael and his brothers."

Mira marveled at Jake's compassion. The fact he worried more about Will's family than himself, was uplifting.

"They're gonna need a lot of people to lean on. It's important…" Jake stopped talking and looked at the Manger that rested outside the church doors. It felt odd that it was still the Christmas season. It seemed like Christmas had been months ago, rather than just the few days that had passed.

Mira watched Jake's face, and something appeared, almost a smile.

Jake squinted, reliving the past, his eyes watering. "Remember that time Will and I slept in the Manger on Christmas Eve and everyone came along and saw us the next morning. You know we didn't make it home that night because of a downpour."

"It was hardly a drizzle," Mira corrected.

"No…" Jake said softly as the tears rolled down his cheeks, "this story belongs to me and Will, and it was a deluge. It rained so hard we were lucky we didn't get swept away in the floods….."

Mira smiled and listened as the story rose and fell like the tides. It was in fact Jake and Will's story, and she was glad it had happened.

Chapter 68

Out of respect, Jim Cowl attended the funeral although it wasn't the true reason he had come to the island. It just happened to be a coincidence that he arrived on the same day. He had other business, and in fact there were two pressing matters he needed to tend to on this visit.

Jim didn't speak to everyone as a whole, as it didn't seem appropriate. Instead, he spoke with a few men, individually, and asked that they spread the word. He wanted everyone to know that he'd be back in seven days, and that he'd be enlisting men for the draft. Jim realized it wouldn't take long for word to spread, and left it at that. His other need was to speak with Mary. And after the service, he headed to the Lea's.

Bess sat in a rocking chair a few feet from the bed Mary lay in, and sewed. The room was quiet and well lit. The curtains were open and the sun shone brightly through. Jim walked into the room and looked at the young girl. Most of the swelling in Mary's face had eased, but the aftermath was nearly as bad. Bruises, now brownish and yellow, covered her entire face like a large distorted birth mark. And stitches, from where Doc Meyer had closed open cuts, looked like large caterpillars along her right eyebrow and across the bottom of her chin.

"Afternoon," Bess said softly.

"Afternoon," Jim replied. "How's she doing?"

"Much better, she stays awake for longer periods and can hold a bit of conversation."

"Good to hear it. I guess there's no way of knowing when she'll wake again. I need to get a testimony from her."

Bess didn't particularly care for the need to do this so soon. She didn't want the girl upset. But she understood life, the difficulties of traversing back and forth to the Island, and the fact he was only doing his job. So she stood, walked to the bed and placed a hand on Mary's forehead. "Mary, Mary," Bess said tenderly.

Mary stirred, her body beneath the covers stretching and awakening. She opened her eyes and smiled when she saw Bess' smiling face.

"There's someone here to see you dear," Bess said with a low and soothing voice. "He needs to talk to you for a few moments. Do you think you can do that?"

Mary's head nodded excitedly, thinking it was Will. She mouthed the word "yes" without making a sound.

Jim moved into view and spoke evenly and directly. "Mary, how do you feel?"

"Fine," she said faintly and with grave disappointment.

"Good. I need to talk to you about what happened. Is that ok?"

Mary only nodded this time.

"Can you tell me what recently happened as well as anything in the past your father or brother may have done to you? I know it may be difficult, but it's something we have to do."

Mary took in a deep breath as Jim pulled a chair close and eased into it. She told the story in unbelievable detail. Most people push trauma deep down inside, but Mary was different. She needed to say these things, and Jim was proud of her.

Jim listened, beginning to end, while taking note. And Mary didn't falter or omit details. Jim didn't show any expression throughout the girl's statement, but grimaced inside as she relayed each story. It had been her life; abuse, rape, and loneliness. And for her, being able to unburden her soul, to explain all that had ever happened, gave her peace. She had always believed that she was wrong, that she had been filthy and disgusting. But as she spoke and the sheriff listened, she knew that wasn't the case. She could see that her father had been the animal. As Mary concluded, Jim's face paled. His eyes filled with pity, but he didn't look away. He wanted her to know everything was okay, and that no one blamed her.

"Mary," Jim said as Mary's head turned away from him, her eyes focusing on the tree outside the window. "I know this was difficult, but I can promise that your father will never harm you again. We have an open and shut case on the abuse. And a charge of murder against Jeff, and conspiracy to commit murder against Leo, will be added."

Mary's head jerked back around. She stared at Jim. "Murder?" She asked with disbelief.

Jim looked at Bess, his hands fidgeting with the pen and paper.

Bess could say nothing.

Jim looked back to the girl. "I'm so sorry; I didn't realize...." His voice was honest and sincere.

Mary's eyes filled with tears that she didn't wipe away. "No, it can't be," she said as she sobbed uncontrollably.

Bess sat on the side of the bed. She leaned over and put her arms around Mary's head as Jim apologized and left.

Chapter 69

The school semester began and Mira found herself back in class and once again buried in a heavy workload. It was also the first time she had seen Sherry since Thanksgiving. She told her everything that had happened.

Mary improved to the point of walking and feeding and cleaning herself. She no longer needed constant care but continued to stay with Bess and Peter, at least for the time being. Two days later, Mary told the Lea's that she'd be going home. She said she felt well enough to care for herself and that she needed to get on with her life. She thanked the Lea's many times for all they'd done, and gave Bess a long hug.

Bess and Peter weren't keen on Mary being alone. They both knew she needed help, as the difficulty of gathering food was in itself a full time chore. But that wasn't all. The girl seemed tormented by dreams and woke often, and throughout the night. Anxiety and panic torched both her mind and body, and no one could help. And now she had decided to return to the house where it all happened. For the Lea's it was unimaginable. So Bess and Peter told Mary that they'd support her decision if she allowed people to help. They wouldn't interfere with her life, and only assist when needed. Mary agreed to all that was asked.

Bess and Mary arrived at her house at ten in the morning. Bess did her best to get Mary settled before leaving. She couldn't help but think that it was a terrible idea.

Mary stood in the kitchen and took notice that the place had been cleaned and the front door repaired. She walked to her bedroom and noticed that that door had also been fixed. The door swung freely, and she gently pushed it close. She would never open it again.

Laura showed up at Mary's door, just after three in the afternoon. She carried a plate of biscuits and a bowl of stew. The front door was ajar and she said "hello" as she walked in. The house was empty. After searching the school and church and coming up empty, she enlisted the help of others.

The evening Will had been injured, Mary promised herself that she'd never again spend a night in the house. And she remained true to her word. As soon as Bess departed, she had done the same.

The afternoon was unseasonably warm for early January. And it was a perfect day to leave. Mary made her way to the Shell Banks and chose a boat with oars. She untied the anchor, which lay on the beach, and climbed aboard. She headed east and then south, leaving the calm waters of the bay for the open Gulf. Mary smiled as she rowed, looking toward the sun that was beginning to set during these short winter days. "It's a beautiful day. A perfect day," she thought. She never again cried for her losses; she understood the way things needed to be. She was finally able to let go of the past, and all the hate that had filled her nineteen years… vanished.

Saul Clark found his skiff two days later on Pelican Island. He reported it to the Sheriff who immediately headed to the island. Jim soon came to the same conclusion as everyone else, though Mary's body was never found. Jim would later send word to Leo and Jeff Gorman of the events surrounding Mary's disappearance, and it was received quite differently by each man. Jeff hung himself in his cell while awaiting trial. And as for Leo, he never said a word as he was told of his daughter's disappearance. He didn't even care. Leo Gorman eventually stood trial and was sentenced to life in prison. He would serve out his days at a State prison in southwest Alabama.

I hope you enjoyed this book

Vaile

ABOUT THE AUTHOR

When I began writing this book, my goal was to

capture how unique the Island is, and how the

generations of locals defined it.

And though the storyline is fictional, the traditions

and love and compassion of the characters is real.

It's their story that needed to be told.

As for me, I've spent a lifetime on the Island and my love for
it has never wavered. My mother's side of the family are all
locals, several generations in fact, and my brothers and myself
were also raised there. I fathered two sons while living on the
Island and I'm glad they both had a chance to enjoy the family
presence it offered. And although I no longer live there
(I now live on the mainland with my wife), I'm fortunate that
my work brings me home most every day.

If you come to the Island, don't be surprised if you can't get
the sand out of your shoes.

www.ingramcontent.com/pod-product-compliance
Lightning Source LLC
Chambersburg PA
CBHW022135170626
46807CB00005B/1948